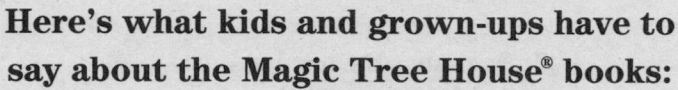

Here's what kids and grown-ups have to say about the Magic Tree House® books:

"Oh, man . . . the Magic Tree House series is really exciting!"
—Christina

"I like the Magic Tree House series. I stay up all night reading them. Even on school nights!"
—Peter

"Jack and Annie have opened a door to a world of literacy that I know will continue throughout the lives of my students."
—Deborah H.

"As a librarian, I have seen many happy young readers coming into the library to check out the next Magic Tree House book in the series."
—Lynne H.

Magic Tree House®

For a list of Magic Tree House® Merlin Missions and other Magic Tree House® titles, visit MagicTreeHouse.com.

MAGIC TREE HOUSE®

#6 AFTERNOON ON THE AMAZON

BY MARY POPE OSBORNE

ILLUSTRATED BY SAL MURDOCCA

A STEPPING STONE BOOK™

Random House 🏠 New York

For Piers Pope Boyce

Text copyright © 1995 by Mary Pope Osborne
Cover art and interior illustrations copyright © 1995 by Sal Murdocca

All rights reserved. Published in the United States by Random House Children's Books, a division of Penguin Random House LLC, New York. Originally published in paperback in the United States by Random House Children's Books, New York, in 1995.

Random House and the colophon are registered trademarks and A Stepping Stone Book and the colophon are trademarks of Penguin Random House LLC. Magic Tree House is a registered trademark of Mary Pope Osborne; used under license.

Visit us on the Web!
SteppingStonesBooks.com
randomhousekids.com
MagicTreeHouse.com

Educators and librarians, for a variety of teaching tools, visit us at
RHTeachersLibrarians.com.

Library of Congress Cataloging-in-Publication Data
Osborne, Mary Pope. Afternoon on the Amazon / by Mary Pope Osborne ;
illustrated by Sal Murdocca.
p. cm. — (The Magic tree house series ; #6) "A First stepping stone book."
Summary: Eight-year-old Jack, his seven-year-old sister, Annie, and Peanut
the mouse ride in a tree house to the Amazon rain forest, where they encounter
flesh-eating piranhas, hungry crocodiles, and wild jaguars.
ISBN 978-0-679-86372-4 (pbk.) — ISBN 978-0-679-96372-1 (lib. bdg.) —
ISBN 978-0-375-89423-7 (ebook)
[1. Rain forests—Fiction. 2. Rain forest animals—Fiction. 3. Adventure and
adventurers—Fiction. 4. Tree houses—Fiction. 5. Amazon River Valley—Fiction.]
I. Murdocca, Sal, ill. II. Title. III. Series: Osborne, Mary Pope. Magic tree house series ; #6.
PZ7.O81167Af 1995 [Fic]—dc20 95003237

Printed in the United States of America
69 68 67

This book has been officially leveled by using the F&P Text Level Gradient™ Leveling System.

Contents

Prologue

One summer day in Frog Creek, Pennsylvania, a mysterious tree house appeared in the woods.

Eight-year-old Jack and his seven-year-old sister, Annie, climbed into the tree house. They found it was filled with books.

Jack and Annie soon discovered that the tree house was magic. It could take them to the places in the books. All they had to do was to point to a picture and wish to go there.

Jack and Annie visited the times of

dinosaurs, knights, pyramids, pirates, and ninjas. Along the way, they discovered that the tree house belongs to Morgan le Fay. Morgan is a magical librarian from the time of King Arthur. She travels through time and space, gathering books.

In their last adventure, *Night of the Ninjas,* Jack and Annie learned that Morgan was under a spell. To free her, Jack and Annie have to find four special things.

In old Japan, they found the first thing: a moonstone.

Now Jack and Annie are about to set out in search of the second thing . . . in *Afternoon on the Amazon.*

1
Where's Peanut?

"Hurry, Jack!" shouted Annie.

Annie ran into the Frog Creek woods.

Jack followed her.

"It's still here!" Annie called.

Jack caught up with Annie. She stood beside a tall oak tree.

Jack looked up. The magic tree house was shining in the afternoon sunlight.

"We're coming, Peanut!" Annie called.

She grabbed the rope ladder and started up.

Jack followed. They climbed and climbed. Finally they climbed into the tree house.

"Peanut?" said Annie.

Jack took off his backpack. He looked around.

Sunlight slanted across a stack of books— books about ninjas, pirates, mummies, knights, and dinosaurs.

The letter M shimmered on the wooden floor. M for Morgan le Fay.

"I don't think Peanut's here," said Jack.

"I wonder where she is," said Annie.

"How do you know Peanut's a *she?*" asked Jack.

"I just know it," said Annie.

"Oh, brother," said Jack.

Squeak!

Annie laughed. "Look, Jack!"

A small pink sock was moving across the

floor. Yesterday Annie had turned her sock into a bed for Peanut.

Annie picked up the tiny lump.

Squeak.

A brown-and-white mouse peeked out of the sock. She looked from Annie to Jack with her big eyes.

Jack laughed. "Hi, Peanut," he said.

"Will you help us again today?" asked Annie.

In old Japan, Peanut had helped them when they'd gotten lost.

"We have to find three more things for Morgan," said Annie.

Jack pushed his glasses into place. "First we have to find a clue that tells us where to begin," he said.

"Guess what," said Annie.

"What?" said Jack.

"We don't have to look very far." She pointed at a corner of the tree house.

In the shadows was an open book.

2
Big Bugs

"Wow," said Jack, picking up the book. "The ninja book was open yesterday. Now this one. Who opened them?"

Jack closed the book and looked at the cover.

It showed a picture of a green forest. The trees were very tall and close together.

On the cover were the words *The Rain Forest*.

"Oh, wow," said Jack.

"Oh, no," said Annie.

"What's wrong?" said Jack.

"I learned about the rain forest in school," said Annie. "It's filled with big bugs and spiders."

"I know," said Jack. "Half of them have never even been named."

"It's creepy," said Annie.

"It's neat," said Jack. He wanted to take lots of notes in the rain forest. Maybe he could even name some unknown bugs.

"Neat? Yuk," said Annie. She shivered.

"I don't get it," said Jack. "You weren't afraid of dinosaurs."

"So?"

"You weren't afraid of the castle guards or the mummy's ghost."

"So?"

"You weren't afraid of pirates or ninjas."

"So?"

"You're not afraid of *really* scary things. But you're afraid of little bugs and spiders. That doesn't make sense."

"So?"

Jack sighed. "Listen," he said. "We have to go there. To help Morgan. That's why the book was left open."

"I know that," said Annie, frowning.

"Plus, the rain forests are being cut down," said Jack. "Don't you want to see one before it's too late?"

Annie took a deep breath and slowly nodded.

"Okay, then, let's go," said Jack.

He opened the book again. He pointed to a picture that showed blue sky, green leaves, and bright flowers.

"I wish we could go there," he said.

The wind began to blow.

Squeak.

"Stay here, Peanut," said Annie as she put the mouse in her pocket.

The wind picked up. The tree house started to spin.

Jack squeezed his eyes shut.

The wind was whistling now. The tree house was spinning faster and faster.

Then everything was still.

Absolutely still.

Wild sounds broke the silence.

Screeeeeech!

Buzzzzzzz!

Chirp! Chirp!

3
Yikes!

Jack opened his eyes.

The air was hot and steamy.

"It looks like we landed in some bushes," said Annie.

She was peeking out of the tree house window. Peanut was peeking out of Annie's pocket.

Jack peeked out of the tree house, too.

They had landed in a sea of shiny green leaves. Outside there were flowers, bright butterflies, and birds. Just as in the book.

"That's strange," said Jack. "I wonder

why we didn't land in a tree. The way we always do."

"I don't know," said Annie. "But let's hurry and find the thing for Morgan. So we can get back home before we meet any big bugs."

"Wait. This seems weird," said Jack. "I don't understand why we landed in bushes. I'd better read about this."

"Oh, come on," said Annie. "We don't even need the ladder. We can just climb out the window."

Annie put Peanut in her pocket. She stuck one leg out the window.

"Wait!" Jack grabbed Annie's other leg. He read:

**The rain forest is in three layers.
Thick treetops, often over 150 feet**

in the air, make up the top layer.
This is called the forest canopy.
Below the canopy is the under-
story, then the forest floor.

"Get back in here!" cried Jack. "We're
probably more than 150 feet above the
ground! In the forest canopy!"

"Yikes!" said Annie. She slipped back into the tree house.

"We *have* to use the ladder," said Jack. He got on his hands and knees. He moved leaves away from the hole in the floor. He looked down.

The ladder seemed to fall between the branches of a giant tree. But Jack couldn't see beyond that.

"I can't tell what's down there," he said. "Be careful."

Jack put the rain forest book in his backpack. Then he stepped onto the rope ladder.

He started down. Annie followed with Peanut in her pocket.

Jack pushed through the leaves.

He came to the understory below the canopy.

He looked down at the forest floor. It was very far away.

"Oh, man," whispered Jack.

This world was completely different from the one above the treetops.

Now that they were out of the sun, it was cooler. It was also damp and very quiet.

Jack shivered. It was the spookiest place he had ever seen.

4

Millions of Them!

Jack didn't move. He kept staring down at the forest floor.

"What's wrong?" Annie called from above.

Jack didn't answer.

"You don't see any giant spiders, do you?" Annie said.

"Well . . . no." Jack took a deep breath.

We have to keep going, he thought. We have to find the special thing for Morgan.

"No spiders. Nothing scary," Jack called. And he started down the ladder again.

Jack and Annie climbed down through the

understory. Finally they stepped onto the forest floor.

Only a few rays of light slanted through the gloom.

The trees were very, very tall and very wide. Vines and moss were hanging everywhere. The ground was covered with dead leaves.

"Before we do anything, I'd better check the book," said Jack.

He pulled out the rain forest book. He found a picture of the dark world under the treetops.

He read:

In the rain forest, many living creatures blend in with their surroundings. This is called camouflage.

"Oh, man," said Jack. He closed the book and looked around. "There're *tons* of creatures down here. We just can't see them."

"Really?" whispered Annie.

She and Jack peered around at the quiet forest. Jack felt unseen eyes watching them.

"Let's hurry and find the special thing," whispered Annie.

"How will we know when we find it?" Jack said.

"I think we'll just know," said Annie. She headed off through the gloom.

Jack followed. They crept between the huge trees and past hanging vines.

Annie stopped. "Wait—what's that?"

"What's what?"

"Listen—that weird sound."

Jack listened. He heard a crackling sound.

It sounded like a person walking over leaves.

Jack looked around. He didn't see anyone.

But the sound got louder.

Was it an animal? A giant bug? One that had never been named?

Just then the silent forest came alive.

Birds took off into the air. Frogs hopped over the leaves. Lizards ran up the tree trunks.

The weird noise grew louder and louder.

"Maybe the book explains it," said Jack. He opened the book. He found a picture of different animals running together. He read:

> When animals hear a crackling sound, they flee in panic. The sound means that 30 million flesh-eating army ants are marching through the dead leaves.

"It's army ants!" cried Jack. "Millions of them!"

"Where?" cried Annie.

Jack and Annie looked around wildly.

"There!" Annie pointed.

Army ants—millions and millions of them—were marching over the leaves!

"Run to the tree house!" cried Annie.

"Where is it?" said Jack, whirling around. All the trees looked the same. Where was the rope ladder?

"Just run!" cried Annie.

Jack and Annie took off.

They ran over the dead leaves.

They ran between wide tree trunks.

They ran past the hanging vines and mosses.

They climbed over thick roots.

Jack saw a clearing ahead. It was filled with sunlight.

"That way!" he cried.

Jack and Annie hurried toward the light. They pushed their way through the bushes.

They burst onto the bank of a river.

They stared at the slow-moving brown water.

"Do you think the ants will come this way?" Annie said, panting.

"I don't know," said Jack. "But if we wade a few feet into the river, we're safe. The ants won't go into the water. Come on."

"Look!" said Annie.

She pointed to a big log rocking at the edge of the river. The inside of the log was dug out.

"It looks like a canoe," said Jack. He listened to the crackling sound in the distance. "Let's get in it. Quick!"

Jack shoved the book into his backpack. Then he and Annie carefully climbed into the dug-out log.

Annie leaned out of it. She pushed away from the bank with her hands.

"Wait!" said Jack. "We don't have paddles!"

"Oops," said Annie.

The canoe started moving slowly down the muddy river.

5
Pretty Fish

Squeak.

Annie patted the little mouse in her pocket.

"It's okay, Peanut. The ants can't get us in the river. We're safe," she said.

"Maybe safe from the ants," said Jack. "But where is this canoe going?"

Jack and Annie stared at the river. Branches spread over the water. Vines and mosses hung down from them.

"We'd better look this up," said Jack. He pulled the rain forest book out of his backpack and flipped through it.

Soon he found a picture of a river. He read:

> **The Amazon River stretches over 4,000 miles from the mountains of Peru, across Brazil, to the Atlantic Ocean. The river basin contains over half of the rain forests in the world.**

Jack looked at Annie. "We're on the Amazon River," he said. "It's more than four thousand miles long!"

"Wow," Annie whispered. She looked at the river. She trailed her hand through the water.

"I have to make some notes—" Jack said. He pulled his notebook out of his pack. He wrote:

The Amazon rain forest is

"Jack, look at those pretty fish with the teeth," said Annie.

"What?" Jack glanced up from his writing.

Annie was pointing at some blue fish swimming near the boat. The fish had red bellies and razor-sharp teeth.

"Watch it!" cried Jack. "Those aren't pretty fish. They're piranhas! They'll eat anything! Even people!"

"Yikes," whispered Annie.

"We better get back on shore," said Jack, putting the books in his backpack.

"How?" said Annie. "We can't go in the water now. And we don't have any paddles."

Jack tried to stay calm. "We need a plan," he said.

Jack stared at the river. The canoe would soon float under some vines.

"I'll grab a vine," said Jack. "And pull us to shore."

"Good idea," said Annie.

As they glided under the branches, Jack stood up.

The canoe rocked. He nearly fell out.

"Balance the canoe," said Jack.

Annie leaned to one side. Jack reached—he missed!

The canoe floated under more branches.

Jack reached for another thick vine.

He grabbed it!

It was cold and scaly. It wiggled and jerked!

"*Ahhh!*" Jack screamed and fell back into the canoe.

The vine was alive!

It was a long green snake!

The snake fell from the trcc. It splashed into the water and swam away.

"Oh, man," said Jack.

He and Annie stared in horror at each other.

"What now?" said Annie, making a face.

"Well . . ." Jack looked at the river. There were no vines up ahead. But there was a big branch floating on the water.

"Grab that branch near you," said Jack. "Maybe we can use it for a paddle."

The canoe floated closer to the branch. Annie reached for it.

Suddenly the branch rose into the air!

It was a *crocodile!*

"Help!" screamed Annie, and she fell back into the canoe.

The crocodile opened and closed its huge, long jaws. Then it moved past the canoe and swam up the river.

"Oh, man," whispered Jack.

A screeching sound split the air.

Jack and Annie jumped.

"Help!" said Jack.

He expected to see another terrible creature.

But all he saw was a small brown monkey, hanging by its tail from a tree.

6
Monkey Trouble

Squeak! Squeak! Peanut poked her head out from Annie's pocket. She seemed to be yelling at the monkey.

"Don't worry, Peanut," said Annie. "He's just a little monkey. He won't hurt us."

But suddenly the monkey grabbed a big red fruit hanging from the tree. He hurled it at the canoe.

"Watch it!" shouted Jack.

The fruit fell into the water with a splash.

The monkey screeched even louder.

He grabbed another fruit.

"Don't throw things at us!" shouted Annie.

But the monkey hurled the red fruit right at them.

Jack and Annie ducked again. And the fruit splashed into the water.

"Stop that!" Annie shouted.

But the monkey only waved his arms and screeched again.

"Oh, brother," said Jack. "I don't believe this."

The monkey grabbed a third fruit and hurled it at Jack and Annie. It landed inside the canoe with a thump.

Annie grabbed the fruit. She stood up and threw it back at the monkey.

She missed. The canoe rocked. Annie almost fell out.

The monkey screeched even louder.

"Go away!" Annie shouted. "You're the meanest thing in the world!"

The monkey stopped screeching.

He looked at Annie. Then he swung away. Into the forest.

"I think I hurt his feelings," said Annie.

"Who cares?" said Jack. "He shouldn't throw things."

"Uh-oh," said Annie. "It's raining now."

"What?" Jack looked up. A raindrop hit him in the eye.

"Oh, no. I don't believe this," Jack said.

"What'd you expect?" said Annie. "It *is* the *rain* forest."

A gust of wind blew the canoe.

Thunder rolled in the sky.

"A river's a bad place to be in a storm,"

said Jack. "We have to get back to shore. Right now."

"But how?" said Annie. "We can't wade or swim. The piranhas, the snake, and the crocodile will get us."

Screeching split the air again.

"Oh, no," said Jack. The bratty monkey was back.

This time, the monkey was pointing a long stick at the canoe.

Jack crouched down. Was the monkey going to hurl the stick at them? Like a spear?

Annie jumped up and faced the monkey.

"Watch it! He's nuts," said Jack.

But the monkey just stared at Annie. And Annie just stared back at him.

After a long moment, the monkey seemed to smile.

Annie smiled back.

"What's going on?" said Jack.

"He wants to help us," Annie said.

"Help us how?" said Jack.

The monkey held out the long stick.

Annie grabbed the other end.

The monkey pulled on the stick. The canoe started floating toward him.

The monkey pulled the canoe all the way to the bank of the river.

7

Freeze!

Jack and Annie jumped out of the canoe.

The rain was starting to fall harder.

The monkey took off. He swung from tree to tree, heading up the riverbank.

He screeched and beckoned to Jack and Annie.

"He wants us to follow him!" said Annie.

"No! We have to find the special thing. Then go home!" said Jack.

"He wants to help us!" said Annie. She took off after the monkey.

The two of them vanished into the rain forest.

"Annie!"

Thunder shook the sky.

"Oh, brother," said Jack.

He dashed after Annie and the monkey. Into the dark forest.

The forest seemed surprisingly dry.

Jack looked up. It was still raining. But the treetops acted like a huge umbrella.

"Annie?" called Jack.

"Jack! Jack!" cried Annie.

"Where are you?"

"Here!"

Jack hurried in the direction of Annie's voice.

Soon he found the monkey. He was screeching and swinging from a tree.

Annie was kneeling on the forest floor. She was playing with an animal that looked like a giant kitten.

"What's that?" Jack said.

"I don't know, but I love it!" said Annie.

Annie batted the animal's paws. It had gold fur and black spots.

"I'd better find out what it is," said Jack. He pulled out the rain forest book and flipped through it.

"Oh, it's so cute," said Annie.

Jack found a picture of an animal with gold fur and black spots. He read:

The jaguar is the biggest predator in the western hemisphere.

"Forget cute," Jack said. "That must be a baby jaguar. It's going to grow up and be the biggest predator in—"

"What's a predator?" asked Annie.

GRRR! There was a terrible growl.

Jack whirled around.

The mother jaguar was coming out from behind a tree. She was creeping over the dead leaves—*right toward Annie.*

"Freeze!" whispered Jack.

Annie froze. But the jaguar kept moving slowly toward her.

"Help," said Jack weakly.

Suddenly the monkey swooped down from his tree. He grabbed the jaguar's tail!

The cat roared and spun around.

Annie jumped up.

The monkey pulled the jaguar's tail again. Then he let go and took off.

The jaguar sprang after him.

"Run, Annie!" cried Jack.

Jack and Annie took off through the rain forest. They ran for their lives!

8
Vampire Bats?

"Wait—" said Jack, panting. "I think we got away."

Jack and Annie stopped running and caught their breath.

"Where are we?" said Jack.

"Where's the monkey?" said Annie, looking back at the forest. "Do you think the jaguar caught him?"

"No, monkeys are fast," said Jack.

Of course, jaguars are fast, too, Jack thought. But he didn't want to tell Annie that.

"I hope he's okay," said Annie.

Squeak. Peanut peeked out of Annie's pocket.

"Peanut! I almost forgot you!" said Annie. "Are you okay?"

The mouse just stared at Annie with her big eyes.

"She looks scared," said Jack. "Poor Peanut."

"Poor monkey," said Annie. She looked around at the forest.

"We'd better check the book," Jack said.

He pulled out the book. He turned the pages, searching for help.

He stopped at a picture of a scary creature.

"Oh, man. What's this?" he said.

Jack read the writing below the picture. It said:

**Vampire bats live in the Amazon
rain forest. At night, they quietly
bite their victims and suck their
blood.**

"Vampire bats?" said Jack. He felt faint.

"Vampire bats?" said Annie.

Jack nodded. "After dark."

Annie and Jack looked around. The rain forest seemed to be getting even darker.

"Yikes," said Annie. She looked at Jack. "Maybe we should go home."

Jack nodded. For once he agreed with her.

"But what about our mission?" said Annie. "What about Morgan?"

"We'll come back," said Jack. "We'll have to be prepared."

"So we'll come back tomorrow?" Annie asked.

"Right. Now which way is the tree house?" said Jack.

"This way," said Annie, pointing.

"That way," said Jack, pointing in the opposite direction.

They looked at each other. "We're lost," they said together.

Squeak.

"Don't worry, Peanut." Annie started to pat the mouse again. But then she stopped.

Squeak. Squeak. Squeak.

"Jack, I think Peanut wants to help us," said Annie.

"How?"

"The way she helped us in the time of ninjas—"

Annie placed the mouse on the leafy forest floor. "Take us to the tree house, Peanut."

The mouse took off.

"Where'd she go?" said Annie. "I don't see her!"

"There!" said Jack. He pointed to leaves rustling on the ground.

A streak of white passed over the leaves.

"Yes, there!" said Annie.

Jack and Annie followed the moving leaves. The streak of white appeared. And disappeared.

Suddenly Jack stopped.

The forest floor was still. There was no sign of Peanut.

"Where is she?" asked Jack.

He kept staring at the ground.

"Jack!"

Jack glanced around. Annie was standing on the other side of a nearby tree. She was pointing up.

Jack looked up.

The tree house.

"Oh, whew," Jack said softly.

"She saved us again," said Annie. "She's running up the ladder. All by herself. Look."

Annie pointed at the rope ladder.

Peanut was climbing up one of the ropes.

"Let's go," Jack said.

Annie started up the ladder. Then Jack.

They followed Peanut all the way up to the canopy of the rain forest.

9
The Thing

Jack and Annie climbed into the tree house.

Peanut was sitting on a stack of books.

Annie patted Peanut's little head. "Thanks," she said softly.

"I have to write some notes about the rain forest," said Jack. "You find the Pennsylvania book."

Annie began searching for the Pennsylvania book—the book that always took them home.

Jack pulled out his notebook.

He had wanted to take lots of notes here. But all he'd written so far was:

The Amazon rain forest is

"It's not here!" said Annie.

"What?" Jack looked up. He glanced around the tree house.

Annie was right. The Pennsylvania book was nowhere in sight.

"Was it here before we left home?" said Jack.

"I don't remember," said Annie.

"Oh, man," said Jack. "Now we can't get back to Frog Creek."

"That means we'll be here when the vampire bats come out," said Annie.

Something came flying through the tree house window.

"Ahhh!" Jack and Annie hid their heads.

Thud.

Something hit the floor. A red fruit.

Jack looked up. The monkey was sitting in the window. His head was cocked to one side. He seemed to be grinning at them.

"You're safe!" said Annie.

"Thanks for saving us," said Jack.

The monkey just grinned.

"I have just one question," said Annie. She pointed at the fruit. "Why do you keep throwing those at us?"

The monkey grabbed the fruit.

"No! Don't throw it!" said Jack. He ducked.

But the monkey didn't throw the fruit.

He held it out to Annie. He moved his lips as if he were trying to say something.

Annie stared into the monkey's eyes. He moved his lips again.

"Wow," Annie said softly. "I understand now."

"Understand what?" said Jack.

Annie took the fruit from the monkey. "This is it," she said. "The *thing* we need."

"What thing?" said Jack.

"One of the special things we're supposed to find for Morgan," Annie said. "To free her from the spell."

"Are you sure?" said Jack.

Before Annie could answer, Jack saw the Pennsylvania book. "Look! Our book!" he said, pointing.

"We found the thing. And now we can see the book," said Annie. "That's the way it works, remember?"

Jack nodded. Now he remembered. The ninja master said they wouldn't be able to find the Pennsylvania book until they had found what they were looking for.

The monkey screeched with laughter.

Jack and Annie looked at him. He was clapping his hands together.

Annie laughed with him. "How did you know to give this to us?" she said. "Who told you to do that?"

The monkey just waved at Jack and Annie. Then he turned and swung away out of the tree house.

"Wait!" said Jack, looking out the window.

Too late.

The monkey was gone. He had vanished below the treetops.

"Good-bye!" called Annie.

A happy screech came from the mysterious world below.

Jack sighed. He picked up his notebook again. He looked at his writing:

The Amazon vain forest is

He had to write *something* before they left. He quickly added—

amazing

Jack put away his notebook. Annie picked up the Pennsylvania book.

"Now it's really time to leave," she said.

She turned to the picture of the Frog Creek woods. "I wish we could go there," she said, pointing at the picture.

The wind started to blow.

The leaves began to tremble.

The tree house began to spin.

It spun faster and faster.

Then everything was still.

Absolutely still.

10
Halfway There

Squeak.

Jack opened his eyes. Peanut was on the tree house windowsill.

"We're home," said Annie.

Jack breathed a sigh of relief.

Annie held the fruit up to the afternoon light.

"What exactly *is* this?" she asked.

"Maybe it's in the book," Jack answered.

He pulled out the rain forest book. He flipped through the pages. He came to a picture of the red fruit.

"Here it is!" he said. He read out loud:

"The mango has a sweet taste like that of a peach."

"Mango? Hmmm," said Annie. She brought the fruit close to her lips.

"Hey!" said Jack, grabbing the mango from her. "We have to put it with the moon-stone."

Jack placed the mango on the M carved into the floor. Next to the clear moonstone.

"Moonstone . . . mango," whispered Annie. It sounded like a spell.

"We're halfway there," said Jack. "Two more to go."

"Then we can free you, Morgan!" Annie called, as if Morgan were nearby.

"How do you know she can hear you?" said Jack.

"I just feel it," Annie said.

"Oh, brother," said Jack. He needed more proof than that.

Squeak. Peanut was looking at Jack and Annie.

"We have to leave you now," Jack said to the mouse.

Squeak.

"Can't we take her with us?" said Annie.

"No," said Jack. "Mom won't let us keep a mouse in the house. She doesn't like mice, remember?"

"How could anyone *not* like a mouse?" said Annie.

Jack smiled. "How could anyone not like a spider?" he said.

"That's different." Annie patted Peanut's head. "Bye," she said. "Wait for us here. We'll be back tomorrow."

Jack patted the mouse, too. "Bye, Peanut. Thanks for your help," he said.

Squeak.

Jack put the rain forest book on top of the book about ninjas.

Then he pulled on his backpack. And he and Annie left the tree house.

They climbed down the rope ladder. They stepped onto the ground.

They started walking through the Frog Creek woods.

Leaf shadows danced in the light.

A bird called out.

These woods are very different from the rain forest, Jack thought.

"There're no jaguars or army ants here," he said. "No little monkeys."

"You know, that monkey was never being mean," said Annie. "He was just trying to give us the mango."

"I know. Actually, nothing was being *mean*," said Jack. "The army ants were just marching. That's what army ants do."

"The piranhas were just being piranhas," said Annie.

"The snake was just being a snake," said Jack.

"The crocodile was just being a crocodile," said Annie.

"The jaguar was just taking care of her baby," said Jack.

Annie shuddered. "I still don't love bugs," she said.

"You don't have to *love* them," said Jack.

"Just leave them alone. And they won't bother you."

In fact, that's true about the whole rain forest, Jack thought. Everyone should just leave it all alone.

"Who cares if the bugs don't have names?" he said softly. "*They* know who they are."

Jack and Annie stepped out of the Frog Creek woods.

They started walking up their street. It was lit with a golden light.

"Race you!" said Annie.

They took off running.

They ran across their yard.

They raced up their steps.

"Safe!" they shouted together, tagging their front door.

Here's a special preview of

Magic Tree House® Fact Tracker

Rain Forests

After their adventure on the Amazon,
Jack and Annie wanted to know more about
rain forests. Track the facts with them!

Available now!

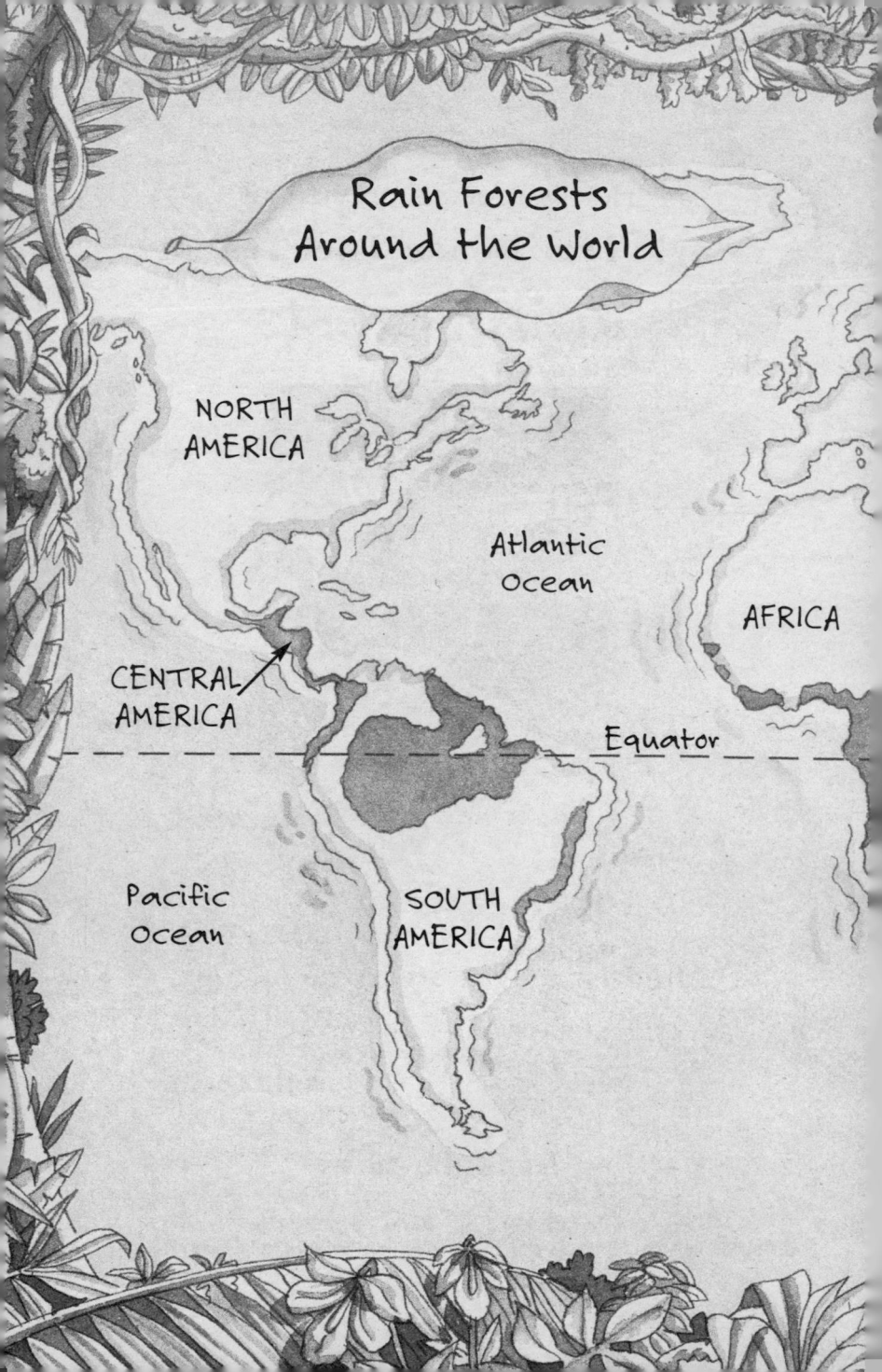

Rain Forests Around the World

NORTH AMERICA

Atlantic Ocean

AFRICA

CENTRAL AMERICA

Equator

Pacific Ocean

SOUTH AMERICA

EUROPE

ASIA

Mediterranean Sea

Madagascar

Borneo

Celebes

New Guinea

Indian Ocean

AUSTRALIA

N

= Tropical Rain Forests

Growing Up in the Rain Forest

Rain forest children learn a lot growing up in the forest. Here are some of their lessons:

1. *What to eat.*

Some rain forest plants and animals are poisonous. Rain forest children learn what's good to eat, and what's dangerous.

2. *How to hunt, gather, and cook.*

Girls learn to find good plants to eat and how to cook them.

Boys learn to hunt animals with spears, bows and arrows, and nets.

3. *How to have fun!*

Most rain forest people tell stories together at the end of the day. They sometimes dance and sing. Rain forest children learn the dances and songs and stories from their parents and other relatives.

TABLE OF CONTENTS

Chapter Four - The Gold Pan & How to Use It

Chapter Five - Testing for "Grade"

Chapter Six - "Sniping for Gold"

Chapter Seven - Processing Auriferous Gravel

Chapter Eight - The Specialties

Chapter Nine - Prospecting as a Business

Chapter Ten - Physical Fitness and Prospecting

Appendix

PROSPECTING & SMALL-SCALE MINING

Foreword

There is great romance and excitement surrounding the business of prospecting, because of the elements of 'luck' and 'chance' that are associated with it. No great outlay of cash is required to get started, yet the potential exists for fabulous monetary rewards. The thrill of a discovery is immeasurable, whether it is a small pocket of gold nuggets worth just a few hundred dollars, or the proverbial million-dollar 'glory-hole'.

Geologists estimate that at least 90% of the earth's accessible gold deposits remain intact, just waiting to be found. Today, prospectors and small-scale miners are making amazing discoveries with the aid of advanced gold pans and sluices, metal detectors, and a variety of portable, powered recovery systems

Many amateur and week-end prospectors develop a secondary source of income from their hobby, and a surprising number become full-time exploration professionals or go on to operate their own commercial mining projects.

There are other important rewards as well, such as the enjoyment of physical exercise, intellectual stimulation, and the peace and tranquillity of the Great Outdoors. All of this, plus the potential for monetary profit is possible with only a modest investment in equipment, coupled with a genuine desire to develop new skills and knowledge.

Introduction

This manual has been prepared with just one idea in mind - to provide information and ideas you can use to locate significant amounts of gold and other valuable minerals. To be sure, as a week-end hobby prospecting is an immensely rewarding experience in itself. But let's face it, for fun or for profit, the 'Big Thrill' is all in the discovery.

With this book, you too can learn the basic skills of prospecting. You will learn how to prepare for successful gold-panning field trips, so as to optimize your chances of quickly finding a workable gold deposit. With perseverance and a little good luck your sampling efforts will eventually be rewarded with additional worthwhile 'finds', and you will begin to achieve a degree of consistency in your gold-hunting activities. This manual explains how to go about evaluating the paystreaks you find, and discusses the viability of the various portable extraction systems used for the different types of deposits you may encounter.

The beginner need not be overwhelmed by the wide scope and complexity of some of the material being presented. The basic skills, such as panning and sniping, will serve you well enough initially, then you can expand your repertoire from there. You certainly don't need an advanced course in geophysics in order to put some gold in your pocket. On the other hand, as some of my more experienced readers can attest, in the prospecting business research and learning rarely goes unrewarded, and there is a true percentage in keeping abreast of the latest techniques and equipment.

That sums up my advice - the rest is up to you. Learn the basics and **find some gold!** Try to be as observant and 'in-tune' with your surroundings as possible, and always keep an open mind as to the wider possibilities. Most of all, have fun. Prospecting is a sort of real-life hide-and-seek game for adults - and the prize is definitely better than a lollipop.

> The best of luck to you.
> See you on the Gold Trail!

Crude placer sluice, Peace River, 1926

The gravel bars containing fine gold supported hundreds of miners during its heyday, but the handmade equipment in use at the time had very poor efficiency (As low as 20%). Today, only a handful of prospectors continue in the tradition, but some of them do very well in places. Gas-powered hi-banker sluices may attain recovery rates of 90% or more.

Average returns of the day were around two or three pennyweight (dwt.), or just under one-quarter troy ounce. With a modern high-performance sluicing system or dredge, today's gold-hunter can do at least as well. With experience, the "Ounce-a-Day" standard used by professionals can be consistently reached.

Modern weekend prospector working placer deposit with a Keene Back Pack Dredge. The Model 2004 (2inch) weighs only 45 lbs, yet with 2-hp it produces 90 gallons per minute and pressure to a 132 ft head. This and other fine dredges are listed in the catalog.

xii

Acknowledgements

For me, the path to becoming a professional prospector has been a rocky one. There were times when, stranded at trails end and broke, I began to question my sanity; "Just what do I think I'm doing on this Godforsaken mountainside, anyway?" At such times a kindly word of encouragement is golden, and I now realize that the treasure I am seeking isn't in the ground - but in all the wonderful souls I have met along the way.

Profound thanks to my former wife, Sandra, who was there at the beginning. An at-heart city girl, she proved herself amazingly adaptable to the outdoor lifestyle. She retained her composure in a face-to-face encounter with a grizzly bear. Another time, in a daring cable-crossing of a precipitous canyon, she calmly disentangled a snagged cable, while dangling suspended, forty feet above a raging mountain torrent. Beautiful and gutsy!

Thanks to Dave McCracken, of Pro-Mack Mining, for encouraging me to get started in gold dredging all those years ago.

Thanks also to Dennis Lieutard, of the Mineral Titles Division, for his fervent support of grassroots prospecting in British Columbia. Mr.Lieutard is a rare breed in officialdom; he tells it like it is whether you like it or not.

Thank you to Bill Barlee, for pointing me in the right direction when I first arrived in B.C. to begin prospecting.

Special appreciation goes to Sid Burget, for his confidence in the Gold Trails concept, and for the long hours of hard work he puts into it to ensure it's success. Thanks as well to Shirley Burget, Sid's wife, for her encouragement and her humor, not to mention that terrific homemade soup she feeds us to sustain us while writing this second edition.

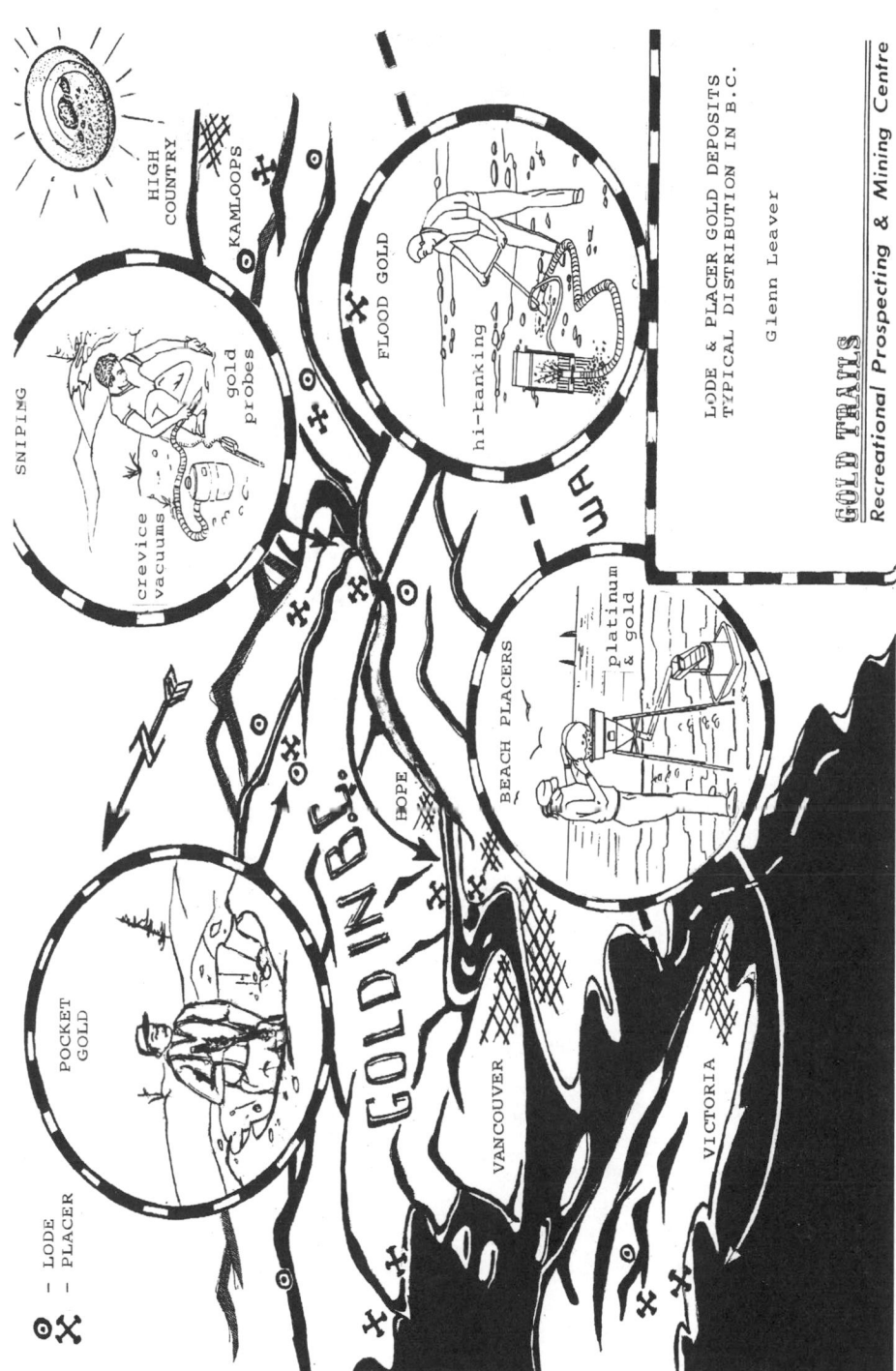

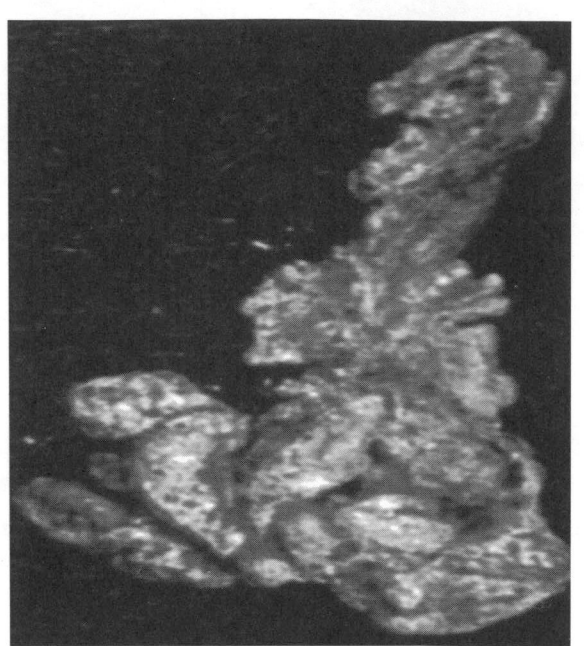

A delicately-formed specimen of crystalline gold, showing *dendritic* characteristics. Early Native American and Egyptian cultures were quick to grasp the connection between the awesome forces which shape our everyday, natural lives and the gift of gold that perpetually washes out of remote mountain areas.

Birthplace of the stars. Iron-nickel meteorites may be part of the puzzle, as some of them have been found to contain high levels of iridium, (a platinum-group metal), and other exotic minerals.

I am intrigued by the fact that the current spate of Mars Global Explorer and Mars Lander missions all have geology experiments on board as scientists are convinced Mars will turn out to be a treasure-trove of mineral wealth. Perhaps the new pioneers are already out there among my younger readers - the next generation of pioneering Martian prospectors, preparing for a new Gold Rush on the High Frontier!

Chapter One

GEOLOGICAL THEORY

"Tears of the Sun" - The Cosmic Connection

According to the Big Bang theory of the creation of the universe, about 14 billion years ago a giant primordial fireball occurred. The fantastic explosion that resulted created an ever-expanding cloud of superheated gasses, which condensed over time into huge galactic nebulae, where the first stars, or 'protostars', were formed. In the cores of those birth stars, densities and temperatures rose under gravitational collapse, eventually igniting another sequence of nuclear chain reactions, resulting in the formation of a second generation of stars, of which Sol, our own sun, is one.

Astrophysicists now have plenty of evidence that all of the heavier elements, including gold, platinum, and the radioactive isotopes, were *transmuted* or 'cooked' from the lighter elements by the tremendous nuclear forces which existed at the very core of exploding stars. Today, we are in the latter stage of this phase, but the process is still going on, and the results of it can be viewed in the night sky as supernova, the scattered remains of exploding stars. This theory accounts for the relatively high concentrations of heavy metals in our own particular region of the galaxy, and it offers us a clue as to why many of the meteorites which fall to earth are found to have very high levels of heavy metals such as iron, nickel, platinum and iridium.

Planetary Mechanics

Heavenly bodies which do not become large enough to burst into nuclear starlight are left circling a star as a part of a planetary system, (solar system). Originally formed from swirling masses of super-hot cosmic dust, the planets have cooled and condensed over time, as they gradually radiate their inner heat off into the vacuum of space. In the case of the larger planets - Saturn and Jupiter, for instance, this process is extremely slow. The 'gas giants' therefore, continue to have very high core temperatures, and are still in a molten state. Small spheres, on the other hand, such as Mercury or our own moon, have long since lost all of their inner heat, resulting in a rocky, stable mass devoid of any inner seismic activity. In the middle are medium-size planets like Venus and Earth, which have retained a molten core, but whose surface has cooled and solidified into a hard, rocky crust. Mars is geologically interesting because, although it appears to no longer have any seismic activity, it's surface is covered with very recent, and very dramatic, volcanic features. This indicates that the 'Red Planet' has only just completed that phase of it's life-cycle, (and maybe gives a hint as to what's in store for us in our own near geologic future).

Plate Tectonics

A useful analogy to the earth is a cook-pot containing a soup or broth. With heat applied, both the interior and the surface of the soup is in a liquid state as it simmers and sputters away. But then, when the pot is removed from the source of heat, something very interesting begins to occur: As the surface cools it begins to congeal, but this doesn't happen all at once. First, there were only a few small patches that have skimmed over. As it cools further, these patches grow in size until eventually, they cover the entire surface. If you look closely, you will observe that small ridges have formed at the margins where the individual patches have floated together.

The earth is similar to a cook-pot in that its internal heat generates convection currents, which cause a slight movement, or *drift* of the skim patches floating on the surface. In geological terms, the earth's "skim patches" are called *tectonic plates*, and their movement on the surface is referred to as *continental drift*. Chains of mountain ranges, or *cordillera* are the equivalent of the ridges we observed. These are formed by a process of *subduction* and *uplift*, where the edge of one moving plate slides under the edge of another, causing it to buckle and raise up.

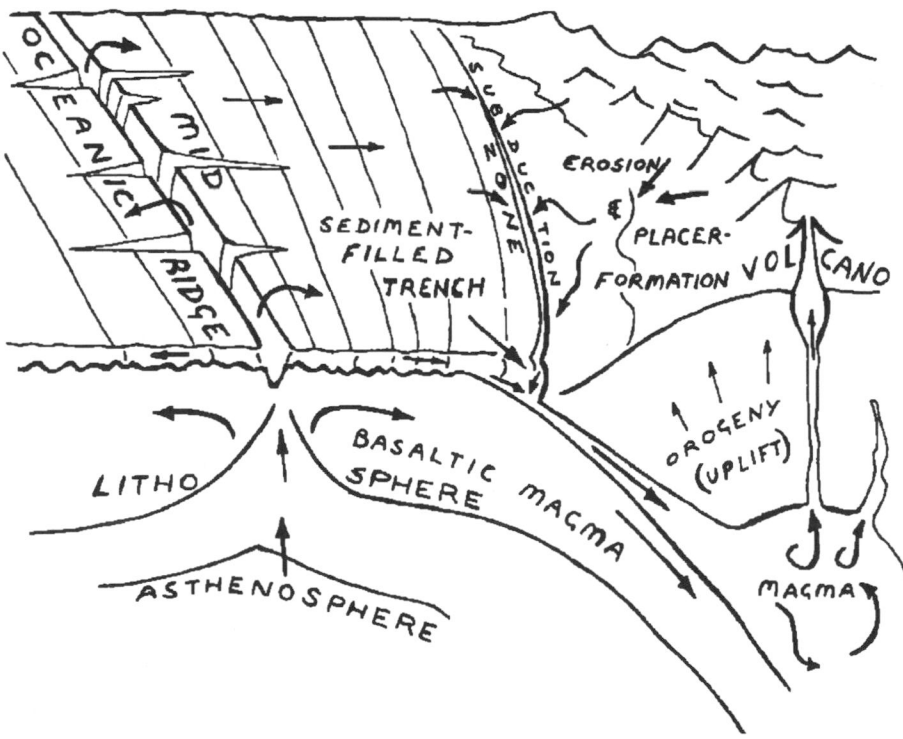

The Formation of Mineral Deposits

Prospectors and geologists need to know about plate tectonics because this process has everything to do with the formation and distribution of mineralized areas.

The margins of the earth's tectonic plates are denoted by the so-called "ring-of-fire" of volcanic activity, and are the weakest areas of the earth's outer crust. Under extreme pressure from below, hot, mineral-bearing solutions are forced upwards, where they impregnate faults and fissures all along the weakened margins, resulting in the formation of valuable bodies of mineral ore at those locations. Places where such orebodies have formed are described variously as gold-belts, silver-belts, and so on, depending on which minerals are predominant.

Giant bodies of molten rock, called *gyres*, or *magmatic chambers*, are continually forming deep below the earth's outer shell. They are forced upwards under intense pressure towards the surface, where they intrude into the thinner and weaker tectonic margins. Cooling as it nears the surface, the magma forms into large bodies of dense, magmatic rock called *plutons*. All along the contact zone, where magmatic rock has intruded and chemically altered the overlying rocks, numerous faults and fissures are opened up. Molten, caustic solutions further decompose the original rock material and, upon their cooling and recrystallization, the mineral lode contained within the solution replaces the material that was originally present. Deposits of this type are described as *replacement* or *vein-type* deposits. Over time, erosional forces break down the less resistant surrounding rock (*country rock*), leaving the pluton exposed and accessible. Across Canada and the United States, most of the large plutons, and many of the smaller ones, have been well mapped and aeromagnetically surveyed, presenting a veritable wellspring of opportunity to the knowledgeable prospector.

4

Glenn's Golden Rule No. 1...

"Gold Is Where You Find It"

This means that, while geological theory can help you to identify local targets to prospect, by itself it can never actually pinpoint a pocket or a paystreak for you, because there are just too many variables to take into account. Actually, this is good news if you're like me and would rather be out in the field instead of spending hours in a musty library. In my experience the people who get out there and just do it are the ones who consistently get good results, even if they don't have an inkling of the geological theory involved.

So what are you waiting for? Grab a gold pan and head for the hills. And don't worry - the theory will catch up with you later.

GOLD TRAILS

Recreational Prospecting & Mining Center

Catalog Items

Gold Trails Catalog Items are featured at appropriate places throughout this manual. All items except "Special Order" items are stocked for immediate shipment. Price list and shipping information are located at the end of this book

The *Gold Trails* Pledge..."*Gold Trails* pledges to deliver only professional, top-of-the-line products and equipment which are *proven successful* in the location and recovery of precious metals."

Video Catalog Items:

GT-V31 (60 min.) Exploring Ancient Placer Deposits

GT-V36 (60 min.) Recovering Fine Gold From Beach Placers

The Formation of Gold Deposits

It appears that precious metals are most commonly taken up and transported in solutions of molten silica, deep inside the earth. This is why gold is usually found in association with the milky-white, translucent mineral *quartz,* which is composed of crystallized silica. However (and this is very important) while it is true that gold is nearly always formed in association with quartz, it does not follow that quartz always contains gold. In fact, most quartz veins are devoid of any minerals at all. It seems that, in order for gold to occur, there have to be some additional, special conditions present during its formation. The principle factor is thought to be the presence of large amounts of iron. For some reason which is still not fully understood, the presence of a body of iron creates an electronic, or electro-magnetic effect, which causes gold to precipitate out of its solution. The best examples of this *electronic effect* are the exquisitely-formed specimens of crystalline gold, telluride gold, and electrum (a silver-gold alloy). Specimens of this type are sometimes referred to as "electronic gold", and are very beautiful indeed.

In applying these theories to the practical search for rich deposits of gold-bearing ore, the field prospector is advised to seek out strongly-formed quartz structures which intrude or intersect an iron dike or some other magnetite-rich rock formation. If you come across that situation, chances are you're on to something pretty good!

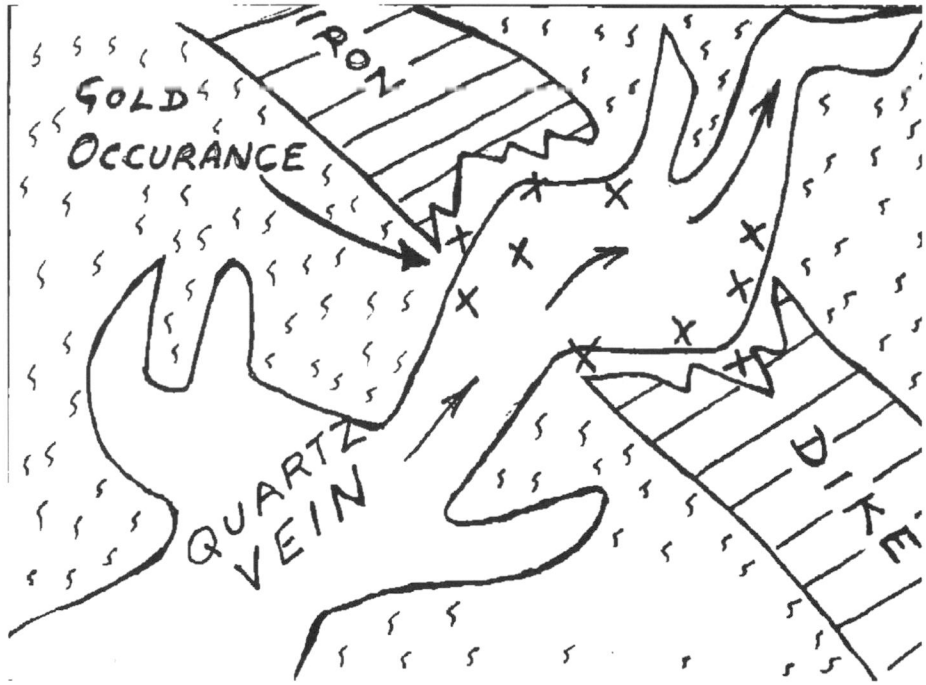

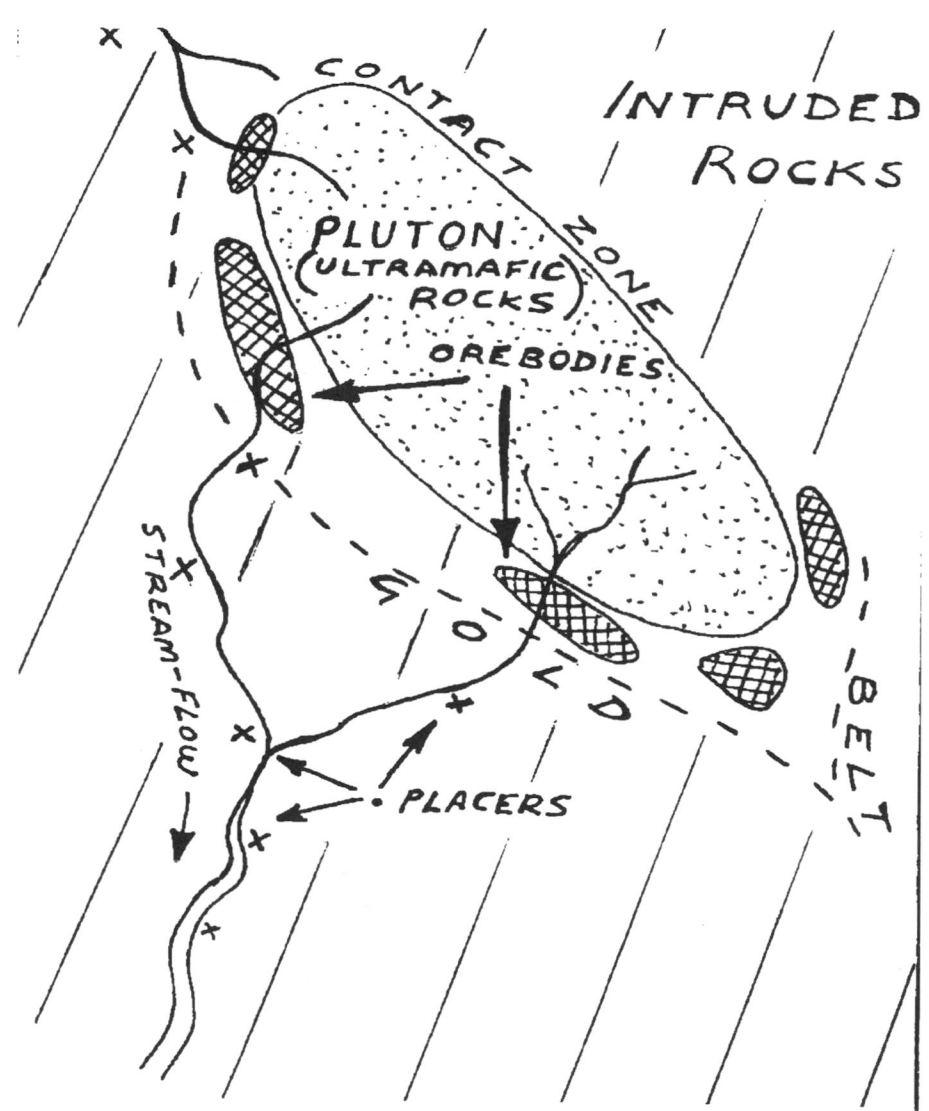

Typical distribution of replacement-vein type deposits and derived placers

Introduction to Mineralogy

If your intention is strictly to locate gold nuggets, all you really need to know is whether or not the creek or stream you intend to prospect has, at some point upstream, "cut-through" a mineral-bearing *host-rock* formation. However, if you decide to prospect for the lode deposits themselves, you can begin by acquainting yourself with what the various types of host rocks and *indicator minerals* look like by obtaining a "Rock and Mineral Sample Set". These are available from **Gold Trails** for just a few dollars, or you might try the Yukon and BC Chamber of Mines, listed in the appendix.

Except for native gold and platinum, which will be described later, mineral identification is something for future research at the library. But since you're going to be in gold country anyway, it's not such a bad idea to get in the habit of rock bashing whenever you encounter interesting looking outcroppings. To start your own mineral collection, concentrate your efforts around rusty, iron-rich zones that have metallic, shiny mineral inclusions. Always label these specimens carefully so that you'll be able to easily re-locate the occurrence if it turns out to be incredibly rich.

Catalog Items

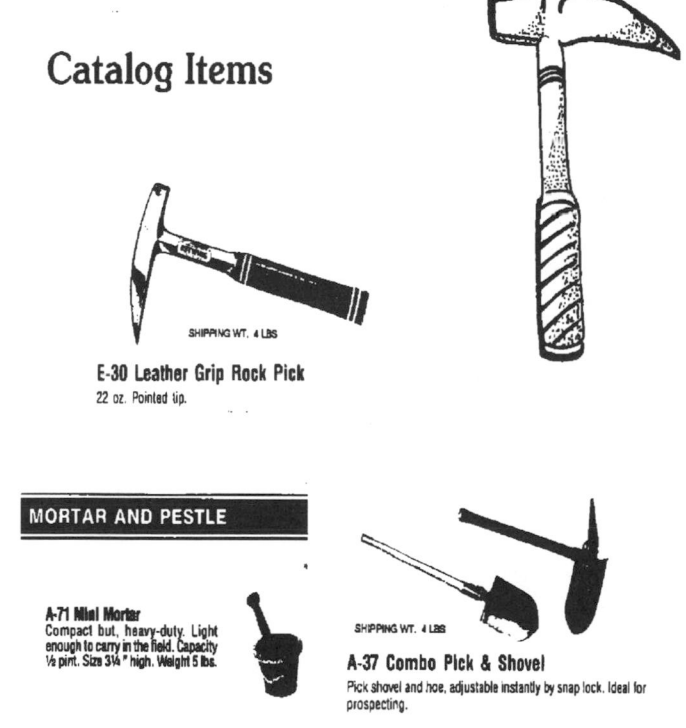

SHIPPING WT. 4 LBS

E-30 Leather Grip Rock Pick
22 oz. Pointed tip.

MORTAR AND PESTLE

A-71 Mial Mortar
Compact but, heavy-duty. Light enough to carry in the field. Capacity ½ pint. Size 3¼ " high. Weight 5 lbs.

SHIPPING WT. 4 LBS

A-37 Combo Pick & Shovel
Pick shovel and hoe, adjustable instantly by snap lock. Ideal for prospecting.

8

"THE ANCIENT RIVER OF GOLD"
by RAYMOND J. WALLACE

FROM THE BITTER COLDS OF ALASKA TO THE TOWERING ANDES OF SOUTH AMERICA the fabulously rich, gold laden, prehistoric, Ancient River of Gold that produced untold millions for the "Forty Niners" is described in easy to read large print.

Less than 100 miles of the Ancient Rivers were discovered and worked by the original "Forty Niners". Due to shifts and faulting in the earth's surface hundreds of miles lie yet undiscovered to the present day prospector. Since the days of the "Forty Niner" erosion has uncovered traces of these prehistoric rivers. With the aid of this book you will at least have the knowledge of where to search for Ancient streams. Once located, whether it be upon a mountain top or the floor of a barren desert, the Ancient River of Gold could be your opportunity for large, beautiful nuggets that even you never dreamed possible.

Over 160 large pages, 8½"x11".
Spiral binding for long life.
Lays flat when opened.
Large print for easier reading.
Bibliography, Index, Appendix.

Read of known locations and some that have long ago been forgotten: Alaska. Alfred Bar, British Columbia. Amazon River, South America. Aztec Gold. Blue Lead. Buffalo Mine. Cascade Mountains. Trinity Mountains. Rocky Mountains. Siberia. Manhattan, California. Gem of the Southern Mines.

The index is a WHO'S WHO in historical gold strikes, locations and forgotten names and places.

RAYMOND J. WALLACE

Catalog Item (B-999)

Most Popular Mining Books

Dredging for Gold: The gold miners handbook. An easy to read, comprehensive book on gold dredging, placer geology, hooka diving, mining law and much more. Fully illustrated with 239 pages.

Gold Mining in the 1990's: The perfect book for the beginner getting started in gold mining. Covers panning, sluicing, dry washing, electronic prospecting and much more. The most advanced mining techniques. Illustrated. 260 pages.

Catalog Items

CHAPTER TWO

PLACER GEOLOGY

Origins of Placer Minerals

Placer deposits, (pronounced plass-er, as in "glass"), are concentrated accumulations of minerals which have been eroded out of the original mineral, or *hardrock* deposit, as described in the previous chapter. Because erosion is the primary factor in the formation of placer deposits, they are most often found in close proximity to running water, along streams and riverbanks, and on ocean beaches, where they are concentrated by the action of waves and tides. Important exceptions to this principle are the *high bench* or *ancient channel* placers, which were originally formed by running water, but which, through geological shifts and uplift, are now left high and dry. Another exception is the desert, or *eolian* (windswept) type of placer. This type has a very limited distribution, found only in a few small areas of the southwestern US.

Many types of minerals - both metallic and non-metallic, may form into placer deposits, but for the purpose of this exercise, let's concentrate on the example of how a *gold placer* is formed...

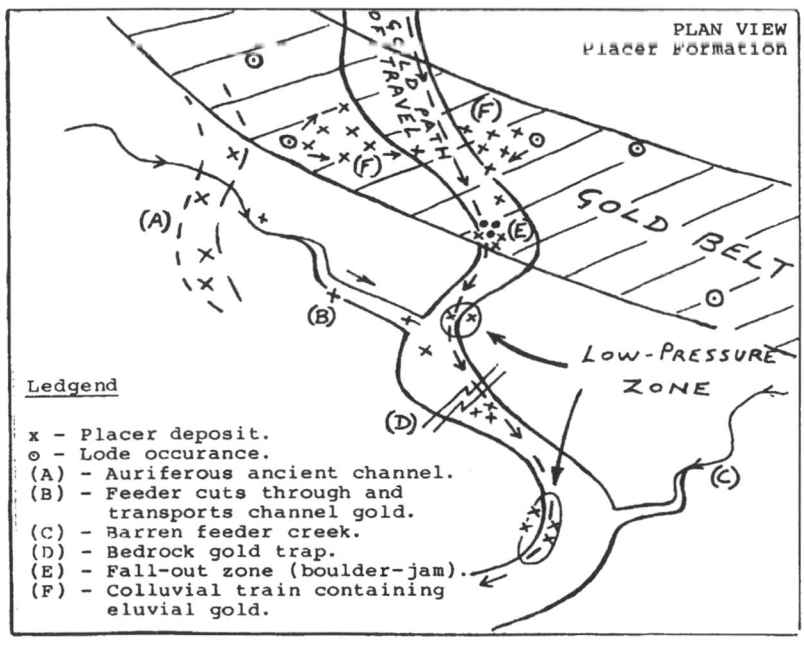

PLAN VIEW
Placer Formation

Ledgend

x – Placer deposit.
⊙ – Lode occurance.
(A) – Auriferous ancient channel.
(B) – Feeder cuts through and
transports channel gold.
(C) – Barren feeder creek.
(D) – Bedrock gold trap.
(E) – Fall-out zone (boulder-jam).
(F) – Colluvial train containing
eluvial gold.

The Genesis of a Gold Placer

As the original *in-situ,* (in place), mineral occurrence is exposed through erosion, the orebody becomes accessible . Although mineral lodes occur anywhere geological conditions are favorable, they are apt to be discovered on exposed hillsides and mountain slopes, since the valley bottoms are usually filled-in with deep layers of silt and gravel. Orebodies which are overlain by deep strata *can* be detected by using specialized techniques such as *geochemical prospecting,* which will be covered later.

Where a vein of mineral ore does outcrop at the surface, the repeated mechanical action of freezing and thawing weakens the mineral bearing host rock. Earth tremors and the chemical leaching action of rain and ground water also contribute to this effect. In some cases, the chemical composition of the host rock, (vein material), is such that it breaks down and decomposes much more quickly than the surrounding *country rock*, so that it forms a shallow depression or "pocket". When this occurs, fragments and particles of gold and heavy minerals settle downwards towards the bottom of the depression, where they can accumulate in very rich concentrations. *Residual Placers* of this type are covered fully in an upcoming segment entitled "Pocket Deposits".In most instances, however, the vein material is harder and more resilient than the surrounding rock, and will withstand the pocket-forming process. It is precisely because it *is* somewhat harder that mineral bodies frequently jut out, or *outcrop f*rom the surrounding topography. In these situations, the vein material simply breaks off and begins to "creep" down the hillside, along with other broken-off fragments of the surrounding country rock. Hillsides which have accumulated significant amount of broken rock are known as *scree,* or *talus* slopes. Individual pieces of rock which contain gold or some other mineral are referred to as *float.*

At this point, the freshly broken rock fragments, as well as the newly released particles of gold, both have a jagged, rough-edged appearance. Then, as the gold fragments continue their down-slope journey, through gravity and erosion, they become spread out, and are distributed in a pattern shaped like an inverted "V", called a *colluvial train.* During this stage of their transportation some of the gold may encounter certain topographical features which act as natural traps. Over time, enough gold may accumulate in such a trap to form what is known as an *alluvial placer.* It is important to note that, at this stage, having traveled some distance from the source, the gold particles and the rocky detritus have had their rough edges smoothed somewhat, and are now characterized as *sub-angular.* (Note: Using a magnifying lens to examine the *character,* (roughness), of the gold is an important skill for the prospector as it often results in a reliable estimate as to the distance to the source).

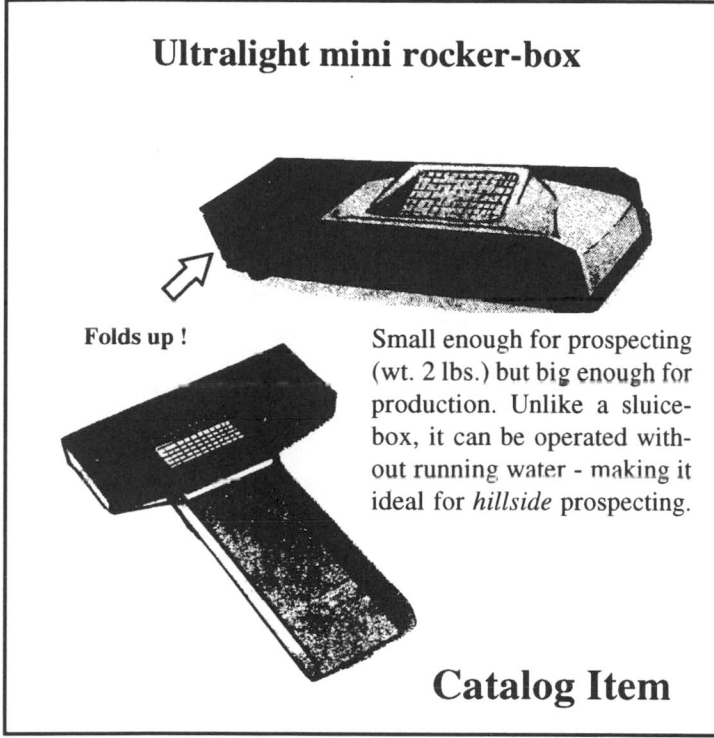

Ultralight mini rocker-box

Folds up !

Small enough for prospecting (wt. 2 lbs.) but big enough for production. Unlike a sluice-box, it can be operated without running water - making it ideal for *hillside* prospecting.

Catalog Item

Eventually, most of the gold finds it's way into a running body of water, where it is transported more quickly. Even in arid desert conditions, much gold is concentrated in dry river bottoms and *arroyos* as a result of flash floods. Once it enters a waterway, *auriferous,* (gold-bearing), rocks and gravel begin a long downhill journey out to sea, forming various types of placer deposits as it goes. As the stream or river cuts through the rocks of the gold-bearing zone, additional lodes are exposed, and each of these will contribute some gold into the watershed. Although there are exceptions, it is quite rare to find placers that are derived from a single source, or *motherlode.* More often, the gold particles that make up any given placer have come from numerous, small, low-grade veins which outcrop at different places along the valley. Once again, the magnifying lens comes in handy for a visual identification, as it will show the distinguishing textural characteristics of individual *colors,* (particles). This in turn may give you some idea of the number and types of contributing lodes that are in the vicinity.

Gold from placers that have formed near their source tends to have a *coarse,* (rough-edged), character. This is the reason why placers in the upper reaches of tributary streams are usually composed of "nuggety" gold, with large individual fragments predominating. Some nuggets may even have pieces of the quartz matrix still attached - a condition which strongly indicates the close proximity of a source.

Stream Placers

The mid-section of a watercourse, where the grade levels off to a more gentle 200 foot-per-mile or so (36 meters per kilometer), is by far the most favorable for the formation of high-grade placers. At this rate of descent, a high proportion of the gold values being transported through the watershed have a chance to "drop-out" and accumulate. This reduction in velocity results in well formed *paystreaks* of coarse (+ 8 mesh-per-inch) gold nuggets which, at this stage in their downstream journey, have taken on a bit more rounded appearance as a result of stream action. Note that in this context, the word "coarse" is used to denote particles of a large (nugget) size. I know it's a bit confusing, but in prospecting, the word "coarse" has a dual meaning; Sometimes it is used to describe "jagged-edged" particles, even when they are very small.

Ancient Channel & High Bench Deposits

I must now interject some amazing facts...

Geologically speaking, the creek that is now running at your feet may not have existed a short time ago. An earlier version of that same watercourse may have been flowing above your head on a bench or terrace ten, fifty or a hundred feet higher up. That older version may have had a completely different character (it might even have flowed in the opposite direction!) and it could contain more or less gold, depending on where its gravels were derived from. (Take a sample with a gold pan and find out).

But wait! What if that old channel had cut through an even older, richer channel remnant further upstream. Then where would the gold lie?

In areas that were subject to valley glaciers during the last ice age, sometimes the higher channels escaped the scouring action of the glaciers, thus preserving extremely rich placer deposits that had accumulated over millions of years.

To make the picture even more confusing, yet another phenomenon has to be taken into account-the *Theory of Deposition...*

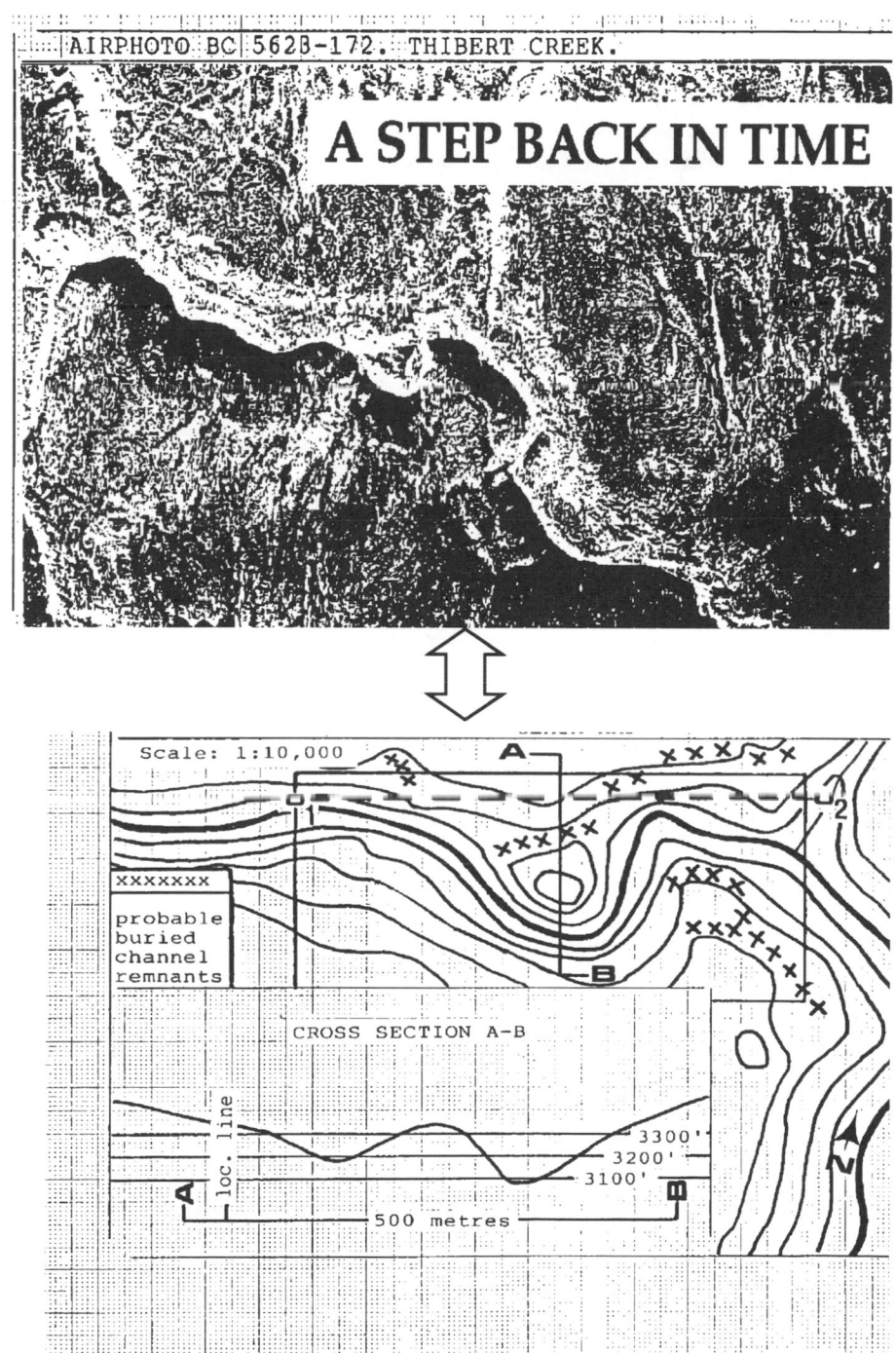

AIRPHOTO BC 562B-172. THIBERT CREEK.

A STEP BACK IN TIME

Scale: 1:10,000

xxxxxxx
probable
buried
channel
remnants

CROSS SECTION A-B

loc. line

3300'
3200'
3100'

500 metres

"Killer" Floods

Up to a few years ago, the conventional wisdom was that placers are formed by more-or-less gradual erosional processes, i.e: annual run-offs. But it is now known to be a much more dynamic, intermittent process, occurring as a result of the tremendous hydraulic pressures generated during extreme flooding. Floods are described as 50-year, 100-year, and 500-year floods, according to their strength and relative frequency. At such times, millions of tons of gravel are ablated, then re-deposited in the watershed. Within days - or even hours - entire gravel bars are physically "lifted" from the streambed and transported downstream in a roiling, semi-fluid state.

In this natural sluicing action, the particles of gold, being six times heavier than the surrounding gravel, eventually work down to the impervious bedrock layer. Where the bedrock offers irregularities and crevices to trap the gold, concentrations occur. These are the river's very own natural riffles!

Because gold from this type of formation tends to be quite heavy and "nuggety", one always tries to inspect the bedrock layer where possible - even if this means hacking your way through several feet of hard, compacted river gravel.

Gold's Path of Travel

You can narrow your search for paystreaks by concentrating your sampling on the *Gold's Path of Travel*. The GPT is an imaginary line connecting the low pressure zones along the river. Being heavy, gold has considerable inertia, and tends to hug inside bends of the river. As you construct this model, project an image of what the river would look like in a stage of extreme high flood. This picture looks completely different from the river's normal state, and you will realize that the low pressure zones are some distance from where you initially thought. The picture is completely changed, and the true GPT (or, should we say *Flood GPT*) suggests targets that are probably some distance from the river's normal water-line. While prospecting along the GPT boundary, pay special attention to those areas where underlying bedrock irregularities are suspected or indicated by local topographic features.

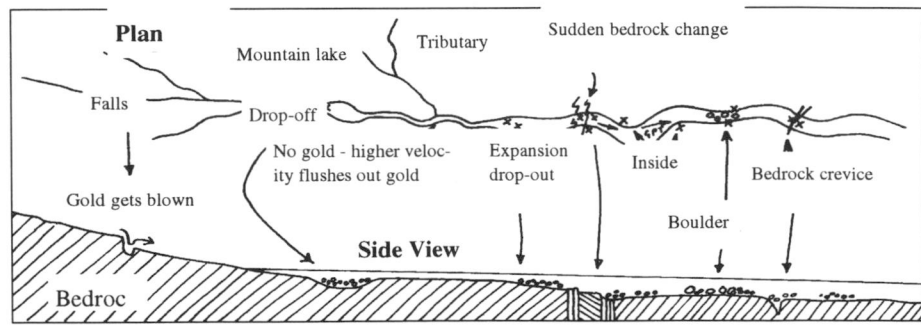

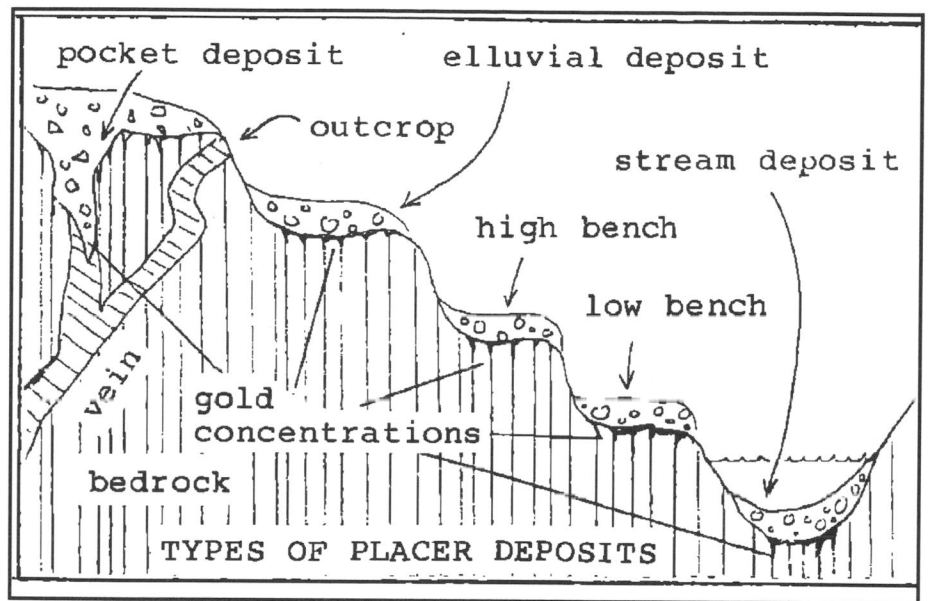

TYPES OF PLACER DEPOSITS

Flood Deposits

Further downstream in the meandering lower reaches of a river, the gold is more finely divided as a result of the pounding action of river cobbles. Thin, flake gold of this type is known as *fine gold*. It can accumulate in significant quantities where conditions are just right, such as where lighter gravels are ablated by successive floods, leaving heavy minerals and gold behind. Most large rivers which drain western Canada and the US have good flood gold deposits along their lower reaches. On the Fraser River, for example, from the town of Hope downstream as far as Herrling Island, the classic type of flood gold deposit can be found on many of the bars.

Incidentally, flood gold deposits are about the closest thing in mining to a *renewable* resource, because they are being continually replenished. Isn't it a shame to think of all that beautiful gold just lying there waiting - only to be swept out to sea with the next spell of bad weather!

Beach Placers

You'd think that, once out to sea, our lovely gold would be lost forever. But no, we get just one last chance, as the now minute grains of *flour gold* get washed back onto the beach with the tide. When storms accentuate tidal action (the so-called *Gold Storms*), beach placers are formed in thin surface layers, or *lenses*. Ancient inland beach-heads may also contain remnants of gold lenses, which can sometimes be profitably worked with a high-efficiency fine-gold plant, preferably one that has a re-circulating sluice.

Gold-bearing lenses within black-sand beach deposits may be only a few feet in extent, or they may go on for miles, as they do at Goodnews Bay and at Nome, Alaska. Extensive beach placers do occur in B.C. waters. Among the more noted producers are: Graham Island, Wreck Bay, Vancouver Island, Mitchell Inlet, Moresby Island, and Brittania Beach, Vancouver North Shore.

CHAPTER THREE

WHERE TO GO - PART ONE

British Columbia - A Prospector's Paradise

We are blessed to live in one of the most heavily mineralized regions on this planet. Located within an immense geological zone known as the Western Cordillera, our hunting ground extends from Alaska in the north, down through the western parts of North, Central, and South America - to the southern tip of Argentina (the *land of silver*.) No matter where you live in British Columbia, or throughout the east or west, for that matter, some interesting mineral deposits are bound to be found close by. These might include some operating mines, as well as hundreds - if not thousands - of abandoned mines and old placer workings.

Some regions are known for a certain type of mineral or geological occurrence. The Yukon and Cariboo districts, for example, are famous for placer gold, while the Kootenay district is known primarily as a silver producer. Base-metal deposits, such as iron, copper, and lead/zinc, occur in many different parts of B.C. Parts of Vancouver Island, and the Highland Valley, near the town of Merritt, are noted for their "kuroko", *(polymetalic)* ores.

Early woodcut depicts sourdoughs ground-sluicing for gold. Notice the two miners on the left working a deep bedrock crevice.

Gemstones

Exciting new diamond discoveries are now being made in Alberta and in the Northwest Territories, and possibilities exist elsewhere. While gem-quality diamonds have not yet been found in B.C., some deposits have been worked for industrial-grade micro-diamond. There have been important discoveries of *Fire Opal* in the Okanagan Valley, and of *Star Sapphire* in the Kootenay District. There have also been reports of rubies and sapphires occasionally turning up in the gravels of gold placers, but these must be considered the exception rather than the rule. Much more common are the valuable lapidary minerals, (sometimes referred to as *semi-precious* stones), which have widespread distribution throughout the region. You won't have to travel too far to find good producing areas for agate, jasper, common opal, rhodenite, and a wide variety of other interesting and valuable mineral specimens. In the past, some of these occurrences have turned out to be commercially viable, as in the case of Ogden Mountain, in the Omenica District, famous for it's world-class jade deposits.

To most people, prospecting means GOLD, so we are indeed fortunate to live in a part of the world which is literally studded with known occurrences of this most noble of precious metals. Nearly every region has it's own gold-producing area. There are even places on the outskirts of Metro Vancouver where the weekend panner can obtain good results. Although the chances of a future discovery the magnitude of a Klondike or a Cariboo are pretty slim, there are thousands of miles of smaller creeks and tributaries which have never been thoroughly prospected, so there is an excellent chance of discovering some small but extremely rich "bonanza" that was previously overlooked.

WHERE TO GO - PART TWO

How to Do Your Research

There is a great allure to the notion of heading off into uncharted territory to locate some previously undiscovered, virgin "glory-hole". If this is your plan, be sure to back it up with some hard geological or historical evidence, otherwise it is probably a mistake. Much better to stick to known mineralized areas that have produced well in the past. It is almost certain that within any given area - even heavily worked areas - some smaller deposits still exist which, for a myriad of reasons, were passed over by previous operators.

Concentrating on the known areas has other advantages as well. Usually, these places have good road access and some nearby facilities. Large amounts of documentation and existing geological reports and maps are available for each of the established gold camps, and you can use this information to your advantage as you begin to develop your own specialized prospecting technique, or, "niche".

To help you decide which gold-producing area to start with, there are several good books available at your library or through your prospecting equipment dealer. These give an overview of the types of deposits found within each area, along with a brief summary of the activities and results obtained from individual gold creeks. Even more detailed information, including descriptions of individual claims, can be gleaned from the pages of the "Annual Reports of the Minister of Mines". These are available for each year since the mid 1880's.

Annual Reports and Government Reports

Annual reports are a fantastic resource for the amateur and professional alike, because they are chock-full of clues about abandoned diggings and mines that for some reason went undeveloped. Perhaps the mine was too hard to get to at the time, but now has a four-lane highway running alongside. Or, maybe the deposit was too difficult to work with the existing technology, but could now be profitably worked with today's portable, small-scale systems.

Some of the Annual Reports may be available in the reference section of your local library. If not, check with your local government agent. Most Gold Commissioners keep a full set in their offices for public viewing.

Armchair Prospecting

All of these research activities come under the general heading of *armchair prospecting*. If you're like me, the idea of reams and reams of dry technical stuff leaves you cold. But, once you get started, you find that this isn't the case at all! Within the pages of those old mining journals are stories of incredible human drama, and wonderful tales of treasures, lost and found. Here's a good example, taken from the pages of the 1878 Report of the Minister of Mines...

376   REPORT OF THE MINISTER OF MINES   1878

"About the middle of last August an exitement (sic) was created in regard to bar diggings on the Upper Stickeen, (sic) distant about seventy miles from Telegraph Creek, and close to where the confluence of the Clap-an (sic) and the Stickeen takes place. The prospects obtained at first, however, did not last, and the transport, etc., of provisions to that locality being attended with great expense that discovery has ceased to be of interest to the mining community.

"Dease Creek being principly in the hands of the Chinese, it is very hard to estimate the returns from it this year. A few claims, worked by white men, have done well, and fair prospects are found in it's hills, which are yet unworked for want of dumpage.

"Only one case of lunacy has come under my notice during the last three years at Cassiar, and that within the past week. The name of the party afflicted is T. O'Brien, a native, I understand, of New York, and a man who is well known throughout the mines in this country. The sympathizing inhabitants of Laketon got up a subscription towards having him taken to Wrangel, en route to Victoria and Portland, where proper medical attention can be had, etc., and the circumstances being brought to my notice, as also the fact of his being entirely destitute, I advanced $50, getting a voucher of receipt for same, on behalf of the Government.

Information Resources

As you can see, Armchair Prospecting can be lots of fun, as well as being a good source of potentially lucrative information.

Because the summer, fall, and early winter, (the low-water season), is the best time for river prospecting, I usually reserve my armchair adventuring for the dead of late winter and the spring run-off, when high water makes panning and sluicing all but impossible. Consider starting your own technical resource library of maps and books, rounded out with a few of the excellent "How-To" videos. I find these tapes to be highly motivational, while delivering expert prospecting instruction right at home.

Maps and Air Photos

Topographical maps and air photos are available through Government Agents, through Crown Publications, listed in the Appendix, or through your prospecting dealer. As well as helping you find your way around the region, topo-maps and air photos can often show surface characteristics that do not reveal themselves at ground level. This is important, because topographic features may reveal hidden targets and clues, such as buried tertiary channels, for example.

The difference between success and failure is most often a case of "being in the right place." It's as simple as that. If there is a secret, it is this: You can get into "guaranteed" gold producing areas by adequately researching your target gold-field, *in advance,* to find out where the action is.

Private and public *archives* provide a deep and reliable geological/historical database, compiled by some of the province's most gifted chroniclers. Locations, methods, production records, large-scale detailed maps, and photographic evidence of gold rush operations, will all help guide you in your initial investigation of an unfamiliar area.

Gold Panner's Manual
Garnet Basque

Garnet's most popular book with 150,000 copies in print. History of the quest for gold; a concise guide to techniques to find and extract gold. This edition is well illustrated with photos and drawings demonstrating the art of panning and gold mining equipment. Extensive glossary.

1-895811-13-9
March 1996 • History, Guide
5 ¹/₂" x 8 ¹/₂" • 108 pages
Softcover • $12.95

Lost Bonanzas of Western Canada
Garnet Basque

Outlaw loot, lost mines and sunken bullion are some of the lost bonanzas in Alberta, British Columbia, and the Northwest Territories. All of the 13 stories have been researched for validity. Do these treasures exist or are they imaginary? Includes 11 maps and 63 photographs.

1-895811-40-6
March 1996 • History, Canada
5 ¹/₂" x 8 ¹/₂" • 160 pages
Softcover • $14.95

Local Knowledge

For those of you who are in it strictly for the outdoor adventure, and have absolutely no intention of trying to navigate your way around the library's geology section - take heart. There is another tried and true method of locating good gold producing areas: *Local Knowledge.*

Catalog Item

WHERE-TO-GO BOOKS

GT-B2 - "Gold Creeks and Ghost Towns" This classic by N.L. Barlee contains detailed accounts of all of BC's Gold Camps, including many interesting lost-mine stories. Illustrated, 191 pages.

Over 200 photos and maps!

Keeping in mind that gold-fever is highly contagious, all you really have to do as you travel through gold country is to simply announce your interest in the yellow metal to one and all. You'll be amazed at the people who will come forward to offer helpful tips and advice as to where to go and what to look for. Sometimes it's possible to develop a good lead before you even get into a new area. Perhaps, among your own family, friends, and contacts, you know somebody who has, "heard a story..." Or, at least, they may know someone from that area who can point you in the right direction.

WHERE TO GO - PART THREE

How to Obtain Permission from Claim Owners

There are literally thousands of spots in B.C., and all over the west, where you can go prospecting with no permit or license required. But you can't go everywhere and anywhere you want, because some areas are covered by private or restricted property, Indian Lands, or existing mining claims, and you will have to get permission first.

To complicate matters, B.C. has, as do most other jurisdictions, two completely different types of mining claims: (1) Mineral Claims, and (2) Placer Claims. The dis tinction between the two types is based on whether the commodity being sought after is in a placer, (gravel) deposit, or in a mineral, (hardrock) deposit, as described in the previous chapter.

Because the titles to the minerals and to the placer minerals are separate and distinct, this can lead to a situation where a Mineral Claim and a Placer Claim can occupy the same ground, and have two different owners. So, if the area you are interested in is covered by a Mineral Claim only, you are free to prospect for placer minerals but not for minerals, (in-place, hardrock minerals, that is), and vice-versa. As you can imagine, this sometimes causes confusion and can result in conflicts between the various mineral-claim and placer-claim holders, and with non-title holders, because of the different interpretations as to what constitutes the respective types of deposits. However, legal proceedings are nearly always avoided by resorting to arbitration by the Chief Gold Commissioner, who is authorized under "The Inquiry Act".

Placer Claim Areas

To cut through the confusion, let's deal first with the issue of Placer Claims, since most people are primarily interested in gold and want to begin their search by panning flakes and nuggets from the banks of a placer creek. As your skills and knowledge increase you may eventually develop an interest in commercial hardrock deposits, but a firm grounding in placer geology is still a necessary prerequisite in any case.

B.C. contains numerous 'Designated Placer Claim Areas", where a claim can be staked by anyone holding a valid FMC (Free Miner's Certificate). Staking cannot take place outside of a Designated Area and so, provided the location in question is on Crown Land and not on private or restricted land, you can prospect for placer gold to your heart's content, because no one actually *owns,* or can have title to, those placer minerals. You can also prospect an area outside a Designated Placer Area which *is* on private land, as long as you obtain permission from the owner first. The map which shows these designated Areas is called the "Index to Placer Titles Reference Map", available at any Government Agents office at no charge.

There are a lot of great gold creeks outside of the Designated Areas. Should you happen to find a workable deposit outside a Designated Area, you can apply to the government for the creation of a new Designated Area. Such an application may or may not be accepted and approved by an Order-in-Council, depending on the circumstances, but many new placer areas have been created in this way over the years, and it could well be worth the effort if a large commercial deposit is involved.

Dealing With Claim Owners

Since most of B.C.'s *historic* placer creeks do lie within one of the Designated Placer Areas, you will need to know how to deal with the claim-owners in that area to get permission.

This is a lot easier than it sounds, and it is highly recommended if you wish to avoid getting a saddle full of buckshot from an irate owner. Joking aside, while it is true that most claim-holders welcome the sight of enthusiastic gold panners on their property, (especially if that someone took pains to show up and report his or her results to the owner), the sad fact is that some people are prone to take advantage of an absentee claim owner. Imagine how the owner feels when, after having invested much time, money, and energy in the property, he or she is greeted one day with the sight of "professional" gold-dredgers, merrily squirreling away precious ounces of his or her gold. Such cases can and do end up in criminal charges, and usually the offending party is blackballed from the area for good.

In gold country, as elsewhere, an honest, personal approach always works best. Start by just driving out to an area and begin asking local service station, restaurant, and motel proprietors about local gold-panning. Ask for the names of local claim owners and track one down to ask permission. Keep your "pitch" short and sweet, because, remember, the owner has probably been through this many times before. The biggest concern may be the claim owner's *liability*, because regular visitors to the claim may have to be registered on an insurance policy. Another major concern most claim owners have is *undisclosed findings* (theft). This is especially a problem on claims that are noted for producing large, specimen-type nuggets. Why would a claim owner take the risk of one, or several, of them walking off without being paid for? Trust is a big factor here, and that's why I keep emphasizing a direct, up-front approach to dealing with claim owners.

Considering all this, it isn't at all unreasonable for the claim-holder to receive a small fee for panning, sniping, or electronic detecting in their claims. Whether or not the owner asks for a fee, *you* should always insist on paying a certain percentage (usually 10-15%) of your finds to the owner. Again, if the claim is exceptionally productive, the owner may feel justified in asking for more - up to 20%, or, "what the market will bear".

The reason for insisting on paying a percentage royalty to the owner is that this now constitutes a *lay agreement* which, in turn, can be the basis for a good future relationship with the owner. If the claim is indeed productive and you wish to return to work it on a larger scale, the owner will be more so inclined if he or she has been fairly paid in the past. Always offer a royalty, no matter how miniscule the "pannings" were. Another bonus in establishing good working relationships with claim-holders is that, as a prospector, you aren't required to have an FMC, as your activities are carried out under the authority of the claim-owner, who *is* licensed.

Owners are impressed when, after concluding your prospecting activities, you mail them a brief, one page *prospecting report*, summarizing the results you obtained. Depending on the type of *Work Program* the owner has in progress, your report may be a useful inclusion to the owner's official Technical Reports, and may even qualify for credit as Annual Assessment Work (more about this in a later chapter.)

Once these issues have been addressed, the owner/prospector relationship can settle down into a wonderfully productive liaison. He or she may suggest where and how to try and, if the tips pay off, you are both winners. Conversely, you may hit upon a discovery or some information that the claim-owner never would have arrived at on his or her own.

Locating an Owner

If there is a specific property that you definitely want to get into, and the claim owner isn't in the area, you will have to have a Government Agent check the computer file for the owner's name, address, and phone number. If you don't have a name to begin with, then you'll have to look up the correct placer claim (tenure) number on the Placer Titles Map, then have the agent cross-reference the owner's name and address.

Verbal permission is usually sufficient for panning, sluicing, and most other "hand operations", but if you plan on using pumps and larger equipment, a written authorization from the owner is preferred. This should be written up at the same time as a Liability Waiver, to protect the claim owner from lawsuits.

"Open" Ground

It's probably occurred to you by now that, at any given time, not all of the lands within the Designated Placer Areas are covered by valid, existing claims. Claims are regularly abandoned, through neglect, or from the owner being deceased. Abandoned claims may lie vacant for some period of time before being re-staked. Not only are you free to prospect these unclaimed areas, but you can stake a claim there yourself if you have a Free Miner's Permit. However, my advice is to get to know an area first by associating yourself with some local claim-holders, and do this before you begin to consider claim-staking opportunities for yourself. This is a potentially lucrative aspect of the exploration business, but it is fraught with risks. Claim staking and ownership are discussed more fully in Chapter 9.

Gold-Panning in a Park or Recreation Area

The Mineral Tenure Act, 1988, which regulates Mineral and Placer Claims in B.C., states that, "no one can stake a claim, or conduct exploration and development within a park or recreation area, without prior authorization." In the Act, no distinction is made between recreational prospecting or systematic testing by a mining and exploration company. Technically, I suppose panning beach sand in a park would be a violation, but in practice this has never happened as far as I know. In my experience, recreational prospecting, rockhounding, etc., is tolerated by park officials. At many campgrounds they are quite enthusiastic about it - to the point of organizing their own gold-panning tours within the park area. Of course, the line has to be drawn somewhere, and no doubt some eyebrows would be raised if you were to crank up a noisy, heavy-duty gold dredge in the middle of a peaceful campsite. This brings us to...

Glenn's Golden Rule No. 2...

"When In Doubt - Check It Out"

If you endeavor to be always open and above-board about your intentions, you will find that most public officials are truly interested in helping the public get the most enjoyment out of our public lands. That is why, should you have the least bit of concern about the appropriateness of your intended prospecting activities within a park area, make a few phone calls and talk to the officers personally. Not only can they help you stay "legal" with your hobby, they may also be able to offer valuable pointers that will increase your enjoyment and success on the trip.

DISCLAIMER: The information presented in this chapter does not constitute a legal opinion or advice. It is a summary of the author's personal experiences on the subject and should be treated as such. Copies of the Mineral Tenure Act are available from your local Government Agent.

Open Communications

Certainly, part of the excitement of gold comes from the aura of secrecy and mystery which surrounds it. But this can be taken too far. Over the years, gold-mining has attracted it's fair share of scoundrels and get-rich-quick artists. Until the mid 1970's, private ownership of gold was actually illegal in the US. The effect of this was the perception by some people that somehow, the gold business is tainted, that prospecting for gold is some kind of fringe activity that's not quite "above board".

In reality, nothing could be further from the truth. Prospecting and mining for gold is a completely legal activity which is actively encouraged and promoted by most, if not all, of the world's governments. Experience has shown that the health of any country's mining industry is completely dependent on the so-called "grassroots sector". That's you and me - the professional, individual prospector, together with the weekend amateurs and hobbyists. Because of the sheer numbers, this group is responsible for by far the largest portion of all the mineral discoveries made each year, and this is why our own Mines Department bends over backwards to support and encourage prospecting wherever the opportunity presents itself. In B.C. This support goes as far as financial awards, through the Prospectors Assistance Program. The government will sometimes pay you to develop and carry out your own exploration program. If you're interested in this, write for an application at the address listed in the Appendix. The tourism sector is also very much in favour of recreation prospecting and our mining heritage, and have even designed entire promotional campaigns around the theme of B.C.'s historic "Gold Rush Trail".

Remote Sensing

Remote sensing is a powerful new tool for the grassroots prospector. It encompasses a wide range of sensing modes, including side-looking radar (ground-penetrating radar), high resolution digitally-enhanced color optics, and infrared imagery. Each mode has it's own particular set of applications. For example, slight color variations in vegetative cover may indicate underlying mineralization. GPR scans are useful for resolving bedrock structure and faulting, and can also be used by placer prospectors to look for old buried channels under up to 200 feet of overburden. In Canada, a recognized leader in satellite data interpretation is:

> Radarsat International Inc.
> 3851 Shell Rd. Suite 200
> Richmond, B.C.   V6X 2W2

Below, native placer-miners at the turn of the century, located near the confluence of the Thompson River and the mighty Fraser.

Taking Notes

As you become acquainted with more and more people who share your interest in prospecting, it's a good idea to record this information in a journal. Years ago, in casual conversation, a stranger told me about a small, unheard-of creek that his grandfather had worked during the 1930's depression. I would have forgotten all about it were it not for the notation I'd made in my diary. Now I'm really glad I did, because this creek has since become one of my favourite "secret" hot-spots that I like to return to year-in and year-out. If this ever happens to you, it's a nice touch to let the person who first tipped you off know about your success. They will certainly appreciate knowing their advice was sound, and who knows, maybe they have even more hot tips up their sleeve they might share.

Where to Go in British Columbia?

Now that we've got all that legal stuff out of the way, you're probably saying to yourself, "OK Glenn, but that still doesn't answer the question: Where *are* the best places to go?"

As a general rule, large bodies of water distribute gold more uniformly than do small creeks, which tend to be "spotty". To optimize your chances of some quick returns from your prospecting, I recommend the following shortlist of B.C.'s "Big Waters". These locations represent hundreds and hundreds of acres of prime prospecting ground...

- The Fraser River

- Thompson River

- Stikine River

- Peace River

- Omineca River

- Wild Horse River

- Columbia River

- Yukon River, Yukon Territory

I would add to this list the major tributaries of these rivers, and the black sand beach placers of Vancouver Island, the Queen Charlotte Islands, and Vancouver-North Shore.

"I'd like to find me a nugget... Just one BIG nugget, so's a fellah can wink at it while he brushes his teeth."

Itinerant Prospector

From: "The Pale Rider", Clint Eastwood, Director

CHAPTER FOUR

THE GOLD PAN & HOW TO USE IT

Background and History

Processing streambed sand and gravel with a gold pan is the oldest method of mining gold and other heavy metals. Archeological evidence indicates that the first gold pans were used by early Minoan cultures and were probably made of wood. Egyptians plied the banks of the Blue Nile, and gave up their "pannings" as offerings to the sun-god, Ra. (Incidentally, a buried channel of the Nile was recently discovered by satellite remote-sensing). Another version of this type of primitive wooden pan, called the "batea", was introduced into North and South America by the Spanish, and is still in use today in remote areas of South America, the Philippines, and in other under-developed regions of the world.

MOTHER LODE. *Irene Leaver, mother of the author, pans for gold and platinum at a scenic spot near Princeton, British Columbia.*

Uses of a Gold Pan

As a prospecting and mining implement, the gold pan has stood the test of time for, despite modern advances in electronic and geochemical prospecting, the gold pan remains the prospector's most important and frequently used tool. The gold pan is the one indispensable tool of the prospector. Whether testing for placer deposits or examining ground-up hardrock specimens for heavy-mineral content, there is no substitute for a good gold pan in proficient hands. When the prospecting phase leads to a discovery and mining begins, the gold pan remains in constant use during the *clean-up* and *final separation* procedures. Here, gold-bearing black-sand concentrates are emptied into your gold pan from the gold vacuum, gold dredge, or concentrator. After panning off the black sand all that remains is your gold, pure and clean, and ready to make into beautiful jewelry pieces with no further processing necessary.

Sampling with a Gold Pan

On the larger gold-bearing rivers - especially in western Canada and the US, there are actually very few places where panning will fail to produce at least a few "colors" of gold, so the beginner can reasonably expect some results the very first time out. The real skill lies in systematically sampling over a large area in order to zero-in on high grade concentrations, or *anomalies*. Search for pockets and paystreaks in areas where there are natural dykes or other bedrock changes. Always check the lowest accessible strata of gravel, since 90% of the gold will occur on this level, immediately above the bedrock. Pay special attention to such obvious gold traps as boulder-jams, (sometimes called boulder-gardens), in bedrock crevices, and in the vicinity of low-pressure drop-out zones.

"Gravity Trap". Hi-Tech panning kit. Includes: Two Gold Pans, Classifier Screen, Gold Snifter, Instruction Book, green color.

Types of Pans

There are still lots of seasoned prospectors around who would rather chew on a blasting cap than give up their trusty, old-fashioned steel gold pan. This is mainly because that's what they're used to and old habits die hard. But molded plastic has now taken over as the material of choice for the modern gold pan, as it has several features and benefits lacking in the old steel version. Not only is plastic durable and won't rust, but you can also use nitric acid or oxalic acid with it, as may be necessary in the separation of some types of ore. A good plastic pan has a bottom lip called a *drop-center* molded into it. Along with the ridges (cheater riffles) along the side of the pan, the drop-center helps trap gold and prevent it from wandering out during the panning. A steel pan cannot be used if you plan on doing any electronic prospecting, for obvious reasons. About the only advantage of a steel pan is that you can heat your concentrates in it to dry them, (or you could cook breakfast in it, for that matter), but this is a marginal benefit. The non-skid surface texture of plastic makes it far superior to metal for recovering the finest gold. Plastic pans generally come in dark colors - green or blue - which also improves visual detection of very fine metallic particles. Black-colored pans do show gold well, but they tend to disguise the amount of black sand present.

This is also a problem in certain types of pocket deposits in which the fine gold particles have a dark stain or coating on them. As well, fine-grained platinum is also hard to see in a black pan, because it too can have a very dark, dull apearance.

GOLD PAN
Klondike 'sure Trap' drop-center gold pan with a lifetime guarantee. Molded side riffles, blue color. 16" diameter.

Practice Panning

It's a really good idea to do some practice panning under controlled conditions at home in order to perfect your technique, or just to keep up your proficiency if you've been away from it for any extended period. Obtain a bag of sample ore which contains real placer gold. (The **Gold Trails** *Paydirt* kit is ideal for this.) Or if you prefer, you can substitute ordinary gravel with bird-shot added in. Use pliers to break off pieces of shot, then flatten the pieces with a hammer to replicate the "flake" characteristic of gold.

Preparation

In addition to the ore-sample, you will need:

1)   A large wash-tub or basin.
2)   Small to medium-size gold pan.
3)   Tweezers, for picking out small flakes and nuggets.
4)   Small sample vial. (Included in the **Gold Trails** *Paydirt* Kit).

Note: So as not to lose any gold down the kitchen sink, the panning is done in a basin or pail. This also makes it easier to save the valuable black sand for future practice sessions.

STEP ONE   Wash your hands, the gold pan, and the basin or tub with mild soap and rinse thoroughly. This removes any oil film which might otherwise interfere with the panning by causing the fine colors of gold to float.

STEP TWO   Place the basin or tub on a countertop or convenient work table and fill with lukewarm water. Next, pour all of the ore sample into the gold pan, then place the pan, submerged, on the bottom of the basin. Next, use your fingers to gently knead the material to make sure all of it is thoroughly wetted and to break up any clumps.

STEP THREE Grasp the pan with both hands and, keeping the pan completely submerged and in a level position, shake the pan from side to side, left to right. This should be done fairly vigorously so as to agitate the sand and gravel *as a mass,* but not so vigorously as to slosh material over the edge. Shake in this manner for about 10-20 seconds. This step causes the gold to work it's way down to the bottom of the pan, gold being about six times heavier than ordinary sand and gravel, and about four times heavier than mineral (black) sands.

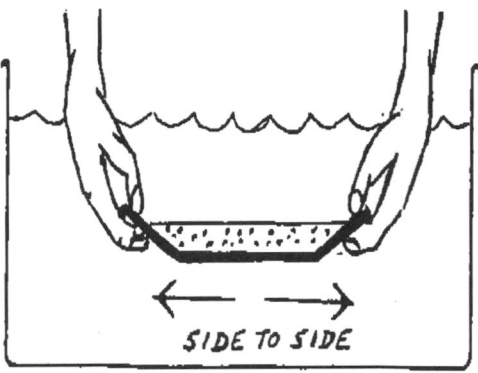

STEP FOUR Still keeping the pan underwater, tilt it forward, but not so steeply that the concentrates pour out. While maintaining this forward angle, gently sift the pan in a circular motion, combined with a gentle "push" each time the pan is moved to the outermost part of the circle.

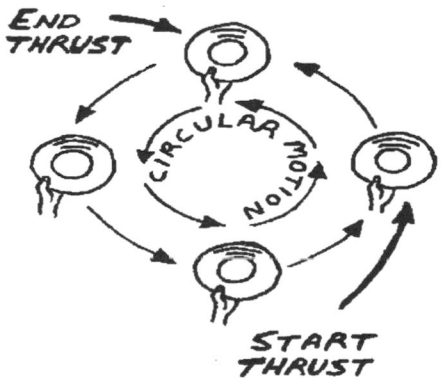

Start Thrust

Each outward thrust will wash a small amount of the lighter surface material out of the lowered side of the pan. Do this for 10-20 seconds. Remember to keep the correct tilt while doing the circular motion. The lip of the pan should always be higher than the junction point, or drop-lip.

PROCEED

Holding the pan level, repeat the shaking procedure outlined in step 3. This ensures that any "wandering" gold settles back to the bottom of the pan. Alternate between the "shaking", and the, "circular-thrust" motions, washing out just a small amount, (about one teaspoon), of concentrate each time.

When only a small amount of material, (about one tablespoon or so), is left, you will begin to notice very small "colors" of gold wandering up to the lip of the pan during your circular washing motion. This occurs as the sand becomes more and more concentrated. In order to keep the gold down you will have to perform the shaking more frequently, and more gently. Tapping the side of the pan at this stage also helps the gold to settle down.

Notice that, although you started out shaking the full pan in a level, *horizontal* position, when only a small amount remains it is helpful to *tilt* the pan slightly forward. This causes the "heavies" to settle down into the lip, or drop-center, of your pan. So, towards the end of your panning you will be performing both the circular-thrust, and the side-to-side shaking with the pan held at a forward-tilt angle.

When you've washed out as much sand as possible, (without letting out too many fine colors), the panning is finished. Now, lift the pan out of the water and, holding it level, (and with a suitably dramatic flourish!), swirl the water around so the gold down in the junction is exposed. Use an eye loupe or magnifier to identify interesting mineral crystals and metallic particles. Tweezers or an eyedropper are handy for picking up small gold flakes or nuggets for your sample vial. Another method is to let your gold bearing black sand dry, then place on a piece of paper and gently blow the black sand to one side. Now you can pick up the gold with the tip of a moistened finger and tap it into the vial. The remaining black sand may still have some good gold values left in it, which will add up in time, so begin to stockpile any residual black sand until you have several pounds, at which time it will be worth your while to do a *secondary* concentration. (More about that later).

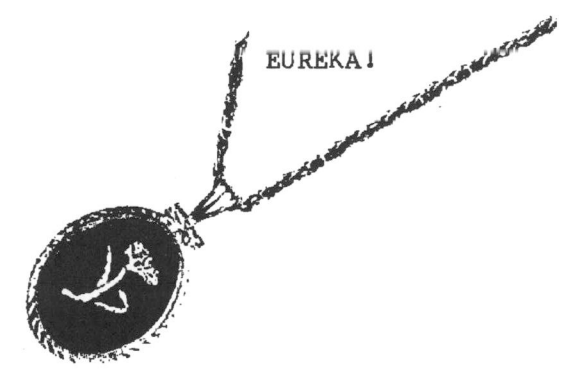

EUREKA!

Tip: Filling the vial with distilled water magnifies the gold beautifully. Another interesting approach is to mount the nuggets or flakes on a favorite piece of jewelry, using a thin coat of clear epoxy cement.

Speed Panning

When you first start, you may need 10, 15 minutes or more to work a full pan. With practice you will reduce this time significantly while still saving most of the fine gold. You will find out that in field work, speed is quite important, because you will want to do lots of sampling and cover as much ground as you can in the time you have. In World Championship Panning (and yes - there *is* such a thing!), time per pan is down to mere seconds. You don't have to be anywhere near this fast, but on a field trip, where time is limited, you don't want or need to waste too much time on any single pan of material.

GOLD TRAILS *"Paydirt!"*
Panning Kit - Perfect for practice panning at home. Includes sample-vial, instructions, black sand, and at least 100 milligrams, (one and one-half grains) of *genuine* Placer Gold!

Panning Under Field Conditions

During in-the-field sampling, you will be testing *bank-run* gravel, which is a bit different from your practice sample. Your practice sample is more like the concentrates from a sluice box or dredge, in that it is made up chiefly of heavy, dense iron sands, which is only four times lighter than gold, whereas bank-run gravel averages about six times lighter. Because the differential in specific gravity isn't as great, it is more difficult, and takes quite a bit longer, with a pan full of black sand than it does with ordinary gravel.

Classification of Gravel

Whatever the recovery method - panning, sluice, dredge, or whatever, *recovery efficiency* is drastically improved if the material is first *classified* into an aggregate of uniform size. Big rocks in amongst the finer sand and gravel impedes the settling-out process, and big pebbles can actually knock gold that has already accumulated right out of the sluice box or pan. Another important reason to always classify your material is that, by *scalping-off* the oversize component prior to recovery, you end up with a much smaller amount of material that needs to be processed for the same amount of gold.

In panning there are two main methods of pre-classifying the sample material. The first method is to use a classifier screen having a one-half to one-inch (12-25mm) mesh. Place the screen directly on top of a submerged pan, shovel in, then, holding both pan and screen submerged, rotate and shake the pan until all the fine sediment falls through. Before discarding the oversize contents of the screen, give them a careful once-over for any large nuggets or interesting mineralized quartz.

Now go ahead and pan the undersize sand and gravel in the normal manner. Some minus-1/2" pebbles will remain, and these can be picked out or raked off with your fingers at intervals during the panning. If you plan on doing a lot of samples in one particular area, it might pay you to introduce a second, smaller screen of about 8-mesh, (8 squares per inch). I've found that multiple screening improves fine gold retention at each successive stage of the recovery process, and cuts down the time it takes by at least half.

The second method of classifying is the manual method, which doesn't require a screen. At the beginning of your panning, as you are kneading the material with your fingers, feel out the larger rocks, swish them around to wash off any adhering clumps of clay, and give them a quick glance as you toss them onto the tailings pile beside you. Proceed to remove successively smaller rocks and pebbles at intervals during your panning. The manual method isn't quite as efficient as screening, but the slight loss of fine gold will have no significant impact on your ability to accurately evaluate the grade of the deposit.

Other Special Panning Applications

Dry Panning, as the term implies, involves panning a concentrate sample from a completely dry batch of gravel. Slightly damp gravel won't work as it tends to clump, but if you need to test a dry gulch or *arroyo,* without having to pack a jug of water and wash-bin, the dry method can be used in a pinch. Because dry-panning isn't nearly as effective as wet-panning, you will have to repeat the "shake-down" procedure much more frequently. Even then, be aware that a dry-panned sample isn't very accurate, because some of the fine gold that may be present will not be able to work down to the bottom. In these situations, really accurate sampling will require you to either pack in some water, or carry your samples out.

As well as testing gravel, the pan can give double duty as the main method of *secondary recovery.* Any concentrates that you develop from your sniping activities - vacuuming, sluicing, or dredging - will be panned to recover the coarse gold. The remaining black sand probably contains some fine gold that you can't pick out with tweezers, so you should save it. Eventually, when you've collected a sufficient amount, it may be economic to recover the remaining fine values with the aid of an *amalgamation kit,* or some type of mechanical extractor such as the Micro Sluice.

38

Catalog Items

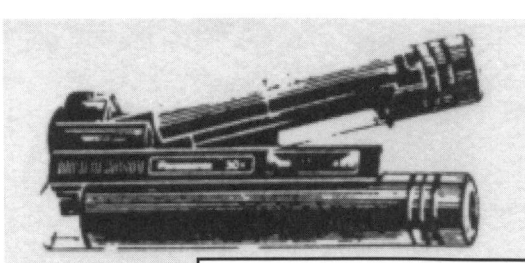

Model MR2 Mercury Retort

A small, compact and efficient retort for separating mercury from gold. Can also be used for cleaning mercury. Comes with a cast iron pot and recirculating water radiator. Heating torch not included. Half pound amalgam capacity. Shipping weight 11 lbs.

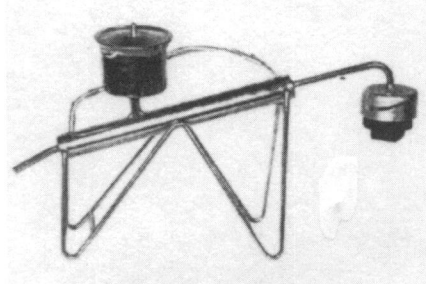

A65A 30 Power Light scope

The new compact pocket microscopes with built-in illumination. Turns off automatically when closed and has rack and pinion focusing. the microscope is furnished with a case and specimen stand. Uses two AA batteries. (batteries not included).

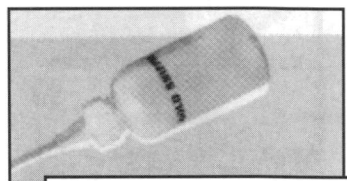

GBS-1 Gold Bottle Snifter

A handy tool for extracting gold and values from a gold pan with suction. Squeeze bottle and release to draw gold into bottle. Ideal for depositing gold into specimen bottles.

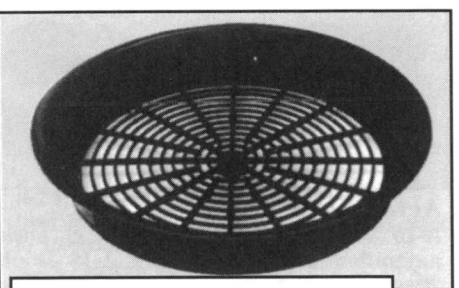

Gold Pan & Relic Sieves

New lightweight sieves of durable plastic, guarnteed against breakage. Model GSP-1 fits over our medium (A-45-14) or inside our large (A-45-16) plastic pans. Model GSP-2 fits snugly over our small plastic pan (A-45-10). Both sieves screen out waste gravels above 3/8" and can cut panning time in half. Can also be used with any type of gold pan of same approx. size as our plastic pans.

SGP-1 16 1/2" diameter

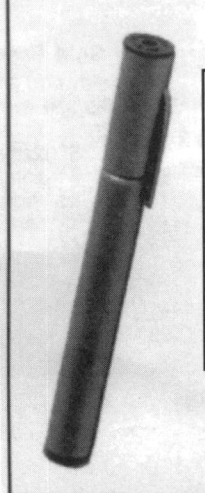

A-62 Field Microscope Combination

8 power telescope and handy 30 power Handy microscope for field use. For microscope, remove lower barrel, insert barrel for telescope. Shipping weight 1

CHAPTER FIVE

TESTING FOR GRADE

The Visual Assay - (Counting the Colors)

You've got to know what you're looking for, right? How will you recognize a bona-fide, economic paystreak when you see it? In this section you will learn how to accurately appraise the colors that appear in your gold pan, then perform some quick, "mental dead-reckoning" to arrive at a reasonable approximation of the *grade* of the material present. "Grade" here is defined as the *richness* of the deposit, expressed as (troy) ounces-per-cubic yard, or grams per cubic meter.

A common mistake among beginners is to become overly impressed by a few fine colors in the pan, wasting valuable field time trying to follow it up. The presence of very fine gold can be a critical clue in some types of pocket-hunting techniques, but is rarely of any consequence in the quest for workable surface placer deposits. By using the following guide, you will know at a glance if the showing in your pan signals an important find.

The following chart specifies the commonly accepted categories of gold particle size...

```
GOLD PARTICLE SIZE COMPARISON CHART
Samples are Actual Size photo reproductions.
```

Size Classification	Sample No	Mesh/In	Grains	Colors/Oz
NUGGET GOLD / COARSE GOLD	1	3	24	20
INLAY GOLD	2	5	5	100
MEDIUM GOLD / PANNING GOLD	3	10	2	240
FINE GOLD	4	16	1	480
VERY FINE GOLD	5	40	.03	16,000
MICRON (Invisible Range)	6	200	.012	40,000
		--	.0005	1,000,00

Measuring Your Sample

The next part of the formula pertains to the volume of gravel per sample-pan. You need to determine approximately how much sample material there is in an average one of *your* pans. Everyone is different. In my case, I like to use a standard, drop-lip 16-inch pan, about one-half to three-quarters full. This works out to roughly 120 cubic inches, and is just a bit more than the volume of a 5-pound, (2.2 kilogram), sack of sugar. Since there are exactly 46,656 cubic inches in a cubic yard, it takes approximately 4,667 cu. in. divided by 120 = 389 of *my* samples to make up one "yard".

In the following examples, we will apply the formula: Average Weight (of gold) per Sample x Average Samples per Cubic Yard.

Example One - Low Grade Deposit

Particles obtained from one pan:
    particle no. 1 -   .05 grain
    particle no. 2 -   .05 grain
Total weight in pan: .10 grain

(Note: Both of the colors found in this pan were matched to the chart and estimated to be in the upper range of the Very Fine category).

The *grade* of the sample can now be solved...
.10 (total sample weight) x 389 (av. pans-per-yard)
= 38.9 grains-per-yard.

Or, this can be expressed in troy ounces as: 38.9/480 (grains in one ounce) = .081 oz/cu. yard.

Now, if this grade was consistently obtained over a wide area, indicating an extensive deposit in the thousands or hundreds of thousands of yards of material, there would be, at least, the *potential* for a profitable, medium-scale heavy-equipment operation. The problem is that most placer deposits are much, much smaller - in the range of a few hundred down to a mere few yards in extent. So in the case of Example One, if the sample came from a gravel bar containing only, say, ten yards of gravel, the sum total gold content of that deposit is only .08 oz x 10 yards = .8 oz. of gold. With small portable equipment, you could process a small deposit like this in three or four days, with time added in for set-up and moving equipment. At current gold prices, ($450 Cdn./oz), the return is only around $90 per day, less gas, equipment costs, etc. Obviously, this doesn't cut it if you're looking for any kind of financial return.

Example Two - Economic Deposit

Some fine-gold deposits do deserve a second look - especially in the case of *beach-sand* or *flood-gold* placers. For instance, suppose, instead of producing an average of only two very-fine colors-per-pan, a new location was now yielding an average of 8 colors of about the same size, (.05 grains each). Using the same formula, we arrive at a total sample weight of:

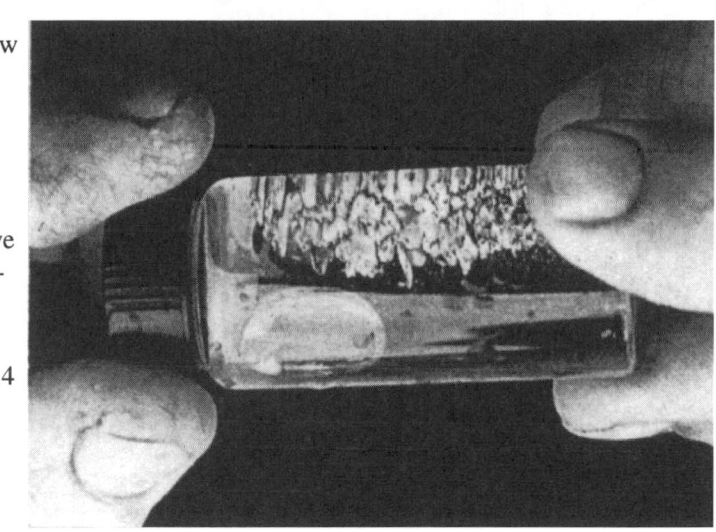

    8 x .05 grain = .4 grain

Multiplied by my standard 389 pans/ yard

= 155.6 grains/yard, or .32 oz/yd (nearly one-third of an ounce).

So, with the same 10 yards of paydirt, the total take would be 3.24 ounces, or about $300 per day or so, at today's prices.

Example Three - High Grade Deposit

Fine gold deposits are so-called because of a general *absence* of coarse gold parti-cles. However, deposits that do contain coarse gold nearly always have some fine gold as well. The presence of coarse gold, *in addition* to the base level, or back-ground level, of fine gold, will really send the Average Grade figure through the roof. Assume that we have a sample identical to our Sample One, (two very fine col-ors), except now, we are also picking up the occasional flake or nugget. If ten sample-pans produce an additional four coarse flakes of, say, five grains each, then we have...

Coarse Gold Component:
5 grains-per-color x 4 colors = 20 grains/10 pans = 2.0 av. grains/pan
Add on the fine-gold component...   0.08 av. grains/pan
Total average weight per pan...   2.08 grains

Again using our hypothetical 10 cubic-yard deposit, the gold content works out to...
389 (av. pans/yd) x 2.08 grains-per-pan = 809.12 x 10 yards = 16.8 oz.

In this example, our five-day work program has resulted in a very respectable
$4,460, before costs.

This 49er checks out his rocker box carefully for those telltale signs
of "color".

Be Selective!

The aim of these ex-
amples is to give you an
idea of what an accept-
able, workable deposit
looks like. "Acceptable"
is a relative term; it is up
to each prospector to
decide for her or him-
self. How much is your
time worth? The point is,
if you're in an area that
yields only a fly-speck
or two from each pan, it
will be impossible for
you to accumulate any
serious amount of gold,
no matter how efficient
your equipment is or
how hard you work. And
really, there is no need
to settle for meager re-
sults because small,
high-grade deposits do
exist in abundance. You just have to be willing to spend the time to find them

Field Trip Pointers

Technically speaking, panning as *exploration work* is classed as 'General
Prospecting'. Under certain circumstances work of this nature can be applied as Annual Assessment Work on a claim. Expenses incurred in General Prospecting may
be deducted for income-tax purposes, so long as there is the intent, and "reasonable
expectation" of a profit.

A Journal, or *Prospecting Diary* provides a good, basic 'chain-of-evidence' for expenses or any other documentation you wish to keep. In British Columbia, as well as most other jurisdictions, the keeping of a Prospecting Journal is highly advised by the government, although it is not strictly a legal requirement. Even on rambling, informal excursions, I recommend that you take the time to make cursory notes of such things as a freehand sketch of the area, claim-post numbers, names of contacts, mileage points, etc. The journal can also include formulas and rough, "back-of-the-envelope" grade calculations. I keep a journal in a watertight plastic pouch, along with any maps I might need on that trip.

Mineral Display Case

Catalog Item

The American River Mineral Display Case is an excellent way to display your collection. Heavy duty, black-hinged case with sky blue foam - practically indestructable. Portable, and stows easily in backpacks. Foam bed holds 5 1/2 inch tweezer, 16 - power magnifying glass, magnet, 1/2 oz, 1 oz, 2 oz, 4 oz vials and three, 1 1/2 inch clear plastic boxes.

Catalog Items

RCBS SCALES

RCBS grain scales are well known for their quality, accuracy, and dependability. Either model will give many years of fine service. They feature a magnetic damper to eliminate unwanted beam oscillation, knife-edge beams on agate bearings for consistent accuracy, tear-shaped pan with pour spout and weighted anti-tip hanger and easy-to-read graduations and deep notches on beam to help prevent errors.

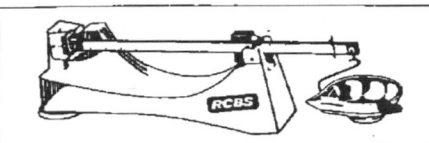

RCBS 5-0-2: Accurate to 0.1 grain, this is the most economical of the series, but is still of superior quality. 505 grain capacity; 2 poises; single beam; Shipping weight 5 lbs.

RCBS MODEL 5-0-5: Features three poise system and magnetic damping. Has agate bearings, improved leveling leg and widely spaced deep beam notches. 511 grain capacity. Sensitivity to 0.1 grain. Shipping weight 6 lb.

RCBSSC--SCALE COVER: A smart accessory to protect the 5-0-5 and 5-0-2 scales when not in use. Soft, vinyl dust

Catalog Item

Electronic Digital Professional Mini Scale ES2
Weighs Grams and Penny weights
This new pocket scale weighs with accuracy of 1/10th. of a pennyweight(0.1). Has low battery indicator and energy saving on/off feature. Easy to use and has an easy to read LCD display. Uses three alkaline batteries included. This new scale has proven to be one of our most popular. Capacity to 64 pennyweight (100 grams) Weighs 6 ounces (170 g) Dimensions 6 1/8" x 3" x 5/8ths. " Shipping weight 1 Lb.

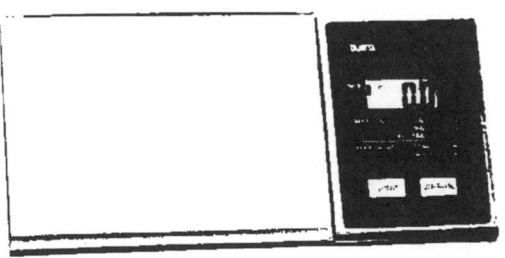

This draws to a close the chapters dealing with panning and sample-testing. A gold pan will take you a long way towards the goal of finding paying amounts of gold, but you've got to stick with it. You'll have to do lots of sampling to consistently find good paystreaks, and panning can be hard work. To do it right, you have to be prepared to cover a lot of ground, ranging far afield through dense brush and rugged canyons. It can be hard on the back too, which is why, if you're at all prone to lower-back strain, you should consider taking a portable seat along. I use an overturned pail, which doubles as a carry-all for heavy tools, and can be strapped to a packboard when hiking.

I enjoy gold panning immensely. There are moments of relaxed tranquility, sloshing around a pan or two amidst beautiful, natural surroundings. Then there are periods of intense concentration and excitement, as you systematically follow up on a promising lead. And, the tangible results of all this - a vial of shiny nuggets to

admire - only deepens the satisfaction of a job well-done.

The Other Important Skill - "Sniping"

The real purpose of panning, or *testing*, as we all realize, is to help us get that much closer to some fabulous cache of gold nuggets, secreted in some out of the way spot, for us, and only us, to discover. Panning skill alone is not enough to quickly and *frequently* locate high-grade paydirt. To achieve consistency, some sort of *strategy* is needed to direct the actual prospecting, or "hunting" of high-potential targets. This comes under the general heading of *Sniping*. It is a revered, age-old art, with a few modern, high-powered twists thrown in...

GOLD TRAILS "Gold Card" - A colorful gift card with mining history on the front and scientific and geological information on the reverse, with a mounted, liquid-filled vial containing at least 1½ grains, (130 milligrams) of *genuine* placer gold. Use as a sample, or makes a great gift for young people and hobbyists.

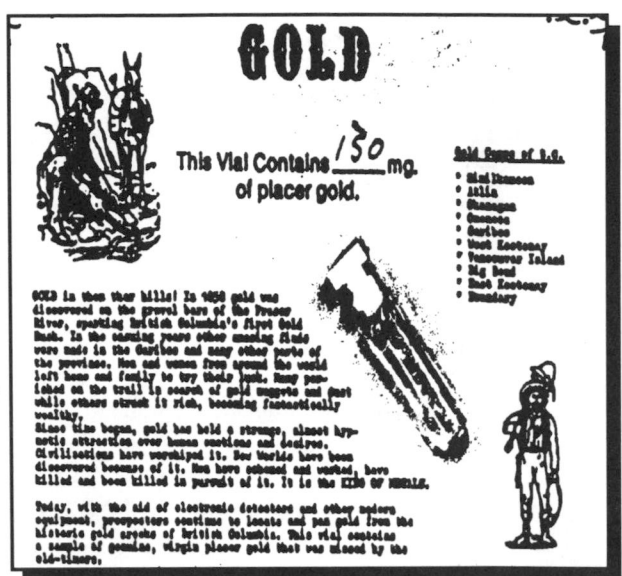

TABLE OF WEIGHTS

Ounces		Dwt.		Grams		Carats		Grains
1	=	20	=	31.103	=	155.5	=	480
.05	=	1	=	1.555	=	7.775	=	24
.032	=	.643	=	1	=	5	=	15.43
.0064	=	.129	=	.2	=	1	=	3.086
.0021	=	.0417	=	.0648	=	.324	=	1

CHAPTER SIX

SNIPING

Let's cut to the chase, shall we? Having digested the more technical information, now we can turn to the fun part - actually digging gold out of the ground!

The techniques described in the next few pages are known collectively as "sniping". There doesn't seem to be any single accepted definition of what sniping is, but I like to think of it as a kind of "mini-mining", involving the recovery of small, but high-grade deposits. The common thread in the various sniping techniques is *mobility*. With the mindset of a guerrilla fighter, the sniper locates a "target", mines it out, then quickly moves on to the next one. Good sniping targets are often located in areas where gold *replenishment* occurs, and so these areas become known to experienced prospectors as *target-rich* environments, which are returned to again and again.

Lets assume you've done your homework, and have located yourself on a good claim on a gold-bearing section of a stream or river. But a full-size placer claim is a hundred acres or more, so where do you start? Obviously, we need to narrow the search area a little more, and the single best way to do is the old-timer's secret technique - "mossing".

Mossing Secrets

Before going into the definition of *mossing*, (which is really a form of geo-chemical sediment sampling), a little background information is in order...

Remember those high-school lessons on Homer's "Iliad", in which Jason and his heroic Argonauts embark on their epic "Quest for the Golden Fleece"? Well, far from being a fanciful adventure story, experts now believe that much of the "Iliad" was based on true events, and that the 'Golden Fleece' were probably actual sheepskins used to line primitive wooden sluice boxes. Sluices were, in fact, used by early Minoan cultures to recover fine gold from the many gold-bearing streams that empty into the Aegean Sea.

The mechanics of a sluice box are dealt with in chapter eight, but for now, think of it simply as an open ended, three-sided box which is set at a slight angle in running water, like so...

Water current carries away the lighter sand and gravel, while the heavier minerals, including gold and platinum, sink to the bottom, becoming trapped in the fibers of the carpet lining. When this lining becomes saturated with gold particles, it is removed and cleaned. Or for more complete recovery, it may be dried, burned and the ashes panned to recover the grains of fine gold.

But what has all this got to do with moss, you ask? Well, the moss that grows

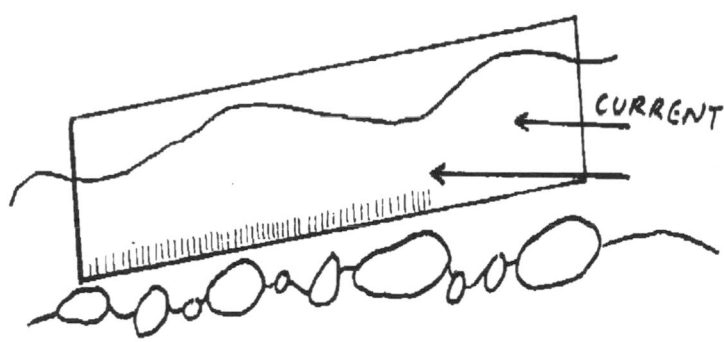

on bedrock and on boulders along the margins of a stream act as nature's very own carpet and, if there is any gold at all in that part of the watercourse - even the finest, minutest gold - the moss will pick it up! Think back to the "Killer Floods" we reviewed in Chapter Three. Did you know that during a flood, one cubic meter of water can hold more than a *ton* of sediment in suspension. That's an awful lot of material passing through, which is being perpetually "scrubbed" by the streamside moss. Furthermore, because moss is such an efficient gold trap, it stands to reason that, in order to qualify as a half-decent prospect, any given location should yield a fairly good showing of fine gold particles in the moss. Otherwise, forget it and move on.

That's what makes *mossing* such a dynamite technique. You only need to pan a few handfuls of moss here and there in order to get an accurate picture of the area's potential for a placer gold deposit. Keep in mind that this mossing technique is suitable only for stream placers, in the presence of running water. It is not pertinent to pocket-type or buried-channel placers, which require different sampling procedures, to be covered later.

Mossing Procedure

1) Select moss growing on an inside bend, preferably on bedrock or a large, flat boulder, somewhere between the high and low water. Select pads of moss which are about one or two inches thick, and avoid very thick, spongy masses that grow on muck, as in this case there is no discernable bottom to act as a barrier to the gold's downward movement.

2) Use a trowel or knife blade to scrape off the moss and deposit the clumps directly into the gold pan. Make sure to scrape right down to the surface of the rock or boulder on which the moss is growing. If it's a boulder that you can pick up, you could actually hold it over the pan in order to scrape off every vestige of adhering roots and sediment with a wire brush. It is this surface-contact layer that holds most of the gold.

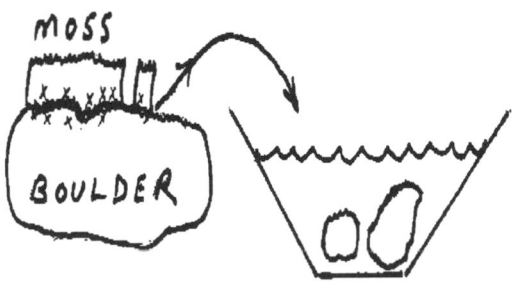

3) Pour water into the pan to completely soak the moss.

4) Use your fingers to break up the clumps of moss, then knead the roots to release all of the fine sediment. Do a thorough job of this, making sure to break up all of the small root-balls and clayey material.

5) Discard the moss that floats to the top. Then, keeping the pan submerged, pan in the same way as was explained for "Panning a Concentrate". Take your time and perform the "shake-down" procedure frequently because, as with a concentrate, sediment from moss will be heavily laden with black sand, and the gold tends to be very fine.

(Note: Because there is likely to be some clay mixed in, which can form a *slime* which can rob the gold, get into the habit of periodically running a forefinger around the drop-center of the pan. This will prevent a coating slime of clay from forming there).

6) As you pan down, make a mental note of how much black sand constitutes that sample. Continue panning until there is about a tablespoon remaining, then "swirl" the contents to reveal the fine colors. Examine, and make notes as to their size, character, and quantity.

On a good section of a gold creek, you will be amazed at the amounts of gold contained within a single handful, or pan-full, of ordinary moss. Ten or twenty fine colors is not unusual. Some places might yield 50, 100, or even 200 colors per pan of moss. Furthermore, fine gold isn't the only product of moss samples. Coarse gold will turn up also, (if there is any coarse gold in the area to begin with). In some spots, the moss will harbor one-eighth to one-quarter inch flakes, and jewelry-size nuggets in abundance, making mossing a potential production-type activity at some locations.

NEWSFLASH:

Yukon Territory, 1980's. *A local equipment dealer reports a successful production-mossing operation on the Stuart River. Two enterprising college women in their early twenties began mining moss with a gas-powered weedeater near Steamboat Bar. After drying the moss on some disused salmon-drying racks, they burned the moss on a large steel plate and then panned the ashes. This operation, which was conducted over a two week period early this spring, yielded 25 troy ounces of fine placer gold.*

On rivers having extensive, moss covered flats, production mossing is sometimes feasible. I recollect that a Boy Scout troop had annual camp-outs at one such location, and never failed to top up the troop's coffers with a good amount of fine gold. I have personally recovered in the range of one-quarter of an ounce during an aftrenoon of mossing on a large river in the Kootenay district. On small creeks, however, you'll find that there just isn't enough moss to support a production operation. More importantly, denuding the banks of a small creek in this manner would be a serious environmental transgression.

The real value of the mossing technique, as I've said, is in testing a handful or two at various locations, as a *sediment sampling* procedure. Having mossed both sides of the river over a certain section, you will have identified one or more high-grade *pay zones* within that section, where the values are relatively higher than anywhere else. THIS is where you will begin sniping in earnest. Locate the nearest bedrock outcrop or, if there is no convenient outcrop, find the nearest big boulder- and go to work!

Glenn's Golden Rule No. 3
Rolling stones gather no moss. But if the moss gathers no gold, be a rolling stone and move on.

On Your TV!

BP077-Modern Gold Mining Techniques-McCracken. McCracken combines years of experience with advanced video effects and demonstrates proper panning, sluicing, moss sampling, fanning, hydraulic concentrating, drywashing, electronic prospecting, and underwater prospecting techniques and equipment used. Includes basics of dredge cleaning, amalgamating, and much more. For the novice exploring a new hobby, or an experienced miner looking for new ways to increase production. Virtually a video encyclopedia. 90 min., VHS,

Catalog Items

BP079-Successful Gold Dredging Made Easy-McCracken. The most important thing to learn in gold dredging is how to find the paystreaks. This follows Dave through a complete day, from startup, to sampling and production, to final cleanup. Covers every important aspect of how to succeed in gold dredging. A valuable visual demonstration. 90 min. VHS,

Bedrock Crevicing

Exposed bedrock outcrops are the sniper's primary target for two reasons:

1) Eighty to ninety percent of all the placer gold occurs on, or just above bedrock.

2) Outcrops are *accessible* -you don't have to dig through a lot of gravel to get to them.

It's true that exposed bedrock is more likely to have received attention from other prospectors before you, but this is not always the case, and the chance of finding a *virgin* bedrock crevice makes it worthwhile, even if you have to sift through a few picked-over areas in the process. (One famous crevice in the Caribou district yielded an amazing 52 troy *pounds* of gold-worth more than $300,000 at today's prices). Also, in my experience, there are actually very few areas that qualify as being genuinely worked-out. A proficient sniper can generally coax an extra nugget or two from even the most popular week-end panning locations. They have a couple of tricks up their sleeve, which I am now about to pass on to you...

By 1856 the Chief Trader at the Hudson's Bay Company, Fort Kamloops, Roderick McLean, had accumulated, "...two pint pickle bottles half full of gold." This gold had been mined during the preceding four seasons by a handful of Nicoamen Indians, whom McLean had supplied with spoons. Spoons? Yes - the best way of digging out the crevices was with an ordinary teaspoon - a method still in use today. But the problem with spoons is you can't get right down into the very bottom of the crevice, where most of the gold is lodged in place. People have even tried tiny, long-handled spoons for this purpose. But still, have you ever tried to lift out small nuggets from a deep crevice with a SPOON? It's practically impossible, which is why so many previously worked-over areas still contain oodles of gold!

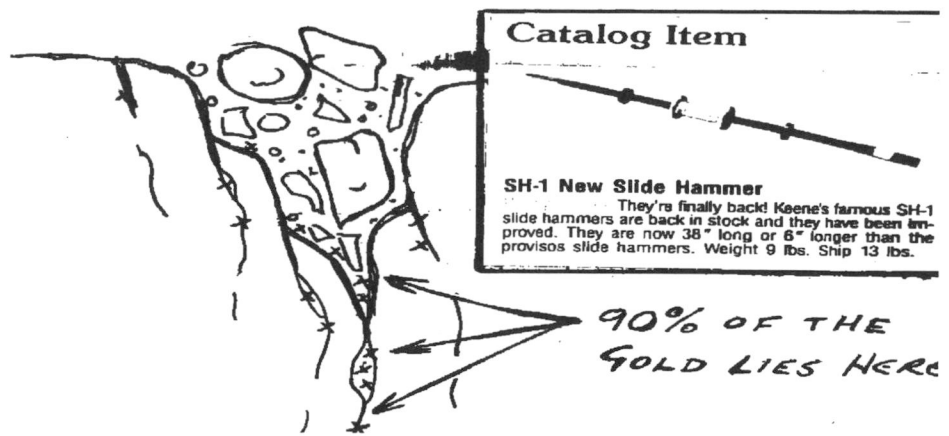

Catalog Item

SH-1 New Slide Hammer
They're finally back! Keene's famous SH-1 slide hammers are back in stock and they have been improved. They are now 38" long or 6" longer than the provisos slide hammers. Weight 9 lbs. Ship 13 lbs.

90% OF THE GOLD LIES HERE

To really do a number on a bedrock crevice, to get to the very bottom and beyond, into the small pockets and expansions which the gold infiltrates, you have to bust the crack wide open with a heavy iron bar. Break away the fractured sides of the crevice and scrub these fragments over your pan or in a tub, in order to collect all of the gold-rich, clayey material adhering to the sides. The example depicted on the previous page ends up looking like this...

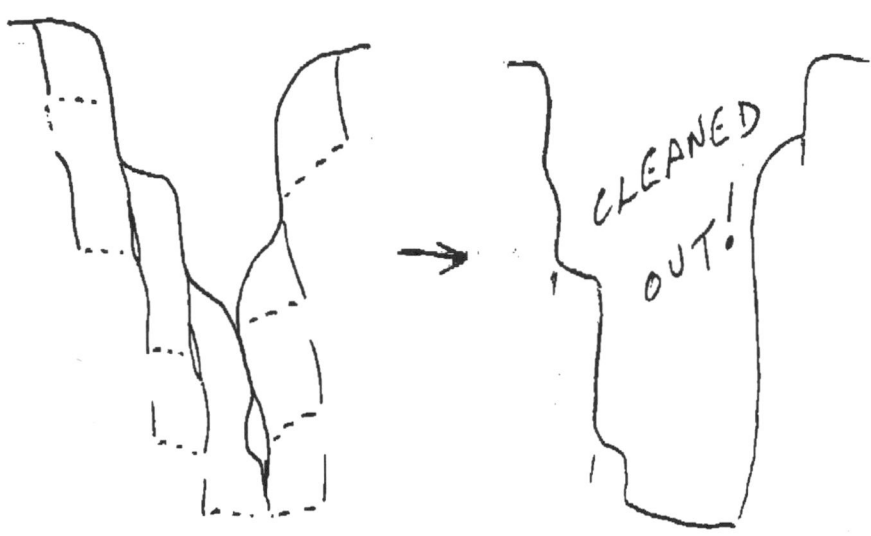

Sniping bedrock crevices really is an art. As you learn the ropes you will begin to appreciate that there are different types of bedrock which require a slightly different approach. For instance, bedrock that is composed of a very hard, resistant granite tends to wear smooth, with only microscopic crevices, if any at all. So even if your mossing indicates an abundance of gold migrating through a particular area, if you find that the bedrock there is smooth and polished, with no holding crevices, it's probably best to pass it by. (This kind of bedrock is called Leaverite, (named after me), because you're supposed to, "Leaverite there - it's no dammed good.")

The best kind of bedrock for trapping gold is slate, with shale a close second. This is a really soft, breakable type of rock which gold can penetrate to depths of three or four feet. For in-between types of bedrock, or composite-type bedrock which is hard in places, you can make headway by using a pick and a gad-pry bar, in the manner of a hammer and chisel.

Some types of bedrock are awkward to work on, as is a submerged crevice in shallow water. One crevicing tool you should never be without is a good quality *ripping* tool such as the Gold Claw. I've watched people hammer and chisel away for hours on a crevice that could have been cleaned out in seconds with a few deft strokes with the claw.

If the areas you work in are noted for having lots of fine gold, you might find a gold suction gun a worthwhile investment. It works like a large syringe, to siphon out every last vestige of gold-rich fine sediment from the bottom of the crevice.

SHIPPING WT. 4 LBS

Gad Pry Bar

Top quality forged tool steel. For easy splitting, prying, raking out crevices. I-beam construction gives super strength. Double polished hammer faces for driving bar either way.

Bulb Snifter/Deluxe Bulb Snifter

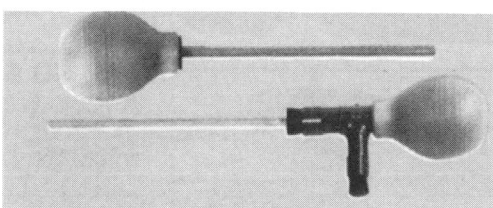

Essential for underwater extraction of small gold nuggets and specimens as well as gemstones. Simply squeeze and retract rubber bulb. Rubber bulb detaches for easy recovery of sample. Deluxe model has reservoir for gold separation from sand.

While crevicing, keep a special lookout for crevices that begin above the water-line then extend out into the bed of the river, because submerged crevices were often left unworked. After removing as much compacted gravel as possible from the submerged crevice, wave your hand vigorously back and forth above the crack. This procedure, called "fanning", will blow out the lighter sand, leaving any gold present remaining at the bottom. Pick out the nuggets with tweezers, or use a suction gun if the particles are very small.

Boulder-Sniping

Suppose the high grade pay zone you located by mossing doesn't have any exposed bedrock outcrops. In this case, your immediate target should be any large boulders embedded in a gravel bar, preferably on an inside bend. Better yet, try to locate a *cluster* of large boulders (called a "boulder jam", or, "boulder garden") as this is evidence of a drop-out zone - a shift from a high pressure to low pressure during floodstage, or an underlying bedrock irregularity. Another consideration is that, in order to get closer to bedrock (always a desirable goal) you can either dig a lot of overburden or you can move one or two large boulders. Moving boulders is easier and less time consuming.

The early history of placer mining in the west is replete with stories of the "Celestials". These were immigrant Chinese miners, skillful enough to eke out an existence on "worked-out" gold creeks long after the whites had become discouraged and moved on. A big reason for their success was their facility at moving very large boulders. I have seen huge, truck-size boulders that have been propped up, in place, so the gravel could be excavated from underneath. It is a marvel to see such feats of engineering, with the wooden cribbing still in place a hundred years later. What a testament to the ingenuity and bravery of those early gold-seekers.

The celestials had discovered an important principle of gold deposition: There is always, always more gold under and around a boulder than there is in the surrounding gravels. This holds true whether the boulder is lying directly on bedrock or is suspended above it in the gravel strata. As well, the gold under a boulder tends to be somewhat heavier, and it's no surprise that most of the very large specimen nuggets have been found underneath a big rock.

"Boys, look for rocks that are red, black, green, and *heavy*." The old-timers used to say. This is good advice, it turns out, because black, red, and green are the predominant colors of *ultramafic* rocks, which *are* heavy, and tend to settle-out in the same places as gold. Another good sign is *cow's tongue*. These are large, flattened rocks that have a wavy, undulating, water-worn top surface. This shape is evidence of having been in place and subject to erosion for a very long time, allowing for the accumulation of a considerable amount of gold. Also, being disk-shaped, the cow's tongue requires extremely high water pressure to move it - yet another sign of a major drop-out zone.

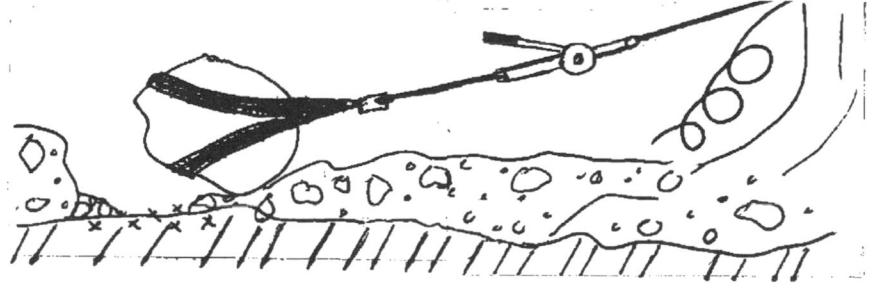

Using A Come-along To Winch Boulders

The lightweight winch, or 'come-along' is a boon to the modern gold miner. With a boulder sling, a length of aircraft cable, and a handy nearby tree for an anchor, you can accomplish in an hour what would have taken a team of sourdoughs a day - and you can do it in safety. Use the snatch-block that comes with the kit to double your pulling power if necessary. You can move some real behemoths with this outfit, so watch your toes while it's

Catalog Item

A-50 BOULDER SLING KIT: Includes 8000 lb. test nylon webbing with slide ring, 50 feet of steel cable and a cable grip for taking up slack in line. Sling kit is a must for moving large boulders.

moving, and be sure to move the rock far enough out of it's hole so there's no chance of it sliding, (or rolling), back in. To be doubly safe, chock the boulder with wooden blocks and leave the cable attached while the hole is being excavated.

Gold Vacuuming

During the past few years *gold vacuuming* has become all the rage in the western US, and is now beginning to catch on worldwide. The reason for the tremendous

success of the gold vacuum is simple - it WORKS! For example, how about the situation we encountered earlier - getting way down to the very bottom of a gold-bearing crevice? With the suction power of a vacuum, you can lift gold-bearing material out of a crevice in a flash. An upholstery attachment can be used to vacuum moss, or even to sweep bare, smooth bedrock with amazing results. If you've never used a vacuum before, you will definitely be impressed by the amounts of gold that can be collected in this way. From a production point of view, it is probably the next best thing to a dredge.

The 12 Volt Electric Vacuum

This inexpensive unit, (about $30 at any hardware store), can be operated with a 12-volt rechargeable power pack, which can be recharged at home or from your vehicle. One charge gives about 20-30 minutes of continuous operation, which is more than enough for an afternoon of intermittent sniping. A solar panel can be purchased as an accessory to the powerpack, and comes in very handy on a remote wilderness prospecting expedition. The 12 volt vacuum can also be hooked up with alligator clips to any 12 volt car or recreational battery, and will give more hours of operation than a power pack but of course, a car battery is quite a bit heavier.

Gas-Powered Production Vacuums

The gas-powered model, (the 'Dry Land Dredge'), is more expensive initially, but you'll appreciate the extra power and duration when you get into a production mode, and the machine will pay for itself in no-time if you're in a halfway decent area. A gold vacuum can increase your sniping productivity at least fourfold so, if you are now up to the level of 4 or 5 pennyweight per day, with a vacuum you should be able to reach the ounce-a-day mark consistently.

DRY-LAND DREDGING

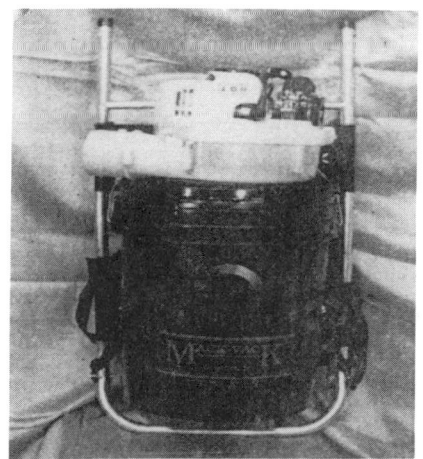

```
MV-1 MACK-VAC

* 2-cycle gas eng.
* Power & Reliability
* Long Crevice Nozzle
* Weighs only 15 lbs.
* Great for backpacking.
```

Catalog Item

Whether you choose to go electric or gas, gold vacuums are very simple to operate. Use it to suck dry or damp material from the crevices. A small whisk is handy for brushing out the bottom of the crack and directing the material towards the suction nozzle.

Underwater Sniping

Underwater crevicing can be very worthwhile, because in many places, the *underwater* crevices have never been touched. The exceptions to this are the very small creeks, which might have been wing-dammed or else completely diverted so as to get to the underwater deposits. But on most larger creeks and rivers - especially those which flow through tight canyons, where diversion wasn't possible - the underwater deposits have remained intact, and they can be very lucrative indeed.

Shallow-Water Sniping

Equipment Required:

1   Rubber boots or hip waders
2   Ripping bar, (i.e.: "gold claw")
3   Gold suction gun
4   Mr. Peeper", or mask-and-snorkel
5   Hand whisk
6   Rake
7   Long tweezers, small spoon
8   Pry-bar and/or slide hammer
9   Small shovel

Procedure

Use the peeper or mask and snorkel to spy out likely looking submerged crevices. Scalp off the overlying gravels and cobbles with a rake. Use the "claw" to loosen up the compacted gravel and pebbles, then use your hand or a whisk to, "fan the crack", and disperse the remaining light sand and gravel. (It helps at this point if there is at least a slight current to wash the material away and improve visibility). Spy the crevice again for any large nuggets sticking out, which you can pick out with tweezers. If necessary, repeat the fanning procedure until you have blown out as much sediment as possible. Finally, use the suction gun to siphon-off the last remaining layer of fine sediment. THIS is where most of the gold will have settled.

Inspect the crevice one last time and, if you suspect it goes deeper or there might be hairline fissures, use your large iron bar to bust it open, as described in the previous chapter.

Big-Water Sniping

You can work underwater more effectively, and in much deeper water, by going whole-hog and donning a wet suit, mask, and snorkel. An inexpensive, farmer-john type wet suit, made from ¼-inch or thicker neoprene rubber, will keep you warm and, because it is very buoyant, you will be quite safe as you float gently downstream, head submerged, hunting down those untouched crevices and virgin glory-holes. To prevent wear-and-tear on the suit, you can use duct tape to secure cloth or rubber kneepads, or wear an old set of oversize coveralls over the suit to protect it from cuts and abrasions on sharp rocks. For float trips of any distance, a heavy-duty canvas knapsack comes in handy as a carry-all. Heavy duty work boots, worn over the soft rubber "booties", are used instead of the traditional frog-man's swim fins.

Admittedly, this style of underwater prospecting isn't for everyone. You should be in reasonably good physical shape if you're going to attempt it. But I know quite a few adventurous types who conduct this sort of float trip every season during the low water of late summer and fall, covering up to two or three miles in a single day - and boy! they sure have some nice gold to show for it.

62

Summary of Sniping Techniques

There's something about sniping that brings out the primitive, carnal aspect of my nature. I suppose it's something like the hunting instinct, but *this* quarry is, in a way, even more elusive than a living, breathing game animal.

What is it about those tiny, glittering fragments of strange metal - cooked in the core of a distant sun, hidden deep in the earth for billions of years, and never before seen by the eyes of man? What is it?

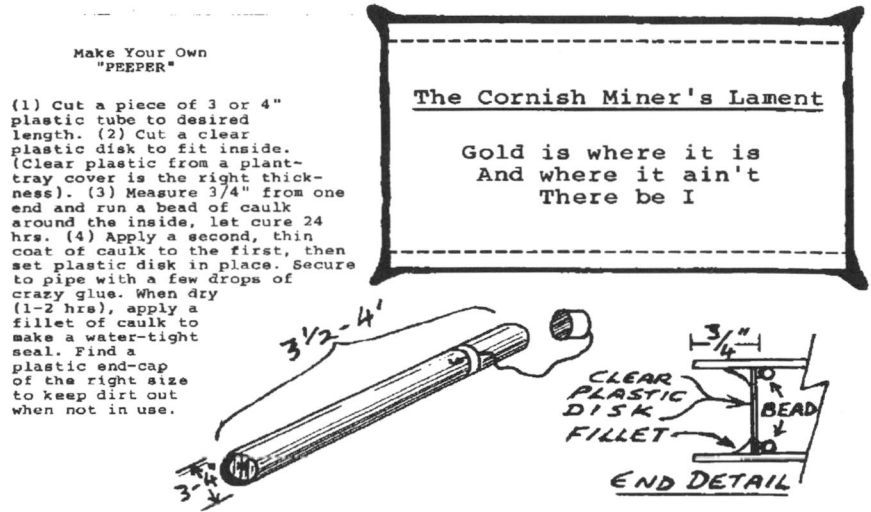

Make Your Own "PEEPER"

(1) Cut a piece of 3 or 4" plastic tube to desired length. (2) Cut a clear plastic disk to fit inside. (Clear plastic from a plant-tray cover is the right thickness). (3) Measure 3/4" from one end and run a bead of caulk around the inside, let cure 24 hrs. (4) Apply a second, thin coat of caulk to the first, then set plastic disk in place. Secure to pipe with a few drops of crazy glue. When dry (1-2 hrs), apply a fillet of caulk to make a water-tight seal. Find a plastic end-cap of the right size to keep dirt out when not in use.

The Cornish Miner's Lament

Gold is where it is
And where it ain't
There be I

Dowsing, etc. - A Nose for the Gold?

I like to indulge myself by thinking I might be one of those people with a special affinity for gold - a sort of "sixth sense". I suppose this is why I'm always on about being "in-tune" with your environment, and that sort of thing.

It's tempting to ascribe such feelings to psychic, (psi), events or to supernatural elements, especially in light of recent hard evidence in the field of parapsychology. Reputable, hard-nosed researchers such as nuclear physicist Stanton Friedman, Jacques Vallee, Paul Devereuux, and even the staid Arthur C. Clarke, have all documented human and animal psi responses in relation to geological activity and unseen "earth forces". Some investigators have gone so far as to suggest that psychic manifestations experienced by ancient cult societies led to the construction of astronomically-based monoliths at certain important "Earth-Line" intersections. The Druid's *Stonehenge* is one oft-cited example of this.

While the specific mechanism behind these strange effects remains obscure, there's no longer much argument that *something* is going on. For centuries, dowsing has been a recognized and accepted method of remote-locating of subterranean water and mineral deposits. Today, in Russia, university curriculum in geology always includes compulsory courses in *biolocation,* an advanced form of psychic remote sensing. All sorts of effects have been reported by experimenters, including piezo-electrically generated electromagnetic manifestations, (the so-called *Earth Lights* of ancient mining lore), ball lightning, strange mists, apparitions and "entities", and hallucinations. To my mind, one of the most compelling bits of evidence in support of geological/psi effects, is the apparent *recognition behavior* which many different types of animals exhibit *in advance* of seismic activity or other geological event.

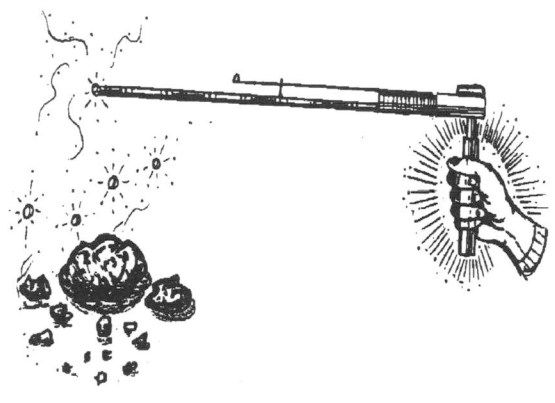

While these are all interesting ideas, in the end I have to throw up my hands and admit that it's more likely that the true explanation will turn out to be a much more mundane one, based on existing knowledge and facts. Probably, because of my enthusiasm for, and enjoyment of prospecting, I am in such a relaxed state as I saunter down the creek-bed that more of the subtle, natural clues and information in the environment is subconsciously creeping in. It's a feeling that's hard to describe - a kind of vague, nonspecific apprehension, perhaps a slight quickening of the pulse. Then, nine times out of ten, a *discovery* is made right away. Most of the time, the finds are fairly modest - a couple of jewelry-sized nuggets or so. Once in a while, though, after having spent time panning good samples over a wide area, it begins to dawn on me that I am in the presence of a considerable amount of heavy metal. If the occurrence appears to be a reasonably accessible surface deposit, then I *really* get excited!

There are a number of dowsing rods, "molecular frequency discriminators", and electronic long-distance "locators" on the market today which claim to enhance human extra-sensory perception for locating minerals. Although some of these devices have a large following of devotees, who swear as to their effectiveness (and often have the results to show for it), we have decided against including them in the **GOLD TRAILS** product line at this time. It seems that the effectiveness of these instruments has a lot to do with the individual "percipient" or operator, so the re

sults cannot be claimed to be *repeatable*. Since "repeatability" is a basic requirement
of the Scientific Method, there is just no way to make claims for these devices that are consistent with the **GOLD TRAILS** pledge...

GOLD TRAILS

Recreational Prospecting & Mining Center

The *Gold Trails* **Pledge...**"*Gold Trails* pledges to deliver only professional, top-of-the-line products and equipment which are *proven successful* in the location and recovery of precious metals

CHAPTER SEVEN

PROCESSING AURIFEROUS GRAVEL - SLUICING & DREDGING

Theory

For a moment, let's reconsider the fundamentals of an economic gold deposit: Grade x Volume. In the preceding chapter we discovered how, because material from a bedrock crevice tends to be highly concentrated, we only need to locate and recover small amounts of this high-grade material, (a hundred pounds or less, let's say), to obtain a satisfactory yield. But dream of the day when you discover a high-grade pocket that contains, not just buckets-full, but ton after ton of rich, nuggety paydirt. If you persevere in the prospecting game long enough, sooner or later you will be rewarded with the opportunity and challenge of a large volume of gold-bearing gravel.

In this chapter - Sluicing & Dredging - I shall outline some of the principles behind small-scale ore processing. The objective here is to make the most efficient use of the small, inexpensive equipment now available, in order to get through larger volumes of material.

The old-timers resigned themselves to shoveling gravel day in and day out. They had to build a cabin nearby and set down roots for a few seasons until the deposit ran out. Even more time was taken up in the construction of crude, heavy wooden sluice boxes, which added further to the miner's labors, and which were not all that efficient anyway. In contrast to that situation, the mobility and access we enjoy today, and the availability of lightweight, high-efficiency sluices, has resulted in the widespread popularity of *weekend mining*.

Catalog Item

Keene Hand Sluices

The standard for light weight prospecting. Both models have improved riffle design for superior recovery in both fast and slow water. New rubber ribbed matting for instant gold recognition and improved fine gold recovery. Improved latching system for quick, easy clean-ups. Model A51 Mini Sluice weighs 5lbs. Dimensions; 36"x 10". Model A52 Hand Sluice weighs 11lbs. Dimensions; 10"x51", with a large 18" flare.

Catalog Item

Eldorado Blue Sluice

From the famous Swedish prospector and inventor, Lars Guldstrun, the inventor of the Gold Spear and the Klondike gold pan.

The Eldorado Blue Sluice has no carpet or cumbersome sluice tray, just reverse and flush for fast clean-ups. The entire 39" length is tough blue plastic with a 4 stage moulded riffle design. It traps very fine gold along with valuable heavy concentrates. With lightweight aluminum sides, it weighs less than 4lbs.

Several years ago, a well known American prospector and author, Carl Fischer, reported the results of one of his own weekend prospecting excursions. He selected a popular site, which happened to be situated close to a large urban center. This place was generally avoided by most other "professional" prospectors, because it had been well worked over, the gold tended to be very fine, and the gravels were universally low grade. By the tone of the article he wrote afterwards, Carl was trying to make a point. He was lamenting the demise of the work ethic, and the tendency of some young people nowadays to avoid hard work, because of the availability of welfare, unemployment insurance, and so on. He was trying to show that small-scale mining is an economically viable alternative.

To prove his point, Carl worked a full eight hour day out on "the digs", then carefully weighed the fine gold he recovered, then extrapolated the results for a one-week period. The result was an income of over $650 per week, in 1984 dollars!

Mr. Fischer sure made his point with me. At the time he was in his eighties.

Sluicing

Sluices are still in use today because they can efficiently process large volumes of gravel. Compared to panning, you can shovel about a hundred times more gravel through a sluice in the same amount of time. The basic sluice, as described in the previous chapter, has changed little, except for the addition of perfectly-engineered, high-tech *riffles*, which have the exact shape and angle for optimum separation of gold and other heavy elements, including gemstones.

There will always be some people who want to save a few bucks by nailing together a homemade wooden sluice box, but in my opinion, this is nearly always a mistake, because it's almost impossible to achieve the results of a manufactured unit. Why re-invent the wheel?

How a Sluice box Works

A sluice works by creating a *vortex*, or, *rotor-wave*, in behind each riffle. Because the water in the space behind each riffle is at a lower pressure than the current flowing over it, heavy particles get trapped there, while the lighter constituents are spun-out and get carried away in the top-current.

The key to setting a sluice box up properly is in getting the right balance between the water *velocity* going through the box, and the *pitch* that the box is set at. If the velocity is too slow, an excess of material will quickly build up. If you try to increase the velocity by increasing the angle too much, gravity will cause the "heavies" to roll out of the box, overcoming the tendency of the vortex to keep them in place. The trick is to find a place in the creek where there is enough flow so that you can set the box at just a slight angle, and the gravel still moves through.

Use rocks to jam the sluice box in place. If necessary, clear out some cobbles from underneath, or use flat rocks to shim the box at just the right angle. To make sure the box is working properly, test it with a few shovelfuls of gravel. You might add a few pennies, BB's, nails, or other little bits of metal to see how it is working. The bulk of the gravel should wash through within about thirty seconds, leaving all of the metal pieces sitting in behind the first two or three riffles. If the gravel isn't being moved quickly enough, increase the angle a little. If that still doesn't do it, try increasing the water flow into the head of the box by positioning some boulders so as to divert more of the creek's current into the box. Make sure the box is perfectly level across the line of the riffles; any slight tilt will cause material to load up along one side or the other.

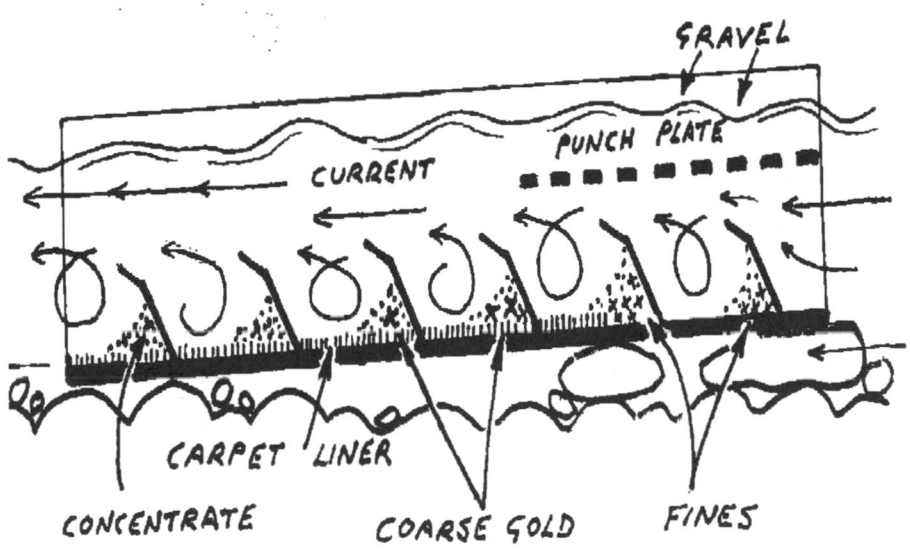

The other important consideration in sluicing is in the adequate *classification* of the gravel, along the same principles outlined in the section on panning. Shoveling bank-run gravel directly into a sluice box is a disaster, because the first large cobble that rolls through will completely disrupt the water flow, and it may very well knock out some of the gold that has already accumulated. To avoid this, shovel the gravel through a screen into a pail, then empty the contents of the pail, a bit at a time, into the sluice. What's good about the pail method is that, as well as properly classifying material, you can set the sluice up at a particular spot and are free to range some distance upstream and downstream to collect samples. By the way, it's much easier to tote two, half-full pails instead of one heavy one because the balance is better for walking on uneven ground. Also, by pre-classifying the material at each sample site, you won't be lugging around a lot of useless oversize rock.

Sometimes everything works out just so, and you find a suitable set-up spot in the creek smack dab next to the deposit you want to work. In this case, it *is* possible to shovel directly into a sluice, provided you set up a *grizzly* screen over the head of the box. You can use any sort of screen with an appropriate, (1/2" to 1 inch), spacing. I've found the racks from an old stove or fridge to be ideal, because the bars go all in one direction, letting the cobbles slide off easier. Use bits of wire to secure the screen, and brace it at about a 45° tilt with some wooden stakes. A tent-shaped grizzly also works well. Whichever configuration you use, remember to keep the rack's cross bars on the underside-so as to present a smooth top surface for the cobbles to roll off.

Adequate classification of gravel is crucial for efficient gold recovery. The more stages of classification the material goes through, the better gold recovery at each stage. One way to effect a *Secondary Classification* in a sluice box is to incorporate a *punch plate* having 1/8th to ¼-inch perforations, located over the head of the sluice. This type of sluice design, called an *undercurrent sluice,* protects the fine material in the lower level from being disrupted by the coarser rock. This feature can be found on all of the better models of sluices and dredges.

In sluicing, nature, unfortunately, does not always cooperate. You will find yourself in situations where the water isn't flowing fast enough, (often the case on large rivers), or the gravel you want to run is located too far from the set-up point. In some cases, you will find a whole section of creek where the gravel is so great that you don't want to waste extra time repeatedly moving and setting up the sluice, even when the water flow and all the other factors are quite suitable. The answer to any of these situations is to provide your own water flow by means of a small, portable gas pump and a length of pressure hose, (up to a maximum of about 100 feet). The technical term for a pump-operated sluice box is *hydraulic concentrator,* but most people prefer the term *"highbanker".* The highbanker has the advantage over a regular river-sluice in that you can set it up very quickly wherever you find yourself, because you can now adjust the water going through, and the angle of the box, which allows you to really fine-tune the device for local conditions, the fineness of the gold, etc.

If you already own a water pump, all you need now is something to spread the flow of water evenly at the head of the sluice, and some kind of grizzly apparatus to classify the gravel. The following arrangement combines both functions...

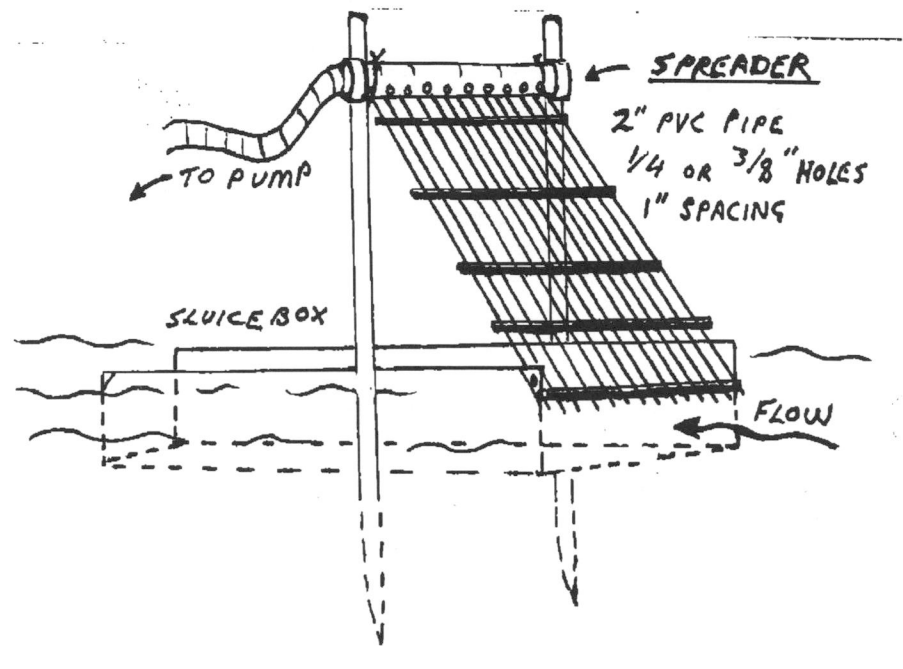

If you intend to begin a small-scale placer operation, and haven't yet purchased a pump, you are in luck, because new on the market are several models of *combination* highbanker/dredges that have interchangeable components. The beauty of these add-on systems is that you can start out with a simple, inexpensive sluice box, to which a lot of bolt-on accessories can be added later. A properly matched pump comes next, then a *conversion kit* which, with the addition of a grizzly-equipped hopper box, turns your basic sluice into a full-fledged highbanker machine. Finally, there is the bolt-on *suction dredge* attachment, which puts you into a whole new league as far as productivity is concerned.

CATALOG ITEM

The versatility offered by a completely integrated system like this cannot be overstated. In one outfit, you have all the equipment necessary for most any placer-mining application. Everything from an ultralight hand-held sluice weighing just a few pounds - to a bank-working machine, all in one package! ....

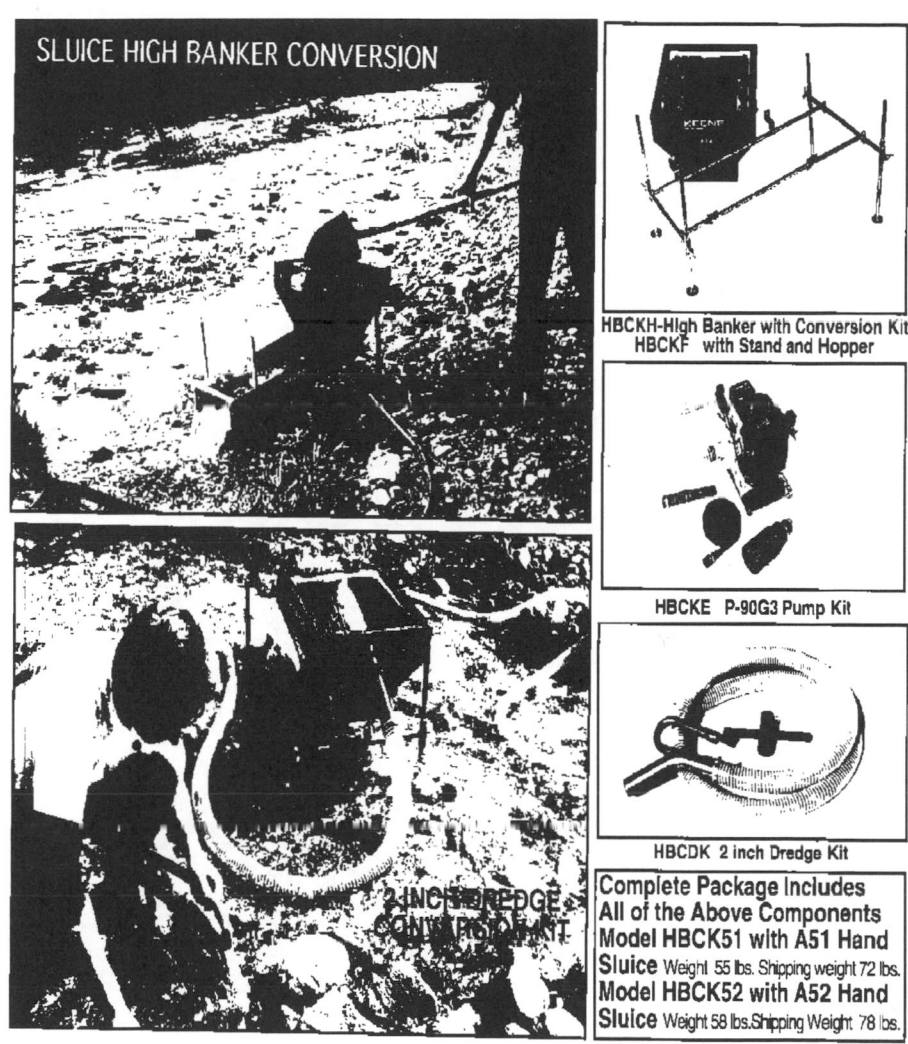

SLUICE HIGH BANKER CONVERSION

HBCKH-High Banker with Conversion Kit
HBCKF with Stand and Hopper

HBCKE P-90G3 Pump Kit

HBCDK 2 inch Dredge Kit

2 INCH DREDGE CONVERSION KIT

Complete Package Includes
All of the Above Components
**Model HBCK51 with A51 Hand
Sluice** Weight 55 lbs. Shipping weight 72 lbs.
**Model HBCK52 with A52 Hand
Sluice** Weight 58 lbs. Shipping Weight 78 lbs.

Dredging Background

No matter how you look at it - dollar for dollar, or pound for pound, today's portable suction dredge is by far the most efficient gold recovery device yet invented. With it, you can recover paying quantities of gold, due to it's powerful, yet lightweight, hydraulic system. It is capable of moving large volumes of gravel, like an underwater vacuum. Just think - no more shoveling!

The Evolution of the Modern Gold Dredge

The suction dredge operates on the *venturi* principle. The civil engineers of ancient Rome were the first to find practical applications for this device, including crude pneumatic drills used in construction work. Centuries later, the Swiss scientist, Bernoulli, made a series of experiments involving the venturi, and laid the foundation for two modern related sciences - hydrodynamics, and aerodynamics. Today, the results of this pioneering work is incarnated in supersonic jet planes and, (lucky for us), in high-efficiency gold dredges and concentrators.

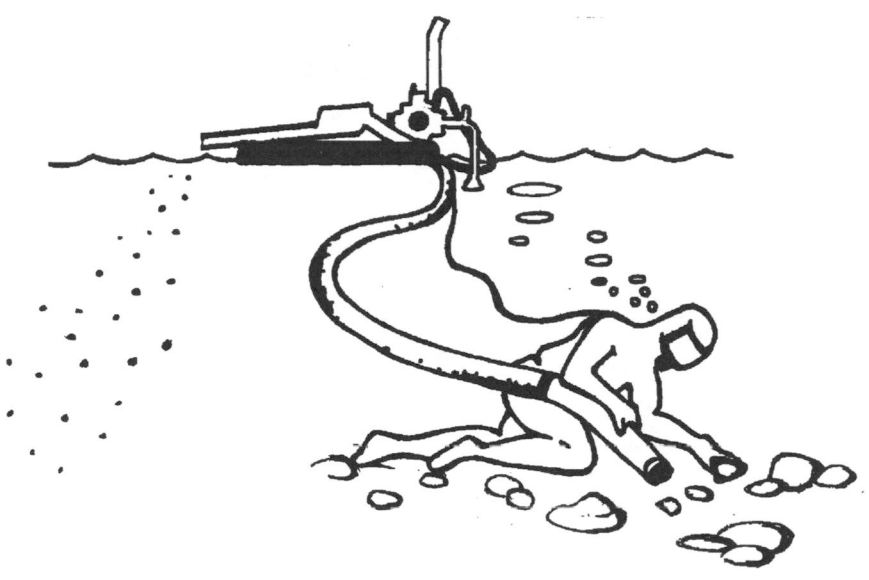

During the last century the same principles were used to operate gigantic *hydraulic elevators* in large-scale placer-mines. Those mines had very deep, unstable deposits that would have been unworkable with any other method. The next development came in the post-World War II period as a result of the popularization of scuba diving by Jaques Cousteau and others, opening up a whole new world for treasure hunters, underwater miners, and recreational prospectors alike.

One of the early enthusiasts was Jerry Keene. He resurrected the hydraulic elevator idea and built several small, portable machines in his garage. They worked so well on the rich gold-bearing rivers of his native southern California that he was soon besieged by prospectors the world over, and Keene Engineering, the world's largest supplier of portable mining equipment, was born. This family business has continued to prosper, and still delivers the superior quality product that Mr. Keene was noted for.

Nowadays, there is a new breed of independent miner, somewhat reminiscent of the early "sourdoughs", called the Professional Dredger. "Professional" is the operative word here. With diesel powered, commercial size dredges of six, eight, or ten-inch intake size, and capable of operating at depths of up to a hundred feet, these are the new pioneers of modern-day Gold Mining. One such individual, the intrepid Dave McCracken, started at a young age, and used the proceeds of his own small gold dredging operation to launch what became a widespread mining organization. Dave is known for the excellent training videos he produces. Under Dave's direct supervision, dredging teams have been trained to work in some of the world's most inhospitable gold hot-spots, from the frigid conditions of the Yukon and Alaska to the steaming rainforests of Venezuela and Costa Rica.

Not all of the professional dredgers become wealthy, but some do, and those who don't all seem to be able to at least make a living at it somehow. One wonders where the next great adventure will be - the fabled upper reaches of the Blue Nile? The impenetrable rain forests of Central America? A multi-million dollar ocean-dredging operation is currently under way in the deep-water gold placers of the Bering Sea, and at this writing, there have been rumors of a fantastic gold strike under the Antarctic ice. In recent years the great hinterland of mother Russia has just begun to open up to western technology, and the vast, uninhabited Siberian Tiaga is beckoning. There's platinum in the Ural Mountains, gold on the Kamchatka Peninsula - magical names, magical places.

Commercial Dredging

Opportunities exist worldwide for commercial, as well as recreational gold dredging. In North America, and in British Columbia, especially, there are great gold rivers that have, literally, never been touched by this kind of mining. It's true that because of our increased sophistication about ecological issues, more effort goes into regulatory compliance than might be necessary in other, less developed jurisdictions. In my opinion, this is a good thing. After all, the environment *must* be protected and, while this does result in an added burden of bureaucratic compliance, the cost is relatively small and is more than offset by our technological endowment, infrastructure, etc. Besides, we need to set an example and show that resource activities need not be at the expense of the environment, but can be conducted *in harmony* with it. Environmental foul-ups, (especially in mining), continue to occur in third-world countries, mostly through ignorance. We have no such excuse.

There are lots of opportunities right in our own backyard for the kind of large, commercial dredging operations I have been describing, and I would never try to dissuade anyone from taking up the challenge. However, there is a big difference between this type of commercial dredging, using monster dredges, and the kind of small, portable, week-end type of operation most of my readers are interested in. For one thing, the type of "backpack" dredging that is within the scope of this book does not, by-and-large, require much in the way of complicated applications and permits. At most, there might be one or two simple forms to fill out, and you won't need the services of a "Howe Street Lawyer" to do it.

Regulations For Small Portable Equipment

Regulatory requirements in western jurisdictions will have small differences from state-to-state, province, or territory. Check the Appendix for a source of information for your particular region. Here I will give some examples of the regulatory environment in B.C. British Columbia is known around the world as being pretty tough when it comes to the environment, and it sets a good example, but what I really like is that here in B.C., the rules are fair and simple, and anyone who exercises good common-sense can understand and comply with them.

In B.C., the Mines Department administers the Mineral Tenure Act. It has authority to issue permits for various "Classes" of exploration and mining activities on Mineral Claims and on Placer Claims. These classes are organized on the general principles of: area of *surface disturbance* involved, and *sample size*, (which dictates the size of equipment to be used).

For example, a "Class A" permit on a mineral claim is available, free of charge, for hand-operations involving minimal surface disturbance. Approved activities include: hand-trenching, small camps, geochemical and geophysical surveys, and surface and underground mapping.

The next category up, "Class B", encompasses light *mechanized* equipment, such as backhoes, drill rigs, and earthmoving equipment for road construction. *Bulk Samples* up to 10 tonnes for a mineral claim, or 2,000 cubic meters for placer claims, are permitted. As of January 1st, 1997, the Resource Use Fee levied on this permit was $100 (subject to change).

Notice that the Class A category, while restricted to "Hand Operations Only", is sufficiently broad to include all types of electronic prospecting, trenching, and geochemical sediment sampling. A small, gas or electric powered, re-circulating sluice or concentrator may be used.

Similarly, the "Class PA" category, for *Placer Claims*, permits hand operations, and is also free of charge. Specifically mentioned in the regulations are:

- hand panning
- hand sluicing
- hand dug pits or trenches
- geophysical surveys
- flagged and blazed lines and control grids

Small pumps, used to deliver water to hand-operated equipment, are permitted. In (Section 42.2) of the Water Act, administered by the Ministry of Environment, provision is made for small diversions of water involved in *prospecting* and exploration (hand operations) and "Water Use Permits" are *not* required. (Note: Most portable equipment has a pump capacity much smaller than the 0.5 cubic foot-per-second unit scale used by the Ministry of Environment. The Keene Mini-Highbanker, for example, delivers 90 US Gallons per Minute, which is the equivalent of 0.2 cfs.)

Although at this time no fees are collected for Class A and Class PA work, the Inspector of Mines has requested that you do submit a "Notice of Work and Reclamation on a Placer Claim". (Or a Mineral Claim, as the case may be.) However, if you intend to explore in an area where prospecting is permitted, but it is not on a mineral claim or a placer claim, the "Notice of Work" permit is *not* required. The operator would do well to keep in mind, however, that to continue to qualify as prospecting and exploration, the Class A and Class PA restrictions will have to be observed.

Screening Pump Intakes

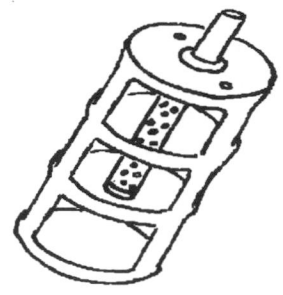

Under Section 28 of the Fisheries Act, any pump intake which draws water from "...any Canadian fisheries waters..." must be fitted with a screen, so as to prevent conflicts in regards to andromedous fish populations. The screen material should be 7-mesh or finer. The size of the screen is to be equal to 10 square meters. Most people set the intake that comes with the pump into a screen or a bucket, to provide additional protection from sand and gravel getting into the pump. As well as protecting the pump, this also protects aquatic life. In the case of "fisheries waters", as described above, you should take the additional precaution of screening-over whatever bucket or drum you are using.

Environmental Aspects of Suction Dredging

Suction dredging gets special treatment from the government. Not too long ago, this type of mining was generally not permitted in British Columbia, although in other jurisdictions - notably in California, where dredging had become very popular - dredging regulations had been developed which were considered quite acceptable, and successful, by environmentalists and miners alike. Because of dredging's growing popularity, various agencies in B.C. decided to have a second look. I was pleased to be involved in several field demonstrations, and worked with other "grassroots" miners to provide supporting documentation for a dredging proposal. The result of these efforts was the development of a set of dredging guidelines, and the issuance of the first (legal) dredging permits in British Columbia. I found that working closely with the various government agencies is the best approach to resolving environmental issues. Most miners are outdoors-type people and are environmentally aware, and although infractions do occasionally occur, (and are nearly always successfully prosecuted), by-and-large miners do a commendable job of policing themselves.

The following are the most recently issued set of guidelines for dredging applications. Be aware that interpretations may differ from region to region, so it's best to clear up any vague issues in advance. Please remember that these agencies do not have the man-power to "baby-sit" each and every placer operation in the province. Do yourself and everyone else a favor by doing your homework before approaching a mining official with a dredging proposal. Come equipped with answers to such questions as: Does this waterway have andromedous, (migratory), fish species? What other native species exist and what are their reproductive cycles? If there are sections of your proposed work-area that have aquatic plant-cover which may provide forage and cover, these should be considered 'biologically active' and left alone. Have these areas been identified and plotted on your mining-plan sketch? Every square inch of your proposed work-site should be well-photographed, with the photos numbered and matched to a location or grid line. For photos of underwater locations, (i.e. a bedrock reef that you want to dredge on), I found that the new disposable waterproof cameras work well and are very inexpensive.

DFO/BCE GUIDELINES FOR THE USE OF SUCTION DREDGES TO "SNIPE" FOR GOLD

The following guidelines apply to the use of portable suction dredges to "snipe" for gold in bedrock canyon areas. The general prohibition on suction dredging in B.C. is not waived, rather, the Regional Placer Mining Coordination Committees may allow portable suction dredges to be operated for sniping on a site specific basis. The following guidelines are offered on an interim basis and the Department of Fisheries and Oceans (DFO) and B.C. Environment (BCE) will follow up these guidelines to assess their applicability and compliance:

a   Canyon site selection for sniping must be true bedrock based, not clay or hard pan.DFO and BCE may limit the number of suction dredges that are operated in a given area.

b   The potential site must be well mapped and photographed. This information must accompany the application. The operation must be confined to the delineated area.

c   Timing on the operation may be confined to after a freshet, and to fall rains. Site specific restrictions on timing may be applied to reflect sensitive fish life history phases.

d   To facilitate agency monitoring the portable system, the portable suction dredge should be painted a fluorescent red/orange in color. The permit number, clearly visible from the air shall be displayed.

e   Equipment is restricted to hand-operated portable units, including suction dredges with intake valve diameter of not greater than 6".

f   No entrainment of fish, under any circumstances, is permitted. While nozzle may remain unscreened, all other intakes must be screened in accordance with DFO guidelines.

g   During sluicing, a tailings bag, approximately 2m x 1m in dimensions and comprised of a nylon type material must be attached to the sluice outfall.

h   During sluicing, the tailings bag and tailings must be deposited on the stream edge outside the wetted perimeter with no discharge to the stream.

i   Removal or shifting of large boulders that may be in the stream bed, or any alteration of the bedrock is strictly prohibited.

j   All fuel and oil products must be stored in a secure manner well removed from the wetted perimeter.

k   Fuel tanks on the suction dredge should be confined to approximately 4 liters capacity.

March 22, 1995 MEMPR Kamloops

Author's Notes: The above guidelines have served well for several years now and are similar to those found in several western states. Dredging is relatively new to BC, and one might expect that they will continue to evolve as more experience is gained. Also, keep in mind that these are only guidelines, and that the rules may be modified, on a *site-specific* basis, at the discretion of the agencies involved. These guidelines are fairly simple and self-explanatory, but one or two may seem a bit confusing, so I would like to add my own personal interpretation, to help clear things up...

d) Some dredgers like to camouflage their outfits so as to avoid having their equipment stolen if they are left unattended at a site. An acceptable alternative to red or orange paint is a red or orange fly-sheet or sock, which can be removed from the dredge when you want to hide it in the bushes.

g) The original tailings containment bag, although still sometimes used, is a fairly primitive affair. The term *"tailings bag"* could now be replaced with the phrase, *"tailings containment system"*, to reflect new developments. For example, the larger-size dredges are often equipped with a *sediment sump* at the sluice's outflow, which diverts sedimented water into a secondary recovery device, such as a "cyclone-type" concentrator, mounted right on the dredge. For small and intermediate dredges, an even more popular solution is to bank-mount the dredge, or to use a suction-equipped high-banker, in which case the "containment system" will be a settling pond to capture the tailings. Both methods have been approved in the past, and they have been found to be very effective in keeping muddied water out of the creek. Note also the wording; "During sluicing..." The expectation is that dredging will be confined to areas of predominantly bedrock outcropping, and does not involve the sluicing of quantities of gravel. In this situation, a bag would not be required because there are, essentially, no tailings to confine. But, although dredging large volumes of gravel is not intended, in practice, the dredger will inevitably run into some narrow seams of gravel while he is working the bedrock. If this gravel happens to have a high clay or silt content, there is a problem, because it will kick up a plume of turbid, sedimented water, and this is not acceptable. So, the proviso is that, "During sluicing...", (of gravel), some form of tailings containment is mandatory.

h) For processing large volumes of gravel, consider a bank mounted dredge or high-banker and a settling pond system as an alternative. A tailings bag will not be required and large volumes of gravel can be handled.

i) Large boulders, (over 1 meter diameter), cannot be moved, but you may be able to prop them up so as to work underneath, if this can be done safely.

j) and (k) Please, please pay attention to your refueling practices - there is just no excuse for sloppy handling in and around the sensitive stream environment!

Summary of Dredging Regulations

If you intend to employ a suction dredge in a professional or commercial mining venture in B.C., you have no option but to go through the approval process. Because these approvals are site-specific, that means either obtaining a claim of your own or finding an amenable claim owner who will cooperate with you on submitting a dredging application. Because this type of equipment is capable of processing large volumes, it is subject to the stringent environmental standards we have been talking about. Dredge capacity is exponential: A 3-inch machine has twice the capacity of a 2-inch, and so on. A commercial, 8-inch suction dredge is capable of moving up to 30 cubic yards of gravel per hour.

Operation of a Suction Dredge

Use the nozzle to draw off gravel and sediment from around boulders, from exposed bedrock and crevices, etc. Oversize, (plus 2-inch) rocks and pebbles are moved by hand or with a rake. Deeper water can be managed by fitting the nozzle with an extension handle, as shown , and even deeper water still can be reached with a wet suit, mask and snorkel.

By comparison, a 2-inch "backpack" style dredge, used mostly for *exploration* work, has a maximum *rated* capacity of only 2 yards-per-hour, but in actual field conditions, 0.2 yard-per-hour is more realistic. I have observed that this type of portable testing equipment is frequently treated as Class PA operations, regardless of the particular operating principles and technical features of the equipment. Rather, the determining factor seems to be the volume/capacity of the equipment, and the total area of surface disturbance of the overall operation. So, if you plan to conduct placer *mining* with a dredge, (as opposed to *sampling* or *prospecting*), you <u>must</u> apply for a permit. The Mines Inspector will send copies of your application to the Ministry of Environment and other interested agencies for their review and input, and it may also be reviewed by a local Placer Advisory Committee. If approved, a Site-Specific Approval will be issued, outlining all of the restrictions and conditions of the permit. You might be assessed a small Resource Management fee, and perhaps a Water Use Permit fee, if a larger size pump is used. As of May 1997, this fee was calculated at "$192 per 0.5 cfs, or fraction thereof." In addition, if you plan to have a large camp or to build roads into the property, you may be required to post a Reclamation Bond upon the property.

I have often had the question posed to me, "What harm can a small dredge do, compared to the millions of tons of material that are moved through a stream during every run-off and freshet?" The answer is, although it's true that immeasurably more material is moved by natural erosion, the *volume* of water is also commensurably greater. Sure, a dredge only produces small amounts of sediment and suspended matter, but if this goes into the stream at normal or low water levels, there isn't enough flow to carry it away. What happens then is that the section of streambed immediately downstream becomes blanketed with a layer of fine sediment, which smothers and chokes all types of aquatic life, including eyed, incubating fish eggs. Placer exploration can be lucrative, but it carries a great deal of responsibility with it. Even when you limit yourself to small portable testing equipment, you must still use good sense in and around a fragile stream ecosystem. Please be careful about refueling, and leave your campsite as you found it.

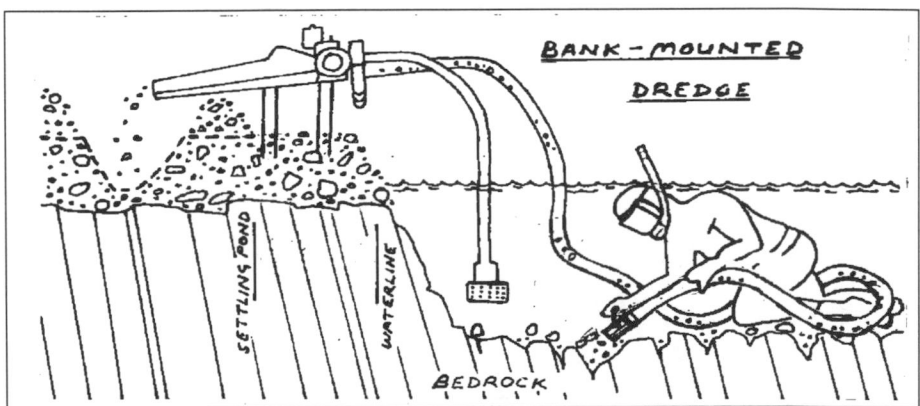

Summary of Exploration Regulations

CLASS A   - Mineral   No fee required. Hand operations. Small camps, geochemical and geophysical surveys.

CLASS PA - Placer   Prospecting. Trenching & Sluicing.

CLASS B   - Mineral   Fees are required. Mechanized Equipment; i.e.: Backhoes, Drill Rigs,

CLASS PB - Placer.   Bulk sampling

More and more frequently, dredging is being conducted as part of an overall program of stream *rehabilitation*, in cooperation with civic and government fisheries enhancement programs. Where prescribed by a supervising Conservation Officer, the dredger can play a useful role in a variety of enhancement activities, such as:

Stream Channelizing - Opening up sediment-choked stream channels to:

- Permit fish better access to rearing and food-producing habitat, better migration.
- Boulder Emplacement - Dredgers can help to position large boulders and other underwater structures to provide cover.

Bank Stabilization - Boulders and Fly-Rock can be positioned so as to:
- deflect water flow, prevent undercutting and erosion of stream banks, etc.
- Spawning-Bed Construction - Tailings from dredges, having been washed and classified, provide excellent spawning-bed material, (pea gravel), which allows for better aeration of incubating eggs.

ABOVE - Snorkel-diving with a backpack dredge. The operator is working the face of a shallow gravel seam, cleaning the bedrock as he goes along.

As a rule of thumb, a 2-inch dredge can comfortably manage 2-3 feet of over-burden; a 3-inch works well at 3-4 feet, and a 4-inch machine down to about 4-5 feet. This formula holds true up to around the 8-inch range. Dredges larger than that can manage deposits of almost unlimited depth, as this size intake can accept a high percentage of the total material in the deposit.

Catalog Items Superb craftsmanship from Proline. All steel parts are zinc plated to prevent rust. Components are jig-built or computer machined, then TIG welded. These are some of the best engineered units we have seen. Available in suction nozzle or power jet configurations.

Specifications - 2.0" Flair Dredge

Engine: Shindaiwa G. P. 45 (2.3 hp, 80 GPM)
Sluice Box .... 10" x 30"
Jet .... 2" x 1.5" slip
Suction Hose .... 2" x 10'
Floatation .... 7" x 26" x 47"
(cross-link polyethylene)
Dredge Capacity .... 2 yards per hour
Weight .... 52 pounds

Dredge-Highbanker Combos These versatile machines come in 1.5", 2.0", 2.5", and 3.0" models, which can be mounted on floats or bank mounted as the situation requires. The 1.5" model weighs just 28lbs and is ideal for testing. The 2.0" model weighs 56lbs and is capable of processing up to two yds. per hour. The 2.5", weighing in at 95lbs can do 5 yds. per hour, and the 3.0" at 155lbs is rated to 8yds per hour. Both the 2.5 and 3.0" models can be equipped with an optional diving compressor.

PROLINE **4.0" Flare Dredge** The 4 inch dredge has always been a popular size due to its ease of operation and portability. However the added suction power and higher production capabilities of this intermediate size make it attractive to the serious gold miner. Equipped with an exclusive "wave" classifier which causes a jiggling action at the front of the sluice. Weighs 208lbs with a capacity to 12yds per hour.

Types of Suction Dredges

In the hand-operated, backpack category there are two basic types: *Power Jet,* and *Suction Nozzle.* The difference is a technical one, having to do with where the venturi is situated on the suction assembly. A power jet has a bit more pulling power per given amount of horsepower, but it's drawback is that it loses it's prime whenever the nozzle is lifted out of the water, and this can be a problem if you are working in the shallows. The power jet version is preferred when the work is at depths over two or three feet. Conversely, the suction nozzle variant is a joy to use in shallow water, because it can never lose it's prime. As an all-purpose machine, the suction nozzle is the best choice.

The 2-inch Keene backpack dredge shown on page two of this manual is equipped with a power jet. On page 85 is another model in a suction nozzle configuration. Both types can be fitted with either the suction nozzle or the power jet system.

Intermediate and Professional Size Dredges

Dredges of 3-inch suction hose diameter or larger are equipped with an air compressor, to supply air to one or two divers at shallow depths, (10-20'). Gold diving in a fast mountain stream is incredibly exciting, but it's not for the faint-hearted. It can be physically demanding, especially when you have to wear lots of extra lead weights to anchor yourself in the current. Cold water can be a factor, due to the extended hours of calorie-burning underwater work that a production operation entails. To avoid the fatigue of cold water, think about equipping the dredge with a good quality *water-heating system.* Several types of devices are available that bolt on to dredge's existing engine; They work by flooding the diver's wetsuit with a constant stream of warm water. By helping you get more hours and more production, these units can, (pardon the pun), be worth their weight in gold. A suit heater is pure heaven - like taking a hot bath all day.

Diving Safety

As I just mentioned, all professional-size dredges, such as the 5-inch Keene model shown here, have compressors capable of supplying air for *two* divers. There's a reason for this...

I strongly recommend two divers, for the added safety, if nothing else. Underwater, boulders can move and shift unpredictably. Some large rocks, dubbed "loomers", may be suspended precariously up in the gravel strata. If you are in the bottom of a dredge hole, and a boulder like this comes down unexpectedly, you stand a good chance of being "loomerized". I was loomerized once, and it wasn't very nice. (But at least it taught me the importance of never going gold-diving alone.) A secondary benefit of the buddy system is that, on many deposits, it is actually more productive to have two people working on one dredge. The second man can more than pay his own way because of the increased efficiency. The "rock man" specializes in removing all of the oversize cobbles and large boulders. This enables the "suction man" (or woman, I suppose) to work much faster, from not having to constantly 'down tools'.

Glenn's Golden Rule No. 4...

"Never Dive Alone"

Catalog Item

MODEL 5109 NEW 5 INCH DREDGE

New "HIGH PERFORMANCE" 5 inch dredge is now one of our most powerful, efficient and portable dredges.

SPECIAL ORDER

SPECIFICATIONS

Engine............	9 H/P Vanguard	Jet................	PJP-5T2
Pump..............	P-350 w/ Oversize Impellar	Suction Hose....SH5 - 5" x 15'	
Compressor.....	T-80	Sluice Box.......	SB-5N 20" x 68"
Flotation...................	PFA 5S	Assembly dimensions..	61" x 101"
Fuel capacity............		Weight................	380 Lbs
Fuel consumption......1/2 Gal Hr.		Shipping Weight..........	480 Lbs
		Capacity................	12 YPH

Clean Up

This is the good part, where you get to empty out the sluice and see how much gold you've got. Some people like to operate a full day before emptying the concentrates. This is fine, provided you watch that the box doesn't become overladen, or that the concentrates behind the riffles aren't becoming compacted. (They will do so if there is a lot of clay in the gravel.)

I prefer to clean up more frequently - at least twice a day, or as much as once every hour, if my main purpose is sampling. To clean up, position a tub or bucket under the tail-end of the sluice, release the riffle catches and swing the riffles out of the way. Slide the carpet and expanded metal screen down into the clean-up tub. Next, splash water into the box, (you can use your gold pan for this), to wash any remaining concentrate into the bucket. Rinse the carpet thoroughly, and reinstall it immediately. (Loose carpets have a knack of floating off when you're not looking.) Proceed to pan down the concentrates in the normal way.

Those Nasty Plug-Ups

Rocks sometimes get lodged inside the suction hose - it's unavoidable. When this happens, try to dislodge the jam by tapping the side of the suction hose with a smooth cobble. If that doesn't free it, you will have to lift the hose completely out of the water, then shake or tap the offending rocks loose. To reduce the number of plug-ups, get in the habit of avoiding flat rocks, or angular rocks that have sharp edges, and don't overload the hose with too much material all at once.

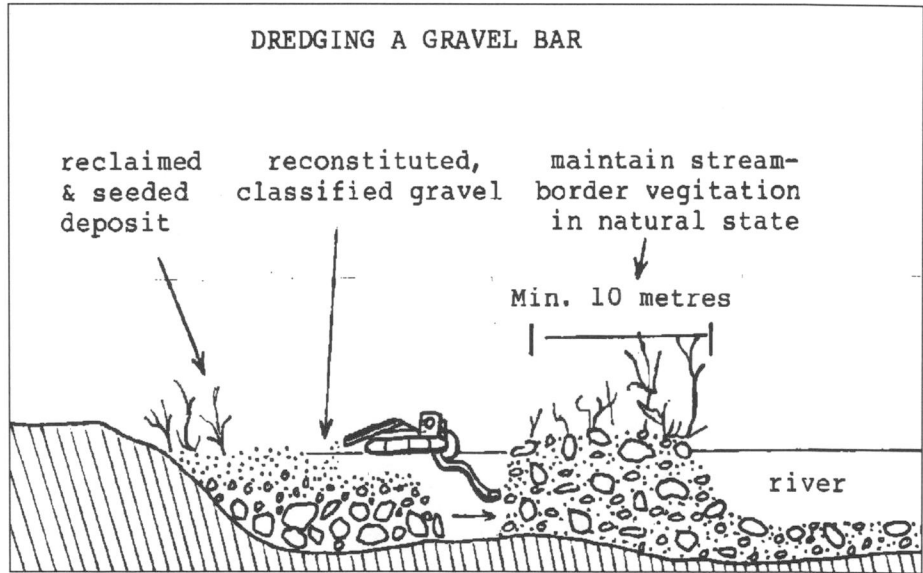

DREDGING A GRAVEL BAR

reclaimed & seeded deposit

reconstituted, classified gravel

maintain stream-border vegitation in natural state

Min. 10 metres

river

Review of Chapter Seven

There are still a lot of misconceptions out there. I am even asked, on occasion, "Isn't dredging illegal?" The answer is no - despite gold-mining's "colorful" past, there is nothing illegal about gold prospecting or dredging. Dredging may be prohibited from some specific locations, because of the potential environmental impact, and, as we have seen, a fairly comprehensive approval process is in place to ensure environmental compliance. From time to time you might run into some ignorant person with extremist views. Don't be put off by these kinds of people, they're just "wannabe's", and they're missing out on all the fun.

In my travels, I have noticed that a high proportion of well-paying stream placers occur in very shallow gravel, from a thin scattering of a few inches up to two or three feet thick. Happily this is the perfect range for a backpack dredge, which can remove light overburden quickly, revealing, (hopefully), rich, nuggety gold trapped in the bedrock underneath.

Secondary Processing

If the operation is a productive one, at some point even a dredging or small hand operation will be producing a large volume of concentrates. When the amount of concentrates gets too much to render down by hand-panning, you will need some sort of *secondary recovery* equipment to make the job easier. And if you eventually get into a small commercial operation, as discussed later in Chapter Nine, then you will definitely need a secondary processing capability.

The entire mining operation, from digging to the final product, can be represented graphically on what is known as a *Flow Circuit* schematic. For big hardrock mines, these diagrams are extraordinarily complicated, involving computerized controls. Large placer mines are much simpler, but still involve at least a dozen elements, from the initial *skip loader,* through the washplant and *trommel,* into a sub-circuit of gravity *jigs* and/or *cyclones,* then onto a series of *concentrating tables*, and finally, to the *amalgamation process.*

You can see from this diagram that, for Secondary Processing in a small operation, you are left with the choice of either a *Micro-Sluice* type of concentrator, or a *Spiral Wheel.* If operated properly, both of these pieces of equipment are capable of complete recovery of gold, from nuggets down to 100-mesh (Very Fine Gold). It's worth repeating here that the key to efficient recovery, regardless of what type of equipment is employed, is CLASSIFICATION. Classify your material, then classify it again. When I am in a production mode, with a lot of concentrates to develop, I like to classify and separate my concentrates through 8, 12, 30, and 100-mesh screens, then I process each batch separately, adjusting the machine for optimum recovery on each batch. In this way, I am capable of recovering close to 97% of the Coarse, Fine, and Very Fine gold, and about half of the remaining Ultrafine, or *Micron* gold. The residual gold loss isn't enough to worry about. I could never understand why some people are so hung up on getting 100% recovery. Even though it's nearly impossible, they will spend thousands of dollars on extra equipment just to get that last one or two percent. To my mind, that's way beyond the point of *diminishing returns* - to the point of being an obsession - and I just don't get it.

Spiral Wheel Concentrators, and Micro-Sluice-type Concentrators are very inexpensive, and can do an excellent job of recovering 90% or more of your recoverable gold. Whichever method of secondary processing you choose, the secret is to experiment with it on your particular type of ore. Send a batch through several different times at different settings, and check the tailings for gold loss on each pass. By practicing in this manner, you will soon discover the optimum configuration for your particular paydirt, and for the different mesh-fractions of your concentrate. Here are a few additional tips...

Spiral Wheel Type Concentrators

1) Feed the wheel slowly and evenly, (an automatic feeder is best).
2) Use the maximum RPM your machine is capable of to take full advantage of centrifugal force. An RPM of about 60 is ideal.
3) Ensure that there is an adequate flow of water over the wheel itself, so that concentrates do not stick to the wheel as it spins.
4) Soft rubber wheels are better at fine gold recovery than are hard plastic ones.

For a small-scale placer operation, down to and including a dredging or hand-mining operation, the Flow Circuit looks like this...

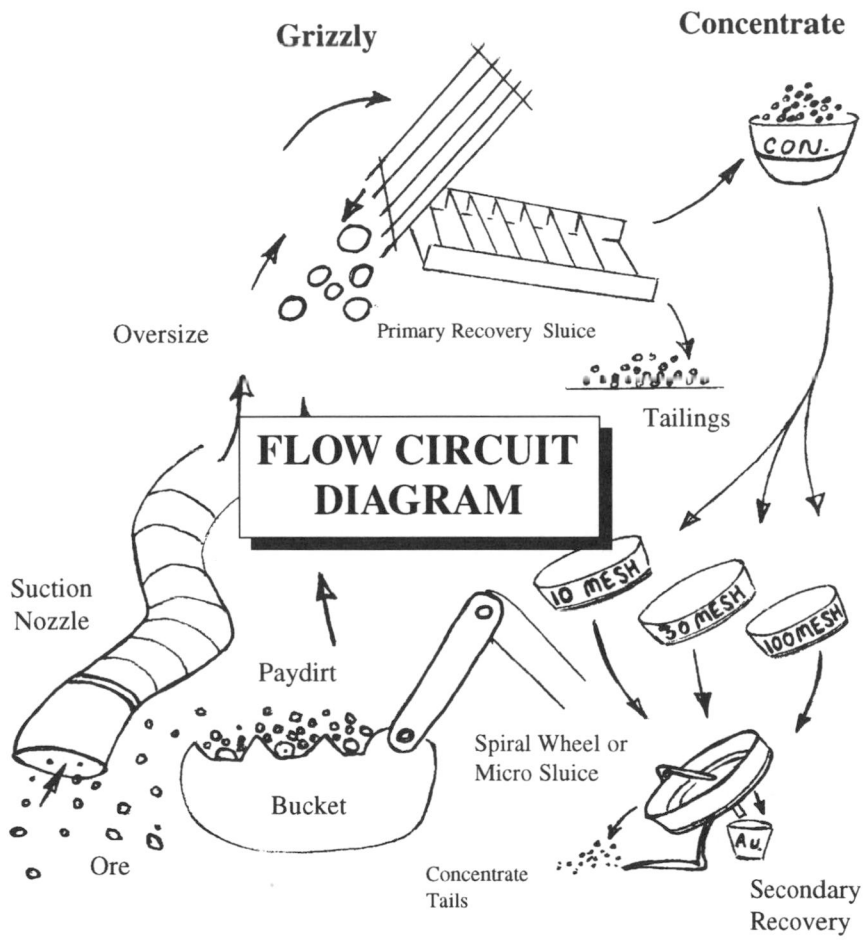

Grizzly

Concentrate

Oversize

Primary Recovery Sluice

Tailings

FLOW CIRCUIT DIAGRAM

Suction Nozzle

Paydirt

Spiral Wheel or Micro Sluice

Bucket

Ore

Concentrate Tails

Secondary Recovery

Micro Sluice Type Concentrators

1) Experiment by first varying the angle of the sluice, then adjust the water-flow.
2) Do not overload the sluice; feed material slowly. (Much more on micro-sluice
     operations in the next chapter.)

For Both Types...

1) Keep the recovery surfaces very clean; remove any scum with a scotch-brite type pad after each use.
2) Add a few drops of a water softener, (green dish soap will do), into the re-circulating bucket. This reduces the water's surface tension and keeps the Very Fine gold from floating on the surface. Be careful not to add too much soap, so as not to create a lot of foam.
3) Operate in a well-lighted area, to improve visibility as you're watching the machine in operation. With practice, you'll be surprised how good you get at watching the gold flow through the machine. Before long, you will be able to see if the machine is operating correctly just from simple observation.
4) Don't forget that, in addition to being excellent secondary recovery devices, these machines are great for in-the-field sampling because they will relieve you of a lot of hard physical work. That's why most of these units are designed to run on a 12-volt battery, for portability. If you're running concentrates at home or in the shop, you could use a 12-volt adapter to run off house current.

And Remember...

Classify, classify, classify...

CHAPTER EIGHT

THE SPECIALTIES

Pocket Hunting

The whole business of *pocket hunting* is something of an enigma, because in many ways it represents one of the best and most exciting opportunities in the field of prospecting, and yet it has been virtually ignored by both amateur and professional practitioners.

I was first exposed to pocket hunting through a pamphlet by R.F. Mayo entitled, "Give Me Liberty", which described the numerous pocket gold occurrences in north-central Washington state. I became interested in this because this area is just across the line from the Similkameen District in southern B.C. - an area quite familiar to me in my search for small-scale gold and platinum placers. So, why haven't I heard of the "pocket deposits" before, I asked myself. At first, I found nothing in the general literature to give me any clues about pocket gold in B.C. Then I came across an excellent booklet by V.Ballantyne entitled, "How to Prospect for Pocket Gold", which cleared up some of the mystery. According to Mr. Ballantyne, ever since the early days of the Spanish "prospecteros", only a handful of placer miners have been aware of the existence of this type of deposit. Realizing they were on to a good thing, those that did know kept their mouths shut. They specialized exclusively in pocket hunting, and they guarded their secrets jealously. At some point, Ballantyne got wind of this activity through a friend, who informed him, (probably over a few drinks), of the exploits of a duo of highly successful pocket hunters that he had been personally acquainted with. Ballantyne learned that, during the 1940's, the two men, Thompson and Gray, had perfected their pocket hunting technique, and had discovered big-dollar bonanzas all over the west and as far north as Alaska and the Yukon. Furthermore, according to these two experts, pocket deposits are downright plentiful, and can be found in almost any area where placer deposits are known to occur.

Again I had to ask myself, "If pocket deposits are so plentiful, why can't I find an account of even one single occurrence in all of British Columbia? This affair had really begun to get my goat, and I resolved to get to the bottom of it. My investigations then turned up an interesting tidbit: Ironically, the seminal work on pocket deposits is by a Canadian geologist, R.W. Boyle, of the Geological Survey of Canada. In his, "The Geochemistry of Gold and It's Deposits" (GSC Bulletin # 280) Boyle offers up several explanations for pocket gold, of which the most likely candidate is the "Enriched Supergene Deposition" theory. Aha! Now that I had the correct technical term for pocket gold, my search of the B.C. Mineral Inventory began to bear fruit. I have since been able to develop files on about a half a dozen individual occurrences and known pocket areas in the province. Still, this is an unbelievably small number, considering their ostensibly widespread distribution. My suspicion is that there is hardly anyone in B.C. or the Yukon actively searching for pockets. (Or, if there are, they are reverting to form and keeping quiet about it).

I imagine old Verne Ballantyne thought he was blowing the lid off a long-held secret when he began circulating his papers on pocket deposits. Well, apparently the idea didn't take hold, so now it's my turn to try to spread the gospel. So, if you want a stab at a big time, bonanza-type discovery, why not join the "secret brotherhood" of the Pocket Hunter. The field is wide open...

Description of Pocket Deposits

A related deposit type, the *residual placer*, or *seam diggings*, is broadly defined as alluvial material that has eroded out of the host rock and has re-concentrated in close proximity to it's original source. True *pocket deposits* are also technically classed as a type of residual placer, (an eluvial placer), by virtue of their having formed from a disseminated hardrock ore. What distinguishes the eluvial category from other placer types is that they have not been transported out of the area by creep or erosion.

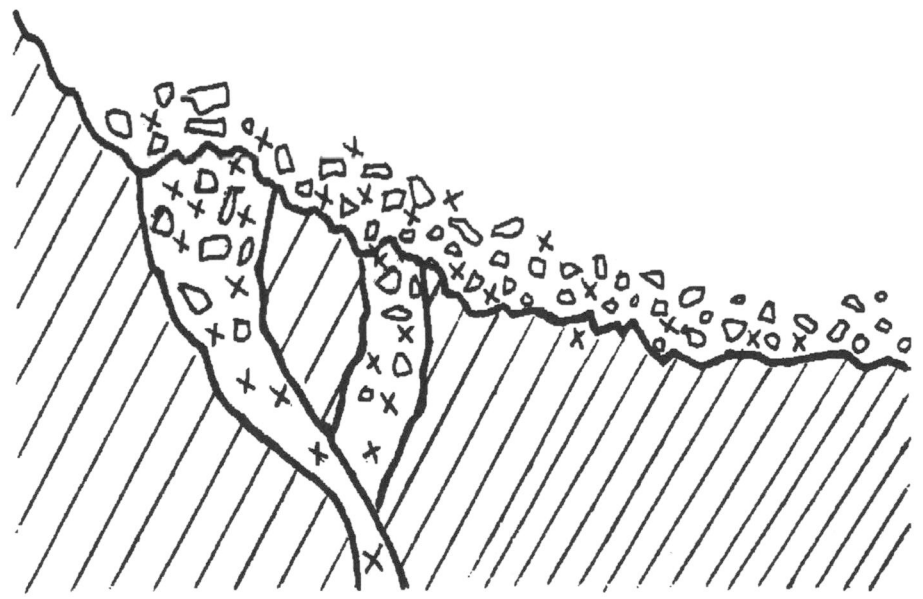

ABOVE: A flat-lying residual placer. The vein outcrops strongly, and is indicated by the presence of rusty, iron-stained, gold-bearing quartz float.

Because they are normally formed in a relatively flat-lying position, residual placers are located in the immediate vicinity of the orebody. The matrix is comprised of fragmented, sub-angular vein material, usually quartz or quartz shale. Similarly, the disseminated particles of gold have a very rough-edged character, and frequently appear in a crystalline or wire form, or as scaly masses. Although most residual placers are quite low-grade, they are a good indication of nearby pockets, which tend to be extremely high grade.

GEOCHEMICAL HALO

Conditions Favorable for Pocket Formation

1) The lode is located in a flat-lying area.
2) The lode is oriented perpendicular to the horizon.
3) The lode is composed of mineralized rocks, which weather at a faster rate than the surrounding country rock, frequently forming a slight depression.

Put simply, the orebody *falls in on itself.* As the vein material breaks down, gold particles are released and begin to migrate *downward,* due to the effect of gravity and mechanical action - frost heaves, earth tremors, etc. Where the side-walls close in, pinching off the vein, the migrating gold begins to collect in rich pockets. Because the gold from a pocket has not been subject to the pounding action of a river, it has a very jagged appearance, and forms in intricate shapes. This feature makes pocket gold highly prized for collections and for jewelry making.

Pocket Hunting Procedure

Use stakes and a marked string line to establish a grid over your target area. The base line should be established at the lowest elevation on the grid. As you traverse the baseline, stop every hundred feet, (a twenty-meter grid is also good), and dig down six inches to a foot for a sample. Collect a ½ to 1 lb. sample, bag it and mark the grid station on a tag with a permanent marker. Next, write the grid co-ordinate on a small wooden stake, to mark the sample site for future reference.

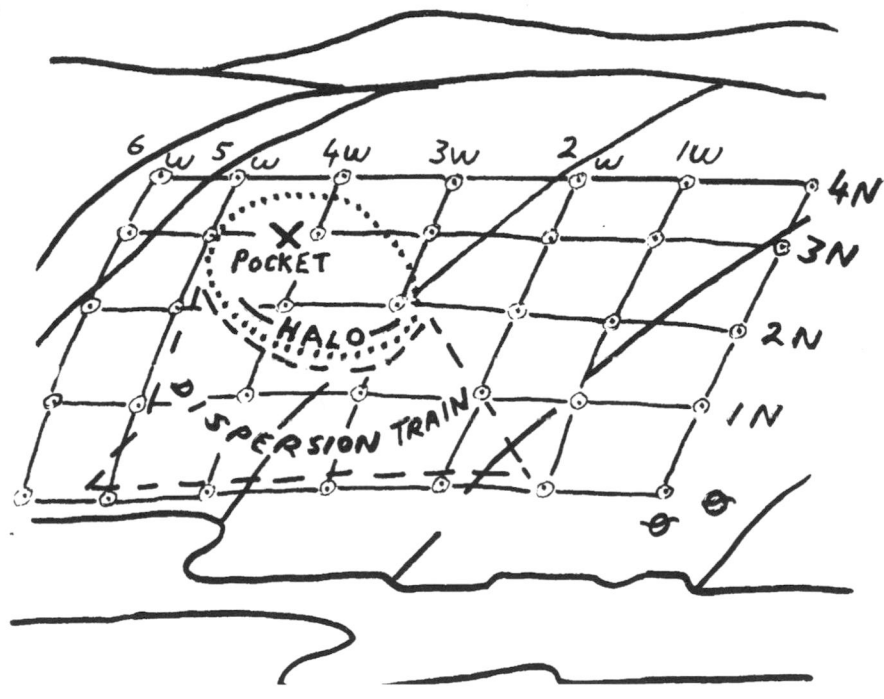

This pocket was located at 3N4W !

It's best to bring all the samples back to a central location - a base camp, as it were, where the samples can be reduced under controlled conditions. Allow the samples to soak a few minutes before panning. Pan the samples as usual, but when you get down to the last teaspoon or so, pour in some clorox bleach and let it sit for a few minutes. A salt-and-vinegar solution, or oxalic acid, could be used instead. These solutions act as solvents and will wash away the black magnesium and iron which stains much of the pocket gold, and you will now be able to identify all of the individual fine colors.

Unlike other types of placers, you won't need to test these samples for *grade*. For this kind of *trace prospecting*, what you're really after is how much gold each sample has, *relative* to all of the other samples in the grid. Grade calculations, therefore, are not needed at this stage - but you will have to count the colors, note their size and character, and mark this information down in a *sample log*. Because halo gold is very, very fine, you will need a good lens of at least 30-power to assist you in the identification.

Having tracked the dispersion train and the geochemical halo which surrounds the pocket, a second, smaller grid is established around the target zone. Repeat the sampling procedure at 10-foot, (3-metre), intervals. By the time you complete this grid, you should be standing right over the pocket!

There are a couple of visual clues to help locate a pocket. First, as the name implies, a pocket often creates a shallow depression in the ground. Secondly, the broken-down matrix of the orebody, called the *gangue*, contains a lot of iron oxides, which stain the ground a reddish-brown or rust color. These dark brown oxides have a loose, fluffy quality, hence it's colloquial name, "snuff". In some western regions, this material may also go by the name of "ochre".

GEOLOGICAL PROFILE

Swauk Creek Enriched Supergene Deposits

Location: Swauk Creek, State
    of Washington, USA.
Surface Geology: Basaltic
    dikes intruding sandstone
    formations.

Host Rocks:
(1) Decomposed Quartz
(2) Quartz and Shale
    (Birdseye Quartz)
(3) Clay Pockets in Sand-
    stone

Commodity Type: Wire Gold,
Telluride Gold.

Mining a Pocket-Gold Deposit

Ok, so you've found your pocket. From here on in, it's all for the pick and shovel. (Good thing most pockets are quite shallow.)

To give you an idea of the size, one pocket, discovered on one of the Gulf Islands, measured just seven feet by seven feet square on the surface, and was six feet deep. It is reported to have produced about $150,000 in gold.

A battery-powered re-circulating concentrator is recommended for pocket mining, as it can be easily packed in and operated in out of the way locations where running water is not available. Pockets do tend to contain a lot of clay, so go slow so as to permit thorough washing of the ore.

Catalog Item - Gold Screw Combo

This combination trommel/automatic panner has been developed and field-tested around the world for nearly 20 years with consistent results. It can handle up to 2 cubic yards per hour of bank-run material, including cobbles up to tennis-ball size. Automatically classifies and concentrates material prior to a final concentration in the spiral panner. Heavy duty, zinc-plated construction, yet weighs only 180 lbs, and breaks down into 6 separate, easily transportable components. Set-up time only 15 minutes.

Beach Placers

Beach Placers occur all along the west coast, from northern California, through Oregon, Washington, B.C. and around the Alaska panhandle, to Nome, on the Seward Peninsula. Gold Beach, Oregon, was a typical beach-mining community. Up to the outbreak of the second world war, small family operations were producing, on average, an ounce of gold per day. At Cape Blanco, one such operation reported a season's take of 50 ounces, plus, "a sizeable amount of platinum", from 700 yards of beach sand.

In British Columbia, a three-mile long concentration was worked at Wreck Bay, producing roughly 1,400 ounces during the three-year period, 1899-1901. Since then, this and many other B.C. beach placers have been worked intermittently, especially after being replenished by a "gold storm". Like the Oregon example I just spoke of, these placers are also noted for their high content of platinum metals. Many smaller beach placers exist which are not noted in the literature. Among those that have been documented are: Toe Hill, Graham Island, and Shuttle Island. Activity has also been noted in the vicinity of Brittania Beach.

Commercial beach placer mines operated at Goodnews Bay, and at the Salt Chuck Mine, on the Alaska panhandle. To date, these locations have produced 647,500, and 661,771 ounces of platinum respectively.

The apparent reason for a relatively high platinum content in beach placers is that platinum, being considerably harder than gold, is more resistant to breaking up, and can therefore accumulate at a faster rate. To identify platinum in your pan, keep in mind that it is just slightly heavier than gold, and it will behave the same way in your pan. In it's natural state, platinum has a steel-grey color, but it may be coated with a dark stain. It has a pitted or scaly texture, and usually presents as minute, rounded pellets or slivers, as compared to the more flattened, flaky shape of finely-divided gold. When I first started prospecting in B.C., I had the opportunity to do some sampling on the Tulameen River, which is noted for it's platinum. My sample had a good showing of gold, and some platinum was also present, but it didn't seem earth-shattering to me so I moved on to another project. Years later, as I was preparing a batch of geochemical samples for the assay lab, curiosity got the better of me and I decided to include the Tulameen sample, to see how well I had visually evaluated the platinum. I was completely unprepared for the results - 84 ounces of platinum per ton of black sand! A single, half-full twenty liter pail of this material contains well over one thousand dollars in platinum. I have since staked this area, and, needless to say, it has become very much a pet project of mine.

Sampling a Beach Sand Deposit

You might find beach lenses in surface layers of beach sand, or in deeper strata on an ancient, inland beach-head. If you select a beach location you won't want to be panning at the ocean's edge in rough surf, so you might want to set up a work station, with a tub of water, at some convenient nearby spot. Collect samples every 50 feet or so, marking each site with a wooden stake as you go. Because beach placers occur as shallow *surface* deposits, (usually, only the top foot or two will pay), what you see in your sample is what you will get when you begin to mine. This means that you will have to evaluate your beach samples *for grade*, in order to zero in on a high-grade lens. A visual assay for platinum is complicated by the fact that some of the platinum is formed *within* the individual grains of magnetite and chromite, (the main constituents of black sand), effectively camouflaging it's presence. If you suspect a good showing, do what I did and have an assay done at a commercial lab. You may have to check around to find one that is equipped to check for all of the major groups of platinum metals, including iridium, osmium, rhodium, and ruthenium. Being hi-tech metals, the platinum group, and some other heavy elements known collectively as "rare earths", are subject to wild fluctuations in market price. Some of these minerals are as precious as gold, commanding hundreds of dollars per ounce. A check should also be made for *titanium,* which is also a major constituent of many black sand deposits, and was recently selling for $4.00 US per pound.

Mining Beach Placers

Because beach placers are most often formed in places that are subject to the full force of westerly winds, conditions are too rough at waters edge for productive sluicing. Here, as with the pocket-type deposits, a recirculating concentrator is the answer, as it facilitates processing under *controlled* conditions. This method is also very sound from an environmental standpoint.

Because there is very little clay in beach sand, a vibrating attachment is not necessary. You can opt for a very simple, inexpensive concentrator, which will run quietly all day from a car battery.

Catalog Items

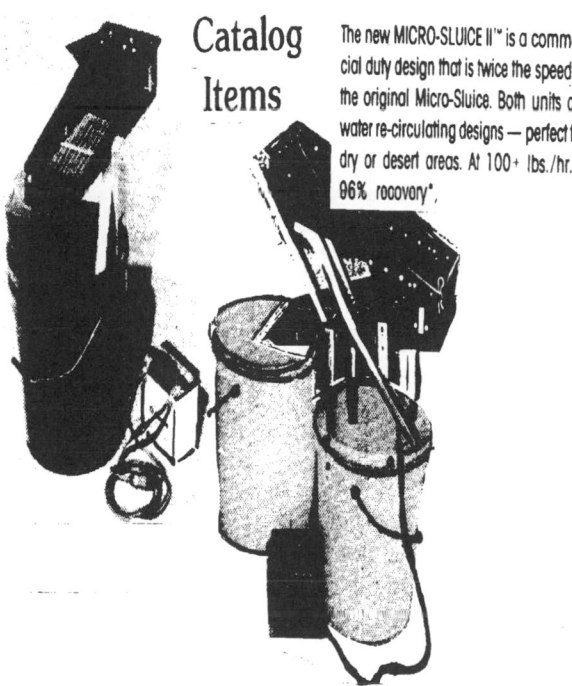

The (original) MIRCO-SLUICE™ will outperform all of the competition in terms of accuracy, speed and/or price (based on data from Goldhound, Genie, D.A.M. & Golden Angel). No other unit will recover more fine gold at the speed & price we offer. So good and unique is our equipment that a U.S. Patent has been issued on the Micro-Sluice and Micro-Sluice II. Made from high impact ABS plastic, all our sluices are OK for salt water placers and are warranteed for one year.

The Micro-Sluice weighs only 5 pounds and will process 50+ lbs/hr. x 98% recovery*.

The new MICRO-SLUICE II™ is a commercial duty design that is twice the speed of the original Micro-Sluice. Both units are water re-circulating designs — perfect for dry or desert areas. At 100+ lbs./hr. x 96% recovery*.

Beach Mining Procedure

When you have located a gold bearing lens, use a rake or scraper to scalp off the top couple of inches of sand, and pile it near your concentrator. This is your feedstock. When you have run this through, go back and peel off another shallow layer, and so on until the gold bearing layer runs out. An automatic feeder is indispensable here, as it will meter-out a full load for you while you are busy scraping up another load. The feeder will also improve fine-gold retention, because it delivers material to the sluice at a constant, controlled rate.

Notice that none of these portable units require dangerous chemicals or harsh leaching agents. Small quantities of mercury can be safely introduced back at home in the shop, provided you use a re-circulating, containment-type system. Mercury has an affinity to gold - sticks to it like glue, in fact - so it comes in very useful where fine gold recovery is a problem. Beach placers produce prodigious quantities of black sand. If the amount of concentrate from your operation starts to become unmanageable, you may need to employ some type of *secondary processing*, to keep up with the volume of black sand. One low cost solution is the vibrator/amalgamator, which can be used with ordinary mercury. For complex ores, the amalgamator improves recovery by *scarifying* the black sand, to break down surface coatings, unlocking the "hidden values" in the concentrate.

Catalog Items

The 'Gold Feeder ' by Gold Screw Many times faster than hand feeding. Controllable spray bar wets material prior to sluicing - no plopping or clumping - less fine gold loss and the most accurate sampling possible. Hopper holds about 20 lbs (9kg). Thoughput is 70 lbs (32kg) per hour. Lightwieght aluminum fold-up design. weighs only 7 lbs.

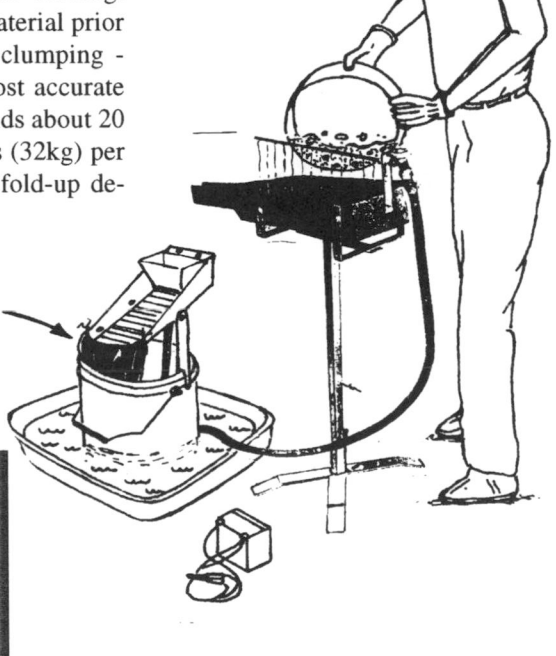

Quality Control
To achieve accuracy in sampling, periodically collect the tailings in a linen or nylon bag, to evaluate for *fine gold loss*. Depending or conditions and type of equipment, recovery rates of 80-90% may be obtained.

Catalog Item

'Quicksand' Mechanical Vibrator. (not shown) Attaches to the micro-sluice products on page 105. Improves recovery and efficiency in difficult or clayey material.

The resultant mercury/gold *amalgam* is pressed or squeezed through a chamois cloth, (do this underwater), to recover the excess mercury. The amalgam ball is then heated in a retort, leaving behind a ball of pure *sponge gold*. Retorting should always be done in a well-ventilated area, as mercury fumes are highly toxic.

Catalog Item

VIBRO-AMALGAMATOR

Model VT-6

- grinds concentrates
- cleans impurities
- polishes rocks & gemstones
- faster than any conventional tumbler
- 6 lb capacity

Gold Screw Automatic Panner

A versatile machine capable of processing bank-run material or super fine gold recovery from concentrates. Bowl angle and water pressure adjustments permit a wide range of operations. The wheel features a cam action which creates a vibration, speeding up and improving gold recovery. Driven by a 12 volt D.C. motor and pump. Trash chute and overflow hose is supplied. Pump stays in clean water at all times. Pail not furnished. Weighs 30 lbs. Shipping weight

Electronic Prospecting - General Information

With the latest advances in electronic circuitry, *metal detectors* have really come of age, for casual recreational prospecting, as well as for professional work, and, more recently, in the day-to-day operations at large mines.

CASE HISTORY: After a long period of dormancy, the famous, "Sixteen-to-One" gold mine in California was re-opened. The new operators had to "bootstrap" the operation, and decided to try to locate hidden, high-grade ore pockets using metal detectors - a method which had not previously been tried in an underground mine. The experiment turned out a great success; within the first three months of re-opening, and working with a skeleton crew, this mine produced more than 2,200 ounces of gold.

We've all seen those funny-looking "metal detector people", who push their way through a crowded swimming beach looking for other people's lost jewelry. Not that there is anything at all wrong with beach-combing or coin and relic hunting, but some of these guys are downright rude to other people and unfortunately, it has given metal detecting as a whole a bit of a bad rap. But the truth is, the metal detector is not just a toy for grown-ups, it is a proven, reliable, and *professional* prospecting tool, and there are many people today who are "swinging a detector" for a living.

Old-timer prospectors are also leery of metal detectors, having been burned in the past by manufacturers who made extravagant performance claims, which the early model detectors couldn't possibly live up to. In fact some of the early BFO-type detectors were so shoddy, you'd have a hard time finding the Titanic if it were buried in your backyard.

The new generation of detectors are a breed apart. For instance, a good VLF/TR machine, (very-low frequency transmitter/receiver), can pinpoint tiny, pinhead size nuggets on the surface, and larger nuggets to depths of two or three feet. Bigger targets, such as conductive bodies of mineral ore, and black sand stringers, can be found at greater depths - 5, 10, or even 20 feet, depending on field conditions and the type of instrument being used.

The secret behind the modern metal detector is it's ability to "cancel-out" the background mineralization in the ground. This is more complicated than it sounds, because the background signal varies greatly from place to place. In fact, background signal noise can change within the space of a few feet. To compensate for this, detectors have a Balance Control, to enable the operator to tune the instrument to the ground on which he or she is operating. Once the detector is tuned to the ground signal at a particular location, the detector will automatically compensate for minor variations at that location. When you move to a new spot, you must re-tune, or *ground-balance* the detector to the new background signal that that location is giving off. Re-tuning is very simple, like bringing in the reception on the radio, it takes about three seconds.

The best detectors are straightforward and simple to operate. Avoid fancy outfits that are laden with a lot of special controls and functions. These are generally overpriced, and the extra features are of questionable value in prospecting work. Besides, you want to be able to use your machine the first time out, without having to spend a lot of time trying to figure out which buttons to press.

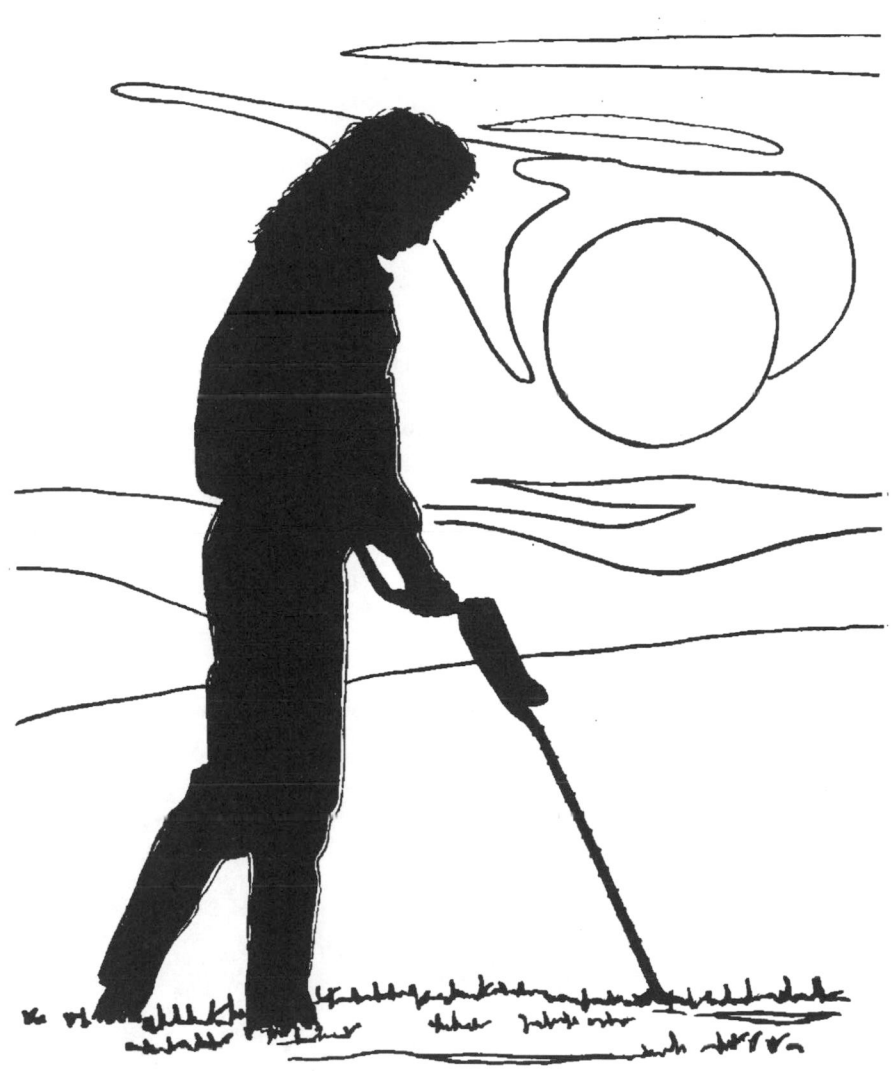

Types of Metal Detectors

The two basic types commonly used in prospecting are the VLF-TR All-Metal type, and the VLF-TR Discriminator type. The All-Metal variety cannot cancel out iron trash, as the discriminator can, but it does have a slight edge in sensitivity, making it the favourite of the two with professional prospectors. Some of the better detectors, such as those described below, combine both circuits in one machine - which gives you the best of both worlds.

The Fisher "Gold Bug 2" is the second generation of a line of powerful, no-frills metal detectors. As with it's predecessor, the original "Gold Bug", it incorporates a special device - the Voltage Controlled Oscillator (VCO) which increases the signal's volume and pitch as the target is approached. The "Gold Bug 2" has a discriminator built in that really works. Discriminator-equipped detectors are especially recommended for specialized work in heavy trash areas or in areas that contain lots of "hot rocks", (magnetic rocks).

Like the Fisher "Gold Bug", the Garrett line of detectors also has extremely high sensitivity, thanks to their proven, 15KHertz "Groundhog" circuit, which can punch through even the most heavily mineralized ground. Garrett's latest entry, the "Scorpion Gold Stinger", is a combination machine, featuring both an All Metal mode and a Discriminator mode, and a variation, the TR Discriminate mode, included especially for ore-testing. This is a really good, deep-seeking detector for the serious amateur or professional gold prospector.

Catalog Item

Find it quicker with three-mode operation. Garrett's famed All Metal circuitry goes deeper, and TR Discriminate mode is available for ore sampling, with Motion Discriminate mode for versatile coin and relic hunting.

Scorpion Gold Stinger™
with 5x10-inch 2D elliptical searchcoil

Your First Detector

When you purchase your first VLF-TR detector:

(1) Assemble as per instructions, installing fresh batteries.

(2) Bench-test and practice. Select an area away from any electrical appliances and metal objects. Set the ground adjust control to the bench-test settings, as per the operators manual. Test prepared samples of different types, including: metal objects, iron filings in a plastic vial, a magnet, a placer-gold sample, a sample of real gold ore.

(3) Practice, practice, and more practice, until recognizing the various signals becomes second nature.

Field Operations With a Detector

Most good detectors have either two or three separate operating *modes*, each with it's own distinct advantage in certain applications. Initially, you should be using the *Automatic* Operating Mode exclusively. Then you can begin to experiment with the other modes as you gain experience and become more confident with the instrument.

In all of the following field applications, the first step is always to ground balance the detector over a neutral spot on the ground, clear of any trash, pull-tabs, nails, etc.

Electronic Nugget Shooting

A metal detector has a waterproof search coil, so it can be operated in or out of the water. Choose a likely looking spot on a gravel bar, and quickly "sweep" an area of about 100 square feet or so, to identify any metallic trash or magnetized "hot rocks". (These are the ones that produce that funny-sounding "rebound" signal.) Once the area has been cleared, the detector is now capable of even greater sensitivity, so ground-balance the detector again, and this time, really *fine-tune* it.

Now, on the second sweep, be alert for any small, soft, fuzzy-sounding blips in your headphones. This is what gold sounds like! After digging all the targets up, use a rake to scalp-off the top two or three inches of gravel from the area you have just done. Sweep the area again, collect any newly-exposed targets, then rake-off another thin layer. Every time you do this you are accessing what is, essentially, a brand new deposit. The presence of any fine gold on the surface is a definite signal to keep on going, because this could indicate concentrations of coarser gold in the deeper strata.

Gold Bug 2 Features

- Conceived, designed, engineered and manufactured specifically for today's electronic prospector
- Powerful 71 kHz operation for extreme sensitivity to small gold nuggets
- Advanced ground rejection circuity for increased depth on large, deep nuggetsin highly mineralized soil
- "IRON DISC" mode for hot rocks and iron ident
- Three auto-tune modes with two retune speends for nugget hunting in almost any ground condition
  - Converts to hipmount

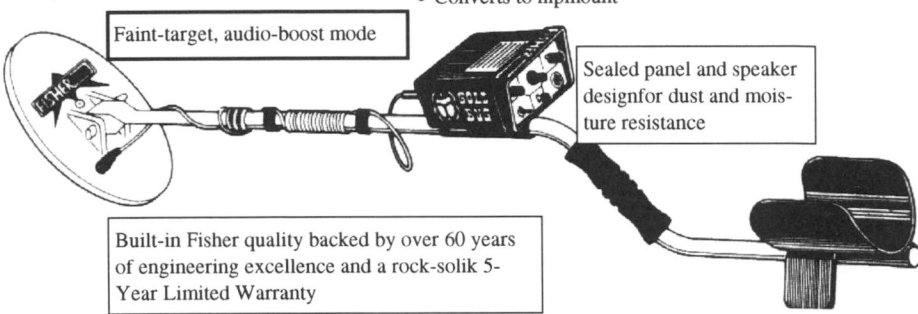

Faint-target, audio-boost mode

Sealed panel and speaker designfor dust and moisture resistance

Built-in Fisher quality backed by over 60 years of engineering excellence and a rock-solik 5-Year Limited Warranty

To be honest, your first time or two with a detector will likely be a bit discouraging. My first experience wasn't so hot, having spent a couple of fruitless afternoons nugget-shooting in a particular area, which I felt certain should have produced some gold. Fortunately, I had a friend who had a lot more experience with a detector, so I went around to ask him what I was doing wrong. He told me I should have been wearing headphones, to hear the tiny gold blips better, but other than that, my technique seemed alright. "Didn't you get any signals at all?" he pressed. I had to think about that. Yes - there was one spot where I'd thought I had a few little blips, but there had been a lot of background static and I wasn't able to pinpoint any of the weak, elusive signals that were trying to get through. "Go back to that spot," he suggested, "and, using the headphones this time, try to *very carefully* adjust the ground balance control. From the way you describe the threshold static, I'll bet you were right over top of a black sand deposit."

I returned to the spot and did what he said. This time, with the headphones, I was able to fine tune the instrument much more precisely. I started to get small, sharp blips right away! I was still confused though, because there weren't just one or two "nugget" signals - there were dozens of them. As I began to dig up the targets, the reason soon became apparent. The detector wasn't registering nuggets, but unbelievably small flakes, and a *lot* of them. As I dug down I uncovered a nice big crevice that was packed-in with black sand. "So my friend was right about that too," I thought, as I feverishly tracked the direction the crevice was going in. Only a small section was accessible from shore, because most of it ran under the creek bed, so I dug up what I could and returned the following weekend with a small backpack dredge. It wasn't a very big crevice - just a few inches wide by a foot and a half deep, and about ten feet long, but it gave up just under six ounces of gold! So, even though it had taken me a while to make my first detector "find", it was a good one, which paid for the cost of my machine several times over. That experience sold me on the metal detector as a bona-fide, professional prospecting tool.

Float-Hunting With a Metal Detector

One of my more recent good finds with a detector, (a Fisher "Gold Bug"), is a beautiful, thumb-size piece of quartz/gold float. The gangue material is a very pretty variety, known as "Smokey Quartz", and the piece contains about 8% by weight of delicate wire gold. I wish I could find the vein this piece came from because the grade of this ore - hold your breath - is 2,700 ounces per ton! A jeweler offered me $2,400 for the piece, (at $1.00 per square millimeter.) He wanted to cut it in thin slices, to use for inlays in fine jewelry. I like it better as a specimen, so I turned the offer down.

Above: In the early part of this century, monstrous bucket dredges scoured the countryside, leaving behind thousands of acres of tailings.

Nugget Shooting the Tailings

In the previous chapter, "Processing Auriferous Gravels", I made reference to the fact that, because of the need to *classify* gravel prior to washing, very large nuggets sometimes get discarded in the piles of oversize waste rock, (tailings).

"Sure, a big nugget is nice to find," you're thinking, "but isn't it a bit like trying to find a needle in a haystack?" It is, but the VLF detector can cut the job down to a manageable size. Consider this formula, postulated by the detector specialist, Steve Voynick...

Average Area of Sweep in 1 Hour: 1800 square feet.
Multiplied by Average Depth of Penetration: 5 inches.
Equals. Total Volume Searched in 1 Hour: 25 cubic yards.

The tailings proposition now begins to look a little more realistic. To take this idea further, let us now make two more assumptions...

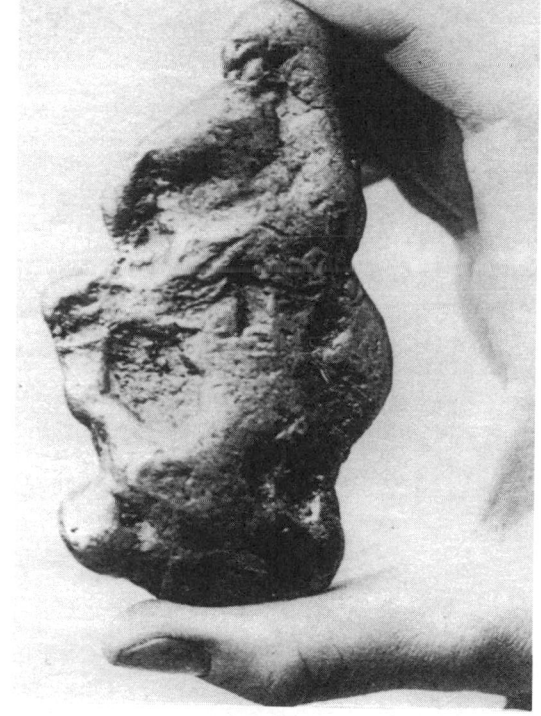

1) Scanning time in one day: 4 hours

2) Amount of Residual Gold in the Tailings: .01oz per yard (a very low concentration)

Therefor: 25 cubic yards per hour x 4 hours = 100 cubic yards per day x .01 oz. per yard residual grade

= 1.0 ounce per day recovered.

Tailings make for a very nice little specialty. There's no brush to hack through, and the tailings areas usually have road access. And, best of all, they PAY!

Metal Detectors on Bedrock

Because they are natural gold traps, you would think that every crevice on every gold creek would have been hunted down and mined out by now. The reason this hasn't happened is simple - most crevices are *hidden* by a shallow layer of overburden. "Out of sight, out of mind," as the saying goes, and the old-timers walked right on by. The VLF detector has changed that forever. Now, we can all be like Superman, with his X-ray vision, and the gold can't hide from us anymore.

As an aside, I have a professional interest in the position that some of the larger mechanized placer operators sometimes find themselves in. Apparently, because of increasingly high operating costs and short mining season, some of the high-volume operations in the north are unable to do a thorough job of cleaning the bedrock; they just can't keep up. The problem is that it is uneconomic to suspend the stripping operation, and let the 'cats' sit idle, while human snipers go our to pick over the temporarily exposed bedrock. Operators in Alaska and the Yukon are beginning to get a grip on this situation by using detectors to quickly scan the bedrock for hotspots. I feel that the process could be further improved by using vacuums *in conjunction* with the detector. Bedrock cleaning is a GOLD TRAILS specialty, and we would be happy to consult with any operators who find themselves in this particular situation.

Abandoned Mines & Underground Workings

At the beginning of this section, I mentioned how metal detectors have become instrumental in the re-opening of some underground mines. However, I must interject a word of caution: Unless you have experience working underground, STAY OUT OF OLD MINES. They can be very dangerous places.

Small hardrock mines can be worked profitably by one or two people, using a portable mill and recovery jig. The grade of the ore in this type of operation has to be quite high, in the range of at least ½ to 1 oz per ton, because the small, portable reduction units are only capable of very small tonnages, from one to eight tons per day. In deciding whether or not to get involved in resurrecting an abandoned working, you must take into account the cost of safely rehabilitating the existing infrastructure, including the *de-watering* of the deeper levels. This can be very expensive, especially in the case of underground placer drifts, where ground-water seepage is a constant problem and is difficult to control. Most likely, the timbering will be rotted and will have to be completely replaced. Figure in the cost of hiring a professional mining engineer, preferably one who specializes in rehabilitating small mines. A good one will earn his consulting fee by providing an accurate, itemized estimate of the re-opening costs, and will prepare an inventory of safety requirements, and any attendant authorizations, permits, etc.

Obviously, re-opening an abandoned mine - even a small one - doesn't exactly fall into the category of "week-end prospecting." However, there *is* one aspect of this business that does fall within the scope of the hobbyist: the *ore dump...*

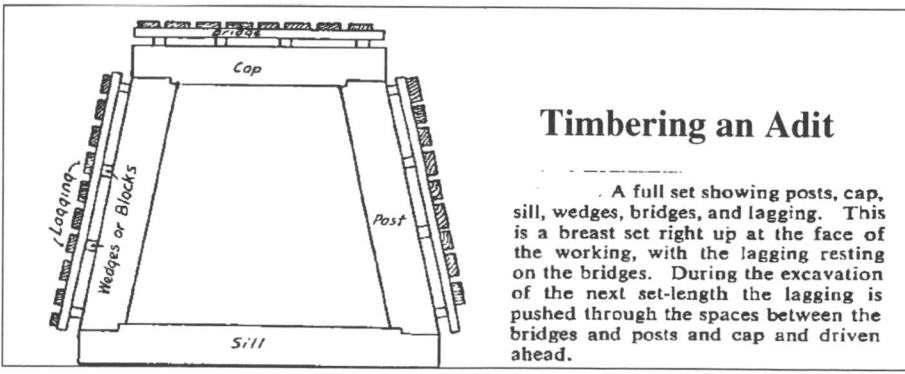

Timbering an Adit

. A full set showing posts, cap, sill, wedges, bridges, and lagging. This is a breast set right up at the face of the working, with the lagging resting on the bridges. During the excavation of the next set-length the lagging is pushed through the spaces between the bridges and posts and cap and driven ahead.

High-Grading Ore Dumps Electronically

An ore dump is not a tailings pile; it is a stack of freshly-mined ore that was stock-piled, prior to being crushed and sent to the smelter. There could be many various reasons why the ore dump was left behind. Perhaps the owner is deceased, or the smelter shut down - who knows? A frequent reason is that, at the outset of both world wars, the government prohibited gold mining as a "non-essential industry", so that mining resources could be applied to recovering strategic metals. Needless to say, after the wars, many of the mine owners did not return, and the mines were never re-opened. In many instances, even the exact location of the mine was lost to posterity. Whatever the reasons, the fact is that intact ore dumps do exist, in surprising numbers, in every gold and silver-producing region in the country.

Look for ore dumps in the vicinity of the *portal* of the mine. There is usually more than one pile, the ore having been *cobbed,* (sorted), into piles of different grades. In this kind of high-grading, you don't actually scan the pile with your detector, you pick through it a piece at a time. Make yourself comfortable and rest the detector's search coil on a clear bit of ground beside you. Now, pass the chunks of ore, piece by piece, over the search coil. The hunks or ore in your hand may look like ordinary rocks, but if your detector suddenly starts sounding off, well, you just *know* it's not an old rusty nail that's in there. In western Australia recently, a detector was used to locate just such a piece of ore. The shoe-box size slab of quartz weighed 28 lbs.-and contained over six and one-half *pounds* of raw gold.

Other Electronic Methods

At the conclusion of this chapter is a chart describing some of the more exotic geophysical methods available. With the possible exception of the *seismograph*, and the *resistivity meter*, these sophisticated methods are beyond the scope of most individual prospectors, and they can be very expensive. I have included some information about them, however, in the event that you run across a geological report that contains the results of one of these kinds of geophysical surveys. Then, you will at least have some idea as to how the data are produced, and how to interpret the results. As I mentioned in the opening chapter of this book, *Aeromagnetic Surveys*, in particular, are widely available, and they may help you to identify all sorts of interesting geological features.

Other Specialties

As you begin your forays into gold country, keep in mind that gold is only one of a host of valuable minerals to be found, (and it is the least common one at that.) While poking around mineralized areas of the country, anything might turn up. Some of the minerals you run across will have economic value, and it's a good idea to get into the habit of collecting mineral specimens wherever you go. Get a mineral book, with color photos, from your public library to help you identify the specimen, or visit your local rockhound club for advice from other prospectors and lapidiarists.

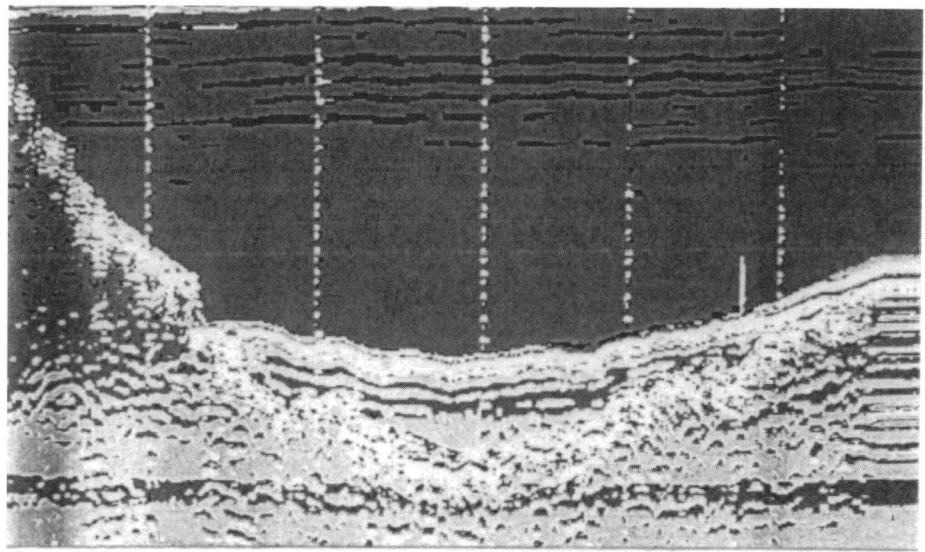

Above: Readout of a placer deposit from a subsurface interference radar. Images are interfaced with a desktop computer to produce digitally enhanced, 3-D color images. Seismic units can produce much the same type of data, and are much less expensive.

Other Types of Economic Mineral Occurrences

INDUSTRIAL MINERALS: kaolin (clay), construction stone, zeolites, magnesite, magnetite, garnet.

BASE METALS: iron, copper, lead/zinc, molybdenum, titanium.

GEMSTONES: Scattered distribution. New discoveries are being brought to light all the time. Outcrops of gem-quality Fire Opal were recently discovered in the Okanagan valley, B.C. Varieties of Jade occur throughout the province. In the Kootenay District, a World-Class deposit of Star Sapphire has recently been announced.

SPECIMEN GOLD & PLATINUM: Large, attractive specimens of electrum, quartz gold, telluride gold, and native platinum are all highly prized by collectors. Quite recently, a brand new mineral, *Tulameenite*, was discovered in the Similkameen District of British Columbia. As far as is known, this native alloy of iron/copper/platinum occurs nowhere else on earth. It's really amazing, but every few years, some one announces the discovery of some brand-new mineral. Perhaps the next one will be named after you!

ROCK & MINERAL SAMPLES: Good markets can be found for even the most common, garden-variety minerals, provided they are of top quality. Universities and private companies purchase large quantities, to include in Rock and Mineral Sets for students.

METEORITES: This is a fascinating specialty, which can also be very lucrative. Meteorites can command very high prices - especially if they contain exotic minerals. The discovery, announced by NASA in 1996, of potential life-forms in Martian meteorites that have landed on earth caused a sensation. Although only a few small fragments of Martian rock have so far been recovered, scientists estimate that the number of these lying unidentified on the surface must number in the hundreds or thousands. I know one "Sky-Rock" hunter who spends days at a time traversing rugged, high-altitude glaciers and snowfields. Apparently, these are good places to look, because any rocks found lying on the barren surface of a snowfield have probably come from above. They stand out against the stark background, which makes them fairly easy to spot. Be cautioned, however, this is mountaineering country, best left to the well-equipped, trained experts.

ARTIFACTS & TREASURE: This deserves a mention, because sooner or later every prospector will encounter some old, abandoned mining camp or pioneer settlement. Going through dead people's garbage may not sound like a very nice thing, but unearthed artifacts can tell you a lot about what was going on at a particular location. If, for example, the community's trash pit is full of fancy bottles, and the remains of expensive, imported canned goods, it's a fairly safe bet that the diggings there were productive. Artifact collecting is a lot of fun, and you can lay claim to such finds, provided they are not taken from private or Indian Lands, or from a Historical or Archeological Reserve.

Radiometric Surveys - A Low-Tech, Low Cost Approach

By and large, electronic surveys are beyond the scope of the individual prospector because of their expense. The one notable exception is the *Radiometric Survey*, using an inexpensive, hand-held geiger-counter. While these instruments are used primarily in the detection of radioactive minerals such as uranium, it is a little-known fact that they can also be used to evaluate placer deposits. The reason behind this is that, while the geiger counter does not register on the gold itself, it can detect some of the other heavy minerals that are associated with the placer gold, including some of the constituents of black sand. Rich placers are likely to carry a relatively higher proportion of heavy Rare Earth elements, which are also highly radioactive. The geiger counter, by itself, cannot tell you how rich a placer is, but by sampling a grid with a geiger counter, you will be able to tell which parts of the deposit have the highest concentration of these heavy minerals.

Conducting a Radiometric Survey

Radiometric surveys are only useful in flat or gently rolling terrain; they become less reliable the hillier it gets. First, lay out a grid of parallel traverses every 100 feet (a 25 meter grid also works well). Try to do your survey in dry weather, as low count anomalies will result from wet ground, which dampens the radioactive count.

At each grid station count the number of clicks registered in a five-minute period. Have the instrument set on the least sensitive scale, and keep it shaded from sunlight as this will also affect the count. A normal, or average background count is about 50 clicks per minute. Little cosmic bursts interfere with the tally, because too many counts arrive at once. All you can do is to estimate the number of sudden counts and keep on tallying.

Once the grid is complete, you will have a fairly good representation of how the heavy minerals are distributed on the deposit. A significant anomaly at two or more stations deserves further examination. A survey of this type does not eliminate the need for physically testing the gravel, but it is a useful, low-cost way of determining the best places to start testing.

Catalog Item

Model hgc-1 Gieger counter. High sensitivity. Three ranges: .2, 2, 20 milliroentgens. Super sensitive meter(50 micro amps). Built-in loud speaker and LED count indicator. Automatic voltage regulation. Sensitive to beta and gamma radiation. Operates 200 hours on one battery.

The "Falcon" Placer Gold Probe

The Falcon is a VLF-TR detector with a very small searchcoil with the capability of detecting tiny flakes as small as one one-hundredth of a grain. That's 48 thousands of an ounce! It can detect such minute particles at a distance of about ¼ inch, and its maximum depth for larger nuggets is about three inches. The Falcon has automatic ground-balancing so it can discriminate between gold and black sand, and it can be adjusted to cancel the black sand out completely. It will even register a single tiny flake of gold embedded in a pile of pure black sand.

I have used mine for low-water sniping on large rivers, and have found it very effective - especially when used in conjunction with a portable gold-vac. It saves a lot of time in locating workable deposits. It weighs just 24 ounces, and you can carry it everywhere with the fanny-pack supplied.

The Goldspear - Electrochemical Potential Method

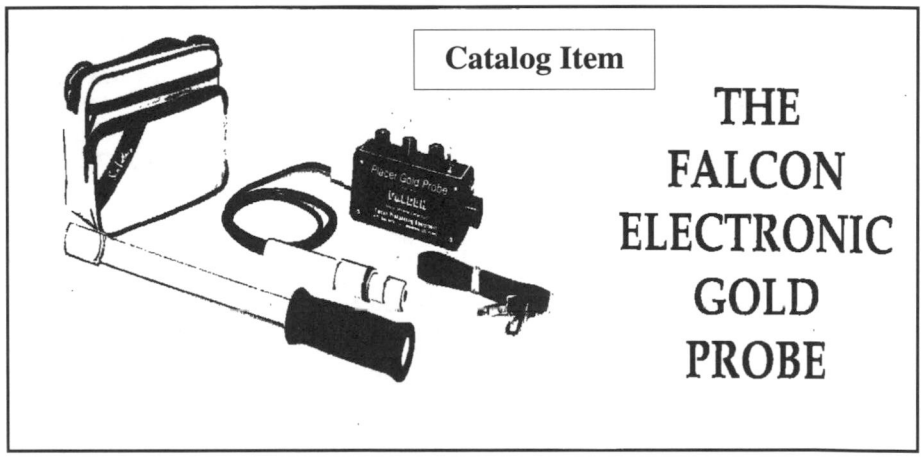

Catalog Item

THE
FALCON
ELECTRONIC
GOLD
PROBE

Every now and then a technical advance is made which promises to completely revolutionize the existing way of doing things. The brand-name "Goldspear" probe is just such a device.

This amazing instrument works on the principle of *electro-chemical potential.* When the probe-head comes into contact with a particle of precious metal, it lets you know about it with a blaze of flashing lights and arcade-type audio signals. The Goldspear can distinguish between: (1) Black Sand. (2) Metallic Minerals. (3) Gold and Platinum. It has different colored lights and a different sounding audio signal for each category. Every time the probe encounters a *single particle*, a signal is made, so you can evaluate the grade of the material you are probing by counting how many signals are produced. The Goldspear can detect micron gold (plus 300-mesh), which is invisible to the naked eye. This feature makes the Goldspear ideal for pocket-hunting because it can find those tell-tale traces in the pockets halo - which are so easily missed by conventional sampling methods. As well, grab-samples take so much time - digging and bagging, packing, panning and examining - probably takes an average of 10 to 20 minutes per sample. With hundreds of samples to get through, you can see why locating a pocket can take weeks, or even months, of sampling. By comparison, a Goldspear "sample" takes all of ten seconds. This is why I have chosen the term "revolutionary" to describe the Goldspear.

Admittedly, the Goldspear isn't cheap, but if you're serious about beach prospecting or pocket hunting, this machine is a real time-saver. You could be out there digging up gold instead of looking for it!

There are some situations where the Goldspear doesn't work well:
1) Deposits that are completely saturated with very finely-disseminated gold.
2) Cemented or hard-packed gravel. (The probe-head cannot be driven very deep into hard ground. To overcome this, a spike can be driven in first, to make a hole for the probe.
3) Deposits that are composed exclusively of very coarse gold. (This is a fairly rare occurrence.)

The only real problem here is with example one. I have come across this situation just once, where there was so much fine gold everywhere that the machine went nuts every time I stuck it in, and so I couldn't properly evaluate the grade of the deposit. In this particular instance, I guess you could call the Goldspear an "overachiever".

Catalog Item

The
GOLDSPEAR

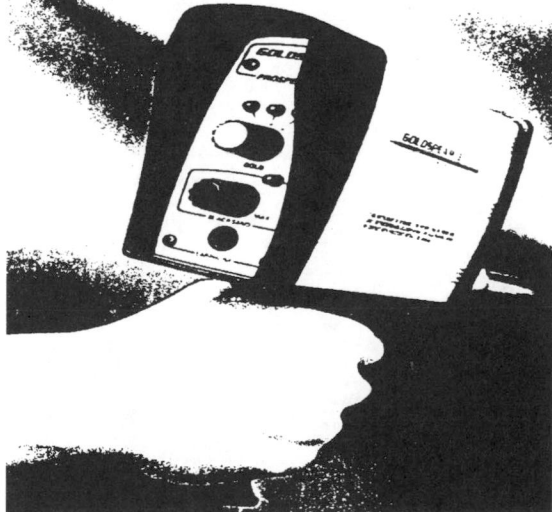

118

<table>
<tr><td colspan="4">ELECTRONIC PROSPECTING</td></tr>
</table>

GEOPHYSICAL DEVICES

Type of Instrument	Cost per km.	Unit Cost	Notes
Potential Field Methods			
1) Gravity Meter	$250 - $600 milligals	$20,000	Ground survey. Measured in
2) Magnetometer	$25 - $100 surveys available for some	$6,000	Air or ground survey. Govt. areas.
3) Self-Potential sulphides.	$75 - $250	$8,000	Measures the field generated by
Electromagnetic Methods			
4) Ohm Meter	——	$25	Measures conductivity of rocks.
5) EM Air or Ground	$100 - $400	$10,000	Operates at 200 - 5,000 Khertz. Survey.
6) VLF-EM or Ground Survey.	$100 - $450	$6,000	Operates at 15 - 25 Khertz. Air
7) VLF-TR	——	$1,200	Metal/Mineral Detector
Electrical Methods			
8) Resistivity Meter	——	$6,000	Ground Survey, to 200'
9) IP-Induced Polarization	$300 - $1,000	$20,000	Produces decay currents to measure sulphides.
Seismic Methods			
10) Seismicmograph	——	$4,000	Maps overburden and bedrock structure.
Radiometric Methods			
11) Geiger Counter	rare earths.	$250	Locates radio-active minerals,
12) Scintillometer	$500 - $1,000 geiger counter.	$10,000	Greater sensitivity than the
Radar Methods			
13) SIR - Subsurface Interferance Radar	——	$8,000	Maps overburden, up to 200' depths.
Electro-Chemical Potential Method			
14) Goldspear (loaming)	$25 - $100	$1,400	ECP probe for surface trace prospecting

CHAPTER NINE

PROSPECTING AS A BUSINESS

From the Grassroots Up

It has been said that in Canada, mining and exploration has created more millionaires than any other business, except for real estate. Billions are spent annually on the never ending search for more and more mineral products to feed the insatiable appetite of our technological society. Even the casual week-end miner is not immune from the lure of the "Big Strike", because in the back of our minds there is the unspoken proposition, "this is how it happens; it could happen to me."

Thoughts like this must have been with billionaire Sir Harry Oakes, Canada's most famous, and some would say, most notorious, prospector and miner. After years and years of grinding poverty in the goldfields of Australia, Africa, and the Yukon, Oakes finally landed in northern Ontario with a sum total of two dollars and sixty-five cents in his pocket. Down but not out, Oakes persevered with his claim-staking, and was eventually able to obtain financial backing for his speculative plans. By 1928, the mines were in full production, and Sir Harry was declared, "The Richest Man in all Canada."

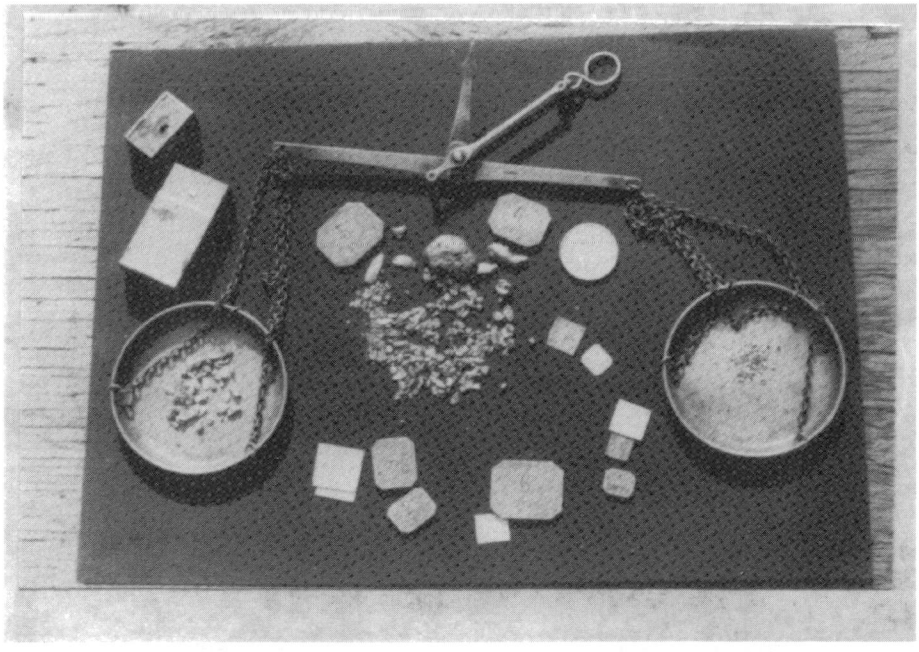

Go Carefully

I'm sure if Harry Oakes were here today, he would agree with me that the key to any successful prospecting venture is to locate the minerals in a *cost-effective* manner. In other words, you have to stretch your limited exploration budget to prospect *targets,* sufficient enough in number so as to result in a winner. In the final analysis, it's all just a numbers game. It's all too easy to get carried away by a good showing - but *please* make sure it's not just "a flash in the pan." I know I sound terribly cliche in this, but you'd be surprised at how many people spend their money on production-type equipment before they are 100% sure that their deposit is big enough or rich enough to support it. Become proficient at each level of prospecting before moving on to the next one. Initial cost for a basic panning and sniping kit is quite low, so you can afford to buy the best. Good equipment will give many years of valuable service if you take care of it. Stick with panning and crevicing until you have found a good showing - one that will reasonably compensate you for the time you have invested. Then you will have to assess the deposit, in terms of what kind of equipment is required to work it. At some locations, the situation might call for a hand-sluice or a gas or electric vacuum, starting at around $40. Other deposits may call for a high-efficiency gas or electric-powered concentrator, ranging anywhere from $250-$1000. A good VLF-TR detector will greatly enhance your exploration capability, and will set you back another $500-$1,000 or so.

The Grubstake Agreement

Amateurs and hobbyists typically finance their projects with their own funds, sometimes supplemented with prospector's assistance grants from the government. For those of us who are unable to personally finance the entire cost of an exploration program, investment partners must be brought on board. In return for providing you with basic equipment, supplies, and operating cash, the *Grubstaker* is cut in for a share of the proceeds that result from whatever is found. Some mining companies will also provide this kind of support. A formal *Grubstake Agreement* is entered into, specifying the *duration*, and the *terms* of the agreement. A 50-50 split is most common in these types of arrangements. In order for the grubstaker to be eligible to deduct the expenses for Income Tax purposes, the Grubstake Agreement must be signed *prior* to the disbursement of any of the funds.

> "Success is going from one failure to the next without a loss of enthusiasm"
>
> **Winston Churchill**

Prospecting Syndicates

This has the same basic structure as the Grubstake Agreement, and can be used where two or more prospectors are involved. The services of a lawyer or a securities broker will be required to write a formal document, or *memorandum,* outlining the financial structure, the details of the proposed work program, and the responsibilities of the principals involved. The Prospecting Syndicate Memorandum should also include a schedule, requiring the submission of progress reports on a regular basis, (at least annually). It used to be that, in B.C., prospecting syndicates were under the purview of the Superintendent of Brokers, but this is no longer the case in this province. Best check to see if formal registration of a syndicate is required in your jurisdiction.

In a prospecting syndicate, it helps if at least some of the members of your investor group can pitch-in in other ways, in actual hands-on operations. Their individual assets and skills can be tapped to help with; bookkeeping, camp cook and helpers, sample crew, technical report writing, and so on. In promoting your prospecting "play" to potential grubstakers and investors, depend solely on your technical and assay reports, and stay away from blue-sky projections. Advance your *geological concept* with a well written proposal, fully documented, and in the correct form. Formats for a Prospecting Program Proposal, and for a Technical Report, are included in the Appendix.

122

You were asking

... about
prospectors and grubstakers

**Revenue Canada
Taxation**

Prospectors and grubstakers are subject to the same general rules as other taxpayers in determining their employment or self-employed income. There are however, certain regulations in the Income Tax Act which apply specifically to activities in these areas.

Prospectors are individuals not corporations who prospect or explore for minerals or develop a property for minerals. They normally work for themselves, on behalf of a group of which they are a member, or for an employer. Grubstakers, on the other hand, are individuals or groups who provide financial backing to prospectors who are searching for or developing mineral rights. The financial backing provided is generally in the form of either a cash advance or the payment of actual expenses.

Expenses of a prospector

As a prospector, you are allowed to claim certain expenses incurred in your search for minerals. These expenses become part of your cumulative Canadian exploration expense pool, which is the total of your expenses from the time you start prospecting.

What expenses may a prospector claim? In general terms, the Income Tax Act allows an expense to be claimed to the extent that it was made or incurred by an individual for the purpose of producing income from a business or property. Therefore, an expense directly relating to your prospecting activities may be claimed, provided you maintain records adequate

to prove that the expenses claimed were in fact incurred. For example, travelling expenses such as helicopter trips must be supported by receipts for the cost of the flight. Expenditures for food, powder, drilling and labour may all be allowed as Canadian exploration expenses, provided they relate directly to the prospecting being done. Satellite and aerial photography, maps and geological surveys could also qualify. The total must be reduced by any personal use included in your expenses, such as personal use of a truck.

Work done on a claim site, such as trenching, digging test pits and preliminary sampling can also be included in the total of your year's expenses. It is important to note that you may not claim as an expense the value of labour you perform yourself.

Capital cost allowance

Certain assets you purchase cannot be totally deducted as an expense. Instead, you may claim a depreciation deduction known as capital cost allowance, which represents a portion of the value of the asset. You may claim capital cost allowance on tools which cost less than $200, at a rate of 100 per cent in the year of purchase. Equipment and machinery costing more than $200 qualify for a rate of 30 per cent a year.

You do not have to claim the maximum deduction available to you in one year on a given asset; any amount up to the maximum may be claimed for a given year. It is important to note, however, that the maximum deduction will be allowed only when the equipment is used solely for prospecting as opposed to personal or some other non-prospecting use.

Canadian exploration expense pool

The total of your allowable expenses for a year (with the exception of capital cost allowance) becomes part of your cumulative Canadian exploration expense pool. At the present time any prospecting expense in the pool incurred after May 25, 1976 may be applied in full against income from any source.

REPRINT

Any expenses in the pool incurred before May 25, 1976, may be deducted only to the extent of

    (i) 30 per cent of the expenses incurred before May 25, 1976,
        or
    (ii) 100 per cent of the income from resource-related activities,

whichever is greater. The balance in the pool not deducted in the current year may be carried forward until absorbed by income in a future year. In addition, as the expense may be applied against income from any source, the pool does not have to continue to accumulate until you eventually receive income from your prospecting activities.

Expenses of a grubstaker

How do the regulations differ for grubstakers? For grubstakers to claim the expenses which have been incurred on their behalf, they must have entered into a written grubstake agreement with the prospector before the prospecting, exploration or development work took place. The grubstaker must have advanced money for, or paid all or part of the expenses of prospecting, or developing a property for minerals; and the mining property must have been acquired under the agreement with the prospector. If the grubstaker is the prospector's employer, then the property must have been acquired through the employee's efforts.

If these conditions are met, the grubstaker is entitled to claim the expenses incurred by the prospector to the extent of the money advanced. However, the grubstaker must be able to prove that the claim is valid by providing, on request, receipts or invoices for the expenses. Of course, the prospector cannot also claim expenses that have been paid for by the grubstaker.

Sale of mining property or claims

When a mining property or a claim acquired through prospecting or grubstaking activities is disposed of, the tax implications arising from the sale will be determined by the form in which payment for the property is received.

If a property is disposed of for cash, the full amount received must be brought into income to the extent that it exceeds the cumulative total balance in the Canadian exploration expense pool. In some cases a property is disposed of for a royalty interest in the property, which has the effect of postponing payment of tax until royalty payments are received. The Supreme Court has held that periodic payments based on the use of, or production from a property should be brought into income even though such periodic payments were instalments on the sale price of the property.

Perhaps the most common method of property transfer used today is the one by which a property is exchanged for shares in a mining corporation. In such cases the following rules apply:
    1) No amount is to be included in the prospector's or grubstaker's income related to receipt of the shares, but
    2) the shares, for capital gains purposes, have an adjusted cost base of NIL to the prospector or grubstaker.

In other words, the prospector or grubstaker will include an amount in income for that property only when the shares are eventually disposed of. As the shares are deemed to have a NIL cost to the individual, the taxable capital gain will be one half of the net proceeds (the sale price minus the costs of disposition, if any).

124

A Bootstraps Approach

Prospecting and exploration is becoming increasingly attractive as a home-based business. Small, individual or family-run ventures, usually operated on a part-time basis, can generate a small but regular cash flow, or can at least break even quickly. If, during the early stages, some losses are incurred, those losses can be applied against future income from the sale of exploration assets, mining claims, or development or production income, etc. Or, (and this is the really good part), exploration expenses can be applied against income *from any other source*. This is a major attraction as far as outside investors are concerned.

Marketing Your Gold

Beyond the basic commodities - the sale of gold or mining property - there is a realm of creative marketing specialties for the entrepreneur to explore. The common element with these various specialties is *added value*. For example, an old diving buddy of mine has progressed to the point where he consistently recovers ½ to 1 ounce every day he goes out. His gross for the year, just from week-end mining, is beginning to look more and more like a regular salary, especially since he found a jeweler to help him sell his nuggets for a retail price. Between them, they make pieces that sell as fast as they can produce them, at a rate of up to 3x spot, or about $1500 per ounce in Canadian dollars. I know that sounds like a lot, but it is actually quite a good bargain for the buyer, since most manufactured gold jewelry sells at around 5x spot. Spot is the current London daily quote listed in the newspapers. As far as I'm concerned, most manufactured jewelry doesn't have near the uniqueness or quality of natural, nugget gold. Most placer gold is between .8 and .95 fine - the equivalent of 21 or 22 carats.

So far, my friend has resisted the temptation to cash in his chips and, (literally), "take the plunge" for a full-time gold-diving career, but I know that he takes great comfort and satisfaction in the knowledge that, if push came to shove, he could do it.

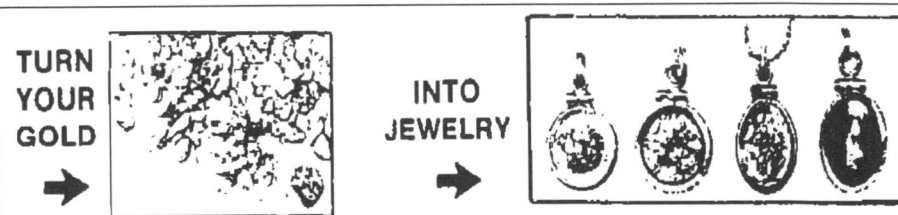

Many prospectors are finding that they can get up to $1000 an ounce or more by making their fine placer gold into jewelry. 12K and 14K gold-filled lockets make attractive earrings, lockets, necklaces, etc.

Catalog Item UY-3

Logistics of a Prospecting Expedition

Logistics involves the planning and support of those aspects of the prospecting program pertaining to physical work, i.e.: where you are going, how you intend to get there, a list of equipment and supplies, etc.

Adequate planning is essential to the success of any prospecting activity, and every eventuality must be carefully considered in advance. Make extensive use of topographical maps, as well as air photos, and be sure to look over your access route *in person* before attempting to transport any equipment. Be wary of the range of climatic conditions you might have to contend with, especially in high-altitude alpine environments. A survival kit, including flares and matches, should be carried whenever your work takes you out of ear-shot of the road. If extended overnight hikes are required, be sure to leave a detailed *trail plan* with a responsible person. If a survival-type firearm is not carried, every person in the group should be equipped with a canister of bear repellent.

You will have to travel very lightly if you are backpacking into remote country. However, wherever possible, try to make your base camp as comfortable as you can, and you will find you can maintain a higher level of gold production. A large, cabin-style tent is ideal. Select one with heavy canvas walls, which will keep the heat in from a small wood or kerosene stove. Folding camp cots are lightweight, and will keep you comfortable, up off the drafty tent floor. You can keep your provisions cool, fresh, and safe from squirrels by storing them in a partially buried galvanized garbage can or similar container.

Access

For the weekend warrior, who doesn't have much time, getting in and out quickly is a major consideration. Fortunately, most areas of B.C. have networks of logging roads, which provide close access to nearly all of the good gold areas. So, unless you have some kind of special "hot spot" in mind, there's really no need to go slogging off into the wilds at all.

Logistics becomes all the more critical the farther off the road you get. For example, if you establish a mining operation a day's hike, (several kilometers, let's say), from the nearest access road, and if, for the sake of argument, you are capable of packing three day's worth of camp supplies, then you would be spending every third and fourth day packing, leaving only two days out of the four for actual mining. This is at the point of diminishing returns, and you would probably decide to search for some other spot, unless the deposit you found is very, very rich. If the deposit *is* just too good to pass up, you might be better off going to the expense of a *fly-camp*, supplied by regular scheduled float-plane or helicopter drops.

Claim Staking Procedure

Staking a mining claim is a lot easier than you might think. The main advantage to staking a claim is that it affords a certain amount of security where a long-term exploration program is indicated, if you are considering making a financial commitment. There are other advantages as well, such as the right to reside on the claim while you are working on it, and the right to apply to use a limited amount of timber for the construction of mine workings. For a complete, step-by-step instructions on claim-staking, obtain a copy of the publication, "Guide to Mineral Titles in British Columbia", available from any BC Government Agent at a cost of $2.00 per copy. Other jurisdictions will have a similar publication, outlining their particular regulations, but the general principles of claim-staking are the same almost everywhere.

Getting Around - Prospecting Vehicles

A camper, van, or small trailer makes an excellent prospecting base-camp. In extremely rugged country, a 4WD jeep or truck is preferable, but in most situations, a regular 2WD pickup, or even a small car, will suffice. You try to get as close as you can, but at some point you just have to get out and hike. After all, that's what prospecting is all about. Find a good deposit first, then you can worry about improving the access later. Whichever vehicle you are using, a winch will get you out of almost any off-road slip-up. Instead of a winch, you could carry a *come-along*, and a length of cable in the trunk.

There are a lot of places where even a jeep can't go - but a small ATV, mini-bike, or trail-bike can. They are the modern equivalent of the old prospector's "burro". If this item is in your prospecting budget, go for it! It does save a lot of time, and it is so nice to have a little two-wheel "buddy" to pack your stuff around on.

The modern-day "Prospector's Burro" . . .

Here is a brief overview of the claim-staking process...

1) Visit the Government Agent, Gold Commissioner, or Mineral Division office and obtain:

    a. A Free miner's Certificate, (Cost: $25) (Note: You no longer have to be a Canadian Citizen to get one of these; non-citizens can obtain one if you are resident in Canada "for not less than 183 days per calendar year, or authorized to work in Canada.")

    b. A copy of the "Titles Reference Map" of the area you plan to stake.

    c. A blank, "Application to Record" form, (free of charge.)

    d. A set of metal "Mineral Claim Tags", or, "Placer Claim Tags", depending on which type you plan to stake. Cost: $2.00 per set.

2) Make a rough plan of how you want to situate the claim, to best cover the targeted area. In B.C., a Placer Claim can be any dimension up to 500 meters wide and 1000 meters in length. A Mineral Claim is made up of *Mineral Claim Units*, each measuring 500 x 500 meters. In locating a Placer Claim, try to orient the *Location Line,* which runs the length of the claim, in a place that is easily accessible.

During a *staking rush*, helicopters are used extensively to transport crews in and out of remote areas rapidly.

3) Claim Posts are now established at either end of the Location Line, like so...

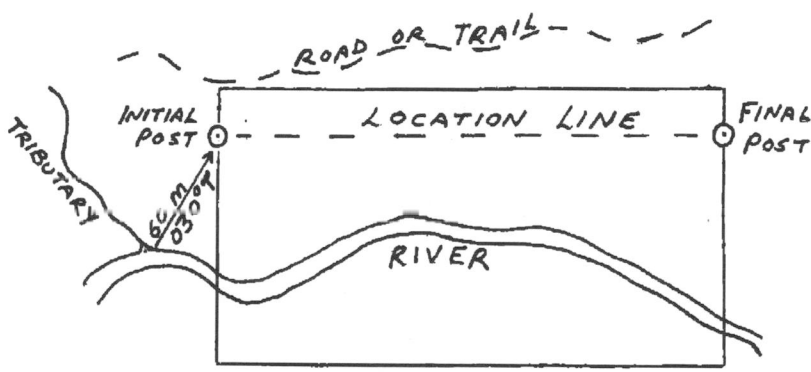

Set up the Initial Post. A legal post can be made of, "either a piece of sound timber, a stump, or a tree cut to the same specifications of a post, or a cairn of stones." See the "Guide to Mineral Titles" for the exact post size dimensions.

4) Imprint <u>all</u> of the required information on the metal tag, and affix it with *broad-head* nails, to the post. (Roofing nails are the best.)
Make sure to record all of the tag information, <u>verbatim</u>, in your notebook or directly onto your application form.

5) Using a compass, pace off the required distance along the

Catalog Item
GPS Personal Navigation Device

Global Positioning System (GPS)

Inaccurate locating of mineral deposits, and staking of claims, has always been the bane of the prospector, because they often occur in remote, poorly charted areas which are lacking in monuments or survey markers. Many a good claim has been lost because of inaccurate staking. This problem is now a thing of the past with the advent of these high-quality, low-cost GPS instruments. Log each interesting outcrop you come across into memory, and the GPS will lead you unerringly back to your discovery. Dozens of other uses, including laying-out super accurate survey grids. And, did you *really* think that prospectors never get lost?

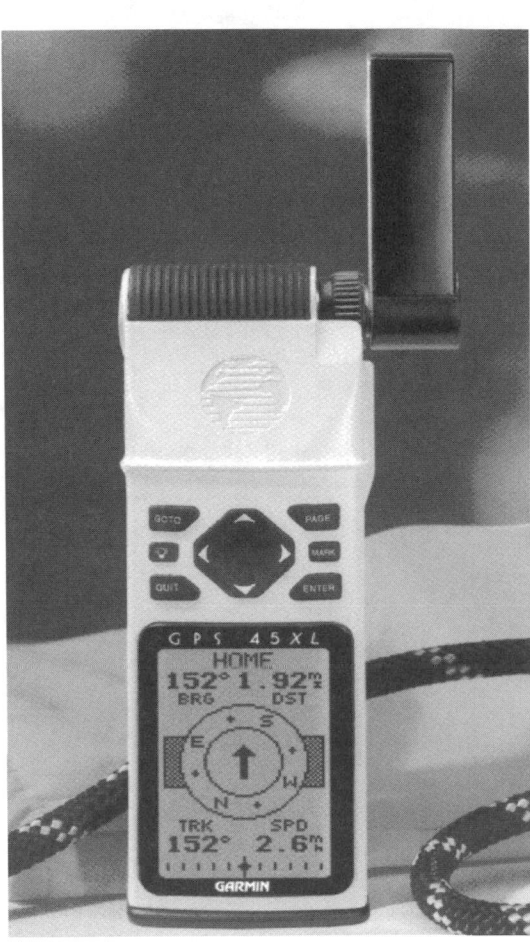

Catalog Item

Hip chain. Distance is measured automatically as you walk. Includes one 1,800 meter spool of bio-degradable thread.

location line, and establish the *Final Post*. In working out the compass headings, bear in mind that your compass is reading according to *Magnetic North*, but your claim sketch is made from maps which are always oriented to *True North*, or *azimuth*. True North is fixed, but Magnetic North fluctuates over time, and it is also different from one location to another. The variance between True North and Magnetic North is known as *Magnetic Deviation*, which can be quite large, (up to 20-30 degrees of arc), and must be corrected for if your staking is to be accurate. Call the Flight Services office at your local airport to find out what the correct Magnetic Deviation is for your area. Measuring the distance along the location line by *pacing* is acceptable, but the locating will be much more precise if you use a string-line or a hip-chain. These can be rented for a few dollars per day from most surveyors or drafting supply house.

6)   Blaze and flag the trees along the location line and clear the underbrush, so the line can be clearly followed.

7)   At the predetermined distance, establish a *Final Post*, impress and affix the Final Post tag, and fill out the rest of the application form. The staking job is complete!

(Note: If you are staking on private property, you must first contact the owner and get permission before you cut down any trees for posts, or blaze or otherwise damage trees. If contacting the owner is not possible, bring along your own posts of 4x4 inch lumber. If the owner does not wish any damage to his or her trees, you may use pickets and extra flagging to mark a line instead of blazing, but this is the only instance where a non-blazed location line is acceptable.)

Applying for a Claim

In B.C., the Gold Commissioner must receive your application *within twenty days* after the staking is completed. The time-frame may be slightly different in other States and Provinces. The Application must be accompanied by a *sketch plan* of the claim, made on a page-size portion of a Titles Reference Map. As of April, 1997, an Application to Record fee of $100 is charged when you apply, and is refunded if, for whatever reason, you are unsuccessful in acquiring title to the claim.

Maintaining a Claim

To legally maintain ownership of a Placer Claim, from year to year, you must:

1) Pay an annual *Recording Fee*, (currently $100 for a Placer Claim, and $100 for each Mineral Claim Unit.)

2) Perform annual *Assessment Work,* to the value of $500, or pay *Cash-in-Lieu* of the assessment work. Trail construction, geochemical surveys, trenching, sampling, etc., all qualify as assessment work. The rates for the various types of work are calculated on the basis of actual costs, or they can be based on the rate schedules found in the Mines Division's publication, "Guide to the Evaluation of Physical Work". In this guide, sluicing gravel is deemed to have a value of "$40 per cubic meter." Therefore, to meet your annual work requirement by sluicing, you would have to move about twelve and one-half cubic meters of gravel. Assessment is accepted on the "Honor System", but you should fully document your work, (including photos), just in case you are called on to prove that the work was actually performed. If the amount of work you did in one year is greater than the annual requirement, ($500), the surplus may be applied to future years, in multiples of $500, to a maximum of ten years.

As a form of tenure, both mineral claims and placer claims are designed to accommodate exploration, bulk-sampling, and small-scale development. Production on a Placer Claim is limited to 2,000 cubic meters of paydirt per year. When production exceeds this amount, conversion to a Placer *Lease* must be applied for.

Glenn's Golden Rule No.5

"Those Who Have the Gold - Rule"

Property Grooming

Some claims are staked for the purpose of immediately re-selling, or *optioning* them to a mining company. Other individuals will put a claim on the market only after they have exhausted the claim's potential for high-grade surface deposits that they can mine themselves. Sooner or later, the deeper hardrock and placer mines become unworkable for the small operator, even though considerable reserves, and value, remains with the mine. At this time, *property grooming* will help you get the best deal on your claim.

Claim grooming consists of carefully mapping the property, and marking all of the outcrops, mineral occurrences, and sample sites with pickets, so they can be easily re-located by the potential buyers and geologist who will inspect the property. On an initial property inspection, try always to personally accompany the prospective buyer. This provides you with the opportunity to qualify the buyer, as well as providing the interested party with full, detailed documentation on the claim, including all of the geological data.

Untested placer claims sell for anywhere from one or two thousand dollars up to around fifty thousand, averaging around ten thousand for a claim that has at least some good history. At the other end of the scale, fully tested claims - those that have *proven reserves*, (based on drilling, trenching, and bulk sampling), are valued as a percentage of the reserves they contain. An open-pit placer operation with 20 million in proven reserves might fetch 2 or 3 million on the open market.

The complicated work of selling a mining claim becomes much simpler if you go through an agent or broker. Sure, they will want their percentage, but we can't all be experts at everything, and maybe you'd rather spend time in the bush looking for gold. Large mining companies, especially, tend toward complicated agreements involving *option-to-purchase, royalty agreements, net smelter returns,* and so forth. More than one mine-finder has found himself on the short end of the stick in these proceedings, and I strongly recommend that you seek legal assistance if a sale reaches this level of complexity.

Mechanized Placer Operations

The advent of low-cost earthmoving equipment is putting mechanized operations within reach of more and more small placer operators. A small, rubber-tired, tracked, or towable backhoe can be had for the price of a small car, and a washplant with feeder starts at around $10,000 US, for a 50 to 80 yard-per-day model.

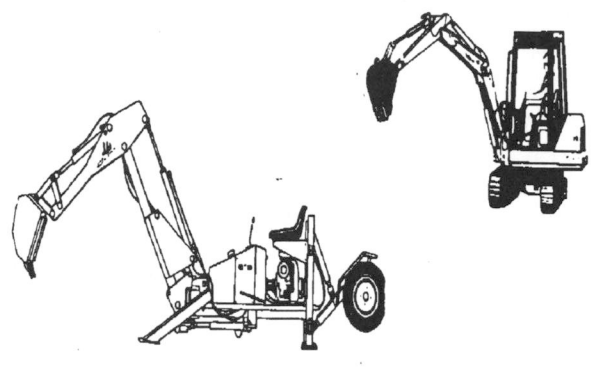

*"Some deposits are too small to interest large mining companies but are rich enough to make mining by one man or a few men practical... Small-scale mining, where practical is a useful phase of the mineral industry because it permits production from deposits that would otherwise probably not be worked and because work of this kind **may show that a deposit is larger and more important than it appeared to be**. (Emphasis added). Possibilities exist for the location and discovery of placers that could be worked for platinum, particularly in the Western Cordillera."*

From: Prospecting in Canada, Lang, 1968

I think that at some time or another, all prospectors dream of operating their own little gold mine. The opportunity is real enough, but it can be risky, even when the deposit appears to be a good-paying one. Before making a production decision on such a prospect, prepare a detailed Cash-Flow Analysis, to avoid any nasty surprises down the road. Each of the following cost categories should be thoroughly researched...

Exploration Costs - geochemical/geophysical surveys

- mapping
- drilling
- bulk sampling

Development Costs

- camp/bunkhouse
- road construction

Capital Costs

- power-plant
- backhoe
- wash-plant/feeder
- secondary recovery circuit

Management Costs - assessment fees

- water use permits
- resource management fees
- reclamation bond

Operating Costs   - fuel

- camp expenses
- equipment maintenance
- wages

Other Expenses

- marketing costs
- refining costs
- training (blasting, 1st-aid)
- commodity royalty
- opportunity cost and cost of financing

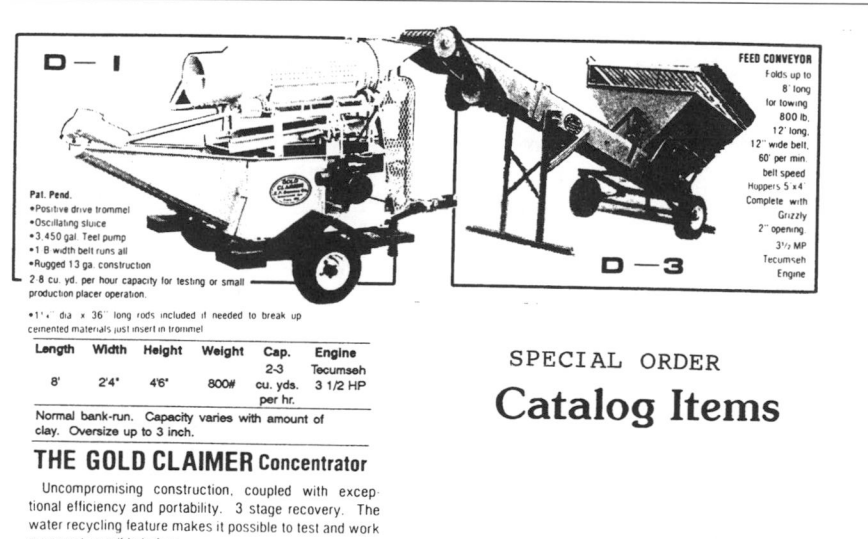

D – I

FEED CONVEYOR
Folds up to
8' long
for towing
800 lb.
12' long,
12' wide belt,
60' per min.
belt speed
Hoppers 5 x 4
Complete with
Grizzly
2" opening,
3½ MP
Tecumseh
Engine

D – 3

Pat. Pend.
- Positive drive trommel
- Oscillating sluice
- 3,450 gal. Teel pump
- 1 B width belt runs all
- Rugged 13 ga. construction

2-8 cu. yd. per hour capacity for testing or small
production placer operation.

- 1' - dia x 36" long rods included if needed to break up
cemented materials just insert in trommel

Length	Width	Height	Weight	Cap.	Engine
				2-3	Tecumseh
8'	2'4"	4'6"	800#	cu. yds.	3 1/2 HP
				per hr.	

Normal bank-run. Capacity varies with amount of
clay. Oversize up to 3 inch.

SPECIAL ORDER

Catalog Items

THE GOLD CLAIMER Concentrator

Uncompromising construction, coupled with excep-
tional efficiency and portability. 3 stage recovery. The
water recycling feature makes it possible to test and work
areas not possible before.

136

The Commercial Placer Mine

"The only financial defense against inflation is ownership of gold and *producing* gold mines. The holders of real money in a deflation will automatically be the only buyer. Everyone else will be sellers of services, inventories, and assets to gain liquidity. As for the producing gold mines, they will be literally digging their liquidity out of the ground. The producing gold mines will be the premier businesses of the deflation."

T.E. Slanker, Jr., Editor, North American Gold Mining News.

It *is* possible to get started in commercial placer gold mining on a very small scale, provided you stick to some basic, time-proven ground-rules, and don't get sidetracked into some wild, pie-in-the-sky schemes. (There are a lot of them out there and sooner or later, they all come crashing down). The two basic rules are:

1) Do not rely on assays, (i.e.: fire assays or AA assays), to determine the value of your potential deposit. These are of value in hardrock mining but are nearly worthless in assessing placers, the reason being that these lab tests will reveal "locked-in" values that you will never, ever, be able to recover. Instead, rely exclusively on gravity methods for your testing, such as: panning, sluicing, and hydraulic concentrating. The result of these testing methods is "gold-in-hand", i.e.: actual, physical gold that you can weigh and measure, and make reliable projections as to what your mine can actually produce. In other words, if you cannot recover the gold in your paydirt by gravitational methods alone, then go find another deposit.

2) Avoid "Microscopic Gold Placers". Microscopic Gold is different from Fine Gold, or even Very Fine Gold, which, as discussed in Chapter Seven, *can* be efficiently recovered with relatively simple methods. There are a lot of placers that have only microscopic, or *ultrafine* gold, and a lot of people have gone broke trying to make them pay. The technology to recover micron gold is on the horizon - there are some good people currently working on the problem - and in the future there may be opportunities in this, but it isn't here yet, so don't get taken in on this one.

Other Income Opportunities

For the past few years the exploration industry in Canada was somewhat depressed, But the exploration business is a notoriously cyclic one, and there now appears to be a new boom underway. New excitement has been sparked by diamond discoveries in Alberta and the Northwest Territories, and there is renewed interest in gold mining in the Yukon and in northern Ontario. Employment opportunities may be available in the area of *contract staking,* in hiring-out on survey and sample-collection crews, and in providing other services to the exploration industry. At the beginning of this, the last decade of the twentieth century, the mineral sector in British Columbia directly employed 18,000 workers, of whom 3,000 were directly involved in mineral exploration, and the number is growing. Each year, on average, around 6,000 individual Free Miner Certificates, (FMC's), were issued in this province, and this number, too, is growing. Claim-stakers locate over 100,000 mineral claim units annually, and a large number of placer claims are also applied for. This activity is expected to continue to increase, along with a steady growth in demand for metals in the future, according to the B.C. Government's Discussion Papers on "A Mineral Strategy for the Province".

Jobs in the mineral sector are relatively high-paying, and young people, especially, should be encouraged by the opportunities present in the field of *geoscience*. To find out about training for this line of work, contact the Association of Engineers and Geoscientists of B.C., listed in the Appendix.

The exciting new field of *geotourism* holds much promise. If you are a good gold panner, and you have access to and knowledge of local mining areas or gold creeks, and if you like meeting people and enjoy teaching, local tours are a good bet. At $20 to $50 per person, small groups of 8-15 participants can be easily accommodated on morning and afternoon tours. Geo tours are definitely an "in thing" these days. They can be quite lucrative - and it's a real fun summer job.

Future Trends in Mineral Exploration

I wonder what the old-time sourdough would think if he could see how things are done today? Prospecting from space-born satellites might seem like pure magic to him. Fifty years from today, I wonder that the technologies of the future would seem equally unbelievable to us; deep-sea robot mining, or prospecting for eolian gold placers on Martian deserts - the possibilities boggle the mind.

What we can be reasonably sure of, however, is an ever-increasing level of technological sophistication and better tools to augment the intuitive skills and creativity of the humble prospector. Technology can be a little intimidating at times I admit, but although the methods change, the will to succeed remains always - and so we adapt.

Prospecting for Space-Age Minerals

A government information circular, "High-Tech Metals in British Columbia", confirms that: "The demand for many of the high-tech metals is expected to increase significantly in the near future, due in part to recent technological innovation."

So what's all the fuss about? Just what are these so-called "hi-tech" metals anyway. (And where can we look for them?) As the name implies, this group of minerals with the funny-sounding names are used in highly specialized technical, medical, and scientific applications. The group includes; Beryllium, Gallium and Germanium, Niobium and Tantalum, the Rare Earths, and Ytrium. They occur primarily in placers, in specialty granites, and in certain types of carbonate-hosted formations, the latter being typical of this province's many lead/zinc/copper occurrences. Research into areas such as this can get pretty heavy-going, technically, but those who do make the effort to educate themselves are likely to be well rewarded. Rare Earth Elements, (REE's), for example, contain cerium oxide and europeum oxide, valued at $750 and $1000 US per pound respectively. In gold and platinum placers, and especially in beach placers, the black sand concentrate should be tested for *rare earths* and for *titanium,* as these could present valuable co-products of the operation.

Earth Science

Lead us on into the mountains

Silver and gold there to find

On rock cragg, in misty vale,

Fortunes lie hidden - ours to devine

Analytical science we apply

Exploring the universe, the atom, the planet

Discover fine metals, mine riches - we try

As we follow the Gold Trail we reach for the summit

Prospecting veins in the earth is the art

Mankind has sought these ten thousand years
Metallurgical man, physics accords;
Transmuting elements The future is here!

CHAPTER TEN

Physical Fitness and Prospecting - How Fit Do You Have to Be?

"Those Who Can, Do - Those Who Can't, Teach."

I never believed that; I think it's a terrible saying. I can still do everything I have written about in this book, but because I have become physically challenged by a form of arthritis the past few years, I have to do a few things differently. I plan my trips much better, and if it looks like there's going to be any real heavy work involved, I make sure to bring along some enthusiastic "associates", to share in my glorious adventure. Disability need not preclude anyone from enjoying a wide range of prospecting activities. The effects of old age or infirmity can be mitigated by eating properly and moderate exercise, and getting out in the fresh air to kick some rocks over is bound to do you good.

There are lots of little tricks to make the physical chores of prospecting a little easier, like setting up a small table for panning, instead of being hunched over in an uncomfortable position at water's edge. John Coombes, a Vancouver native, must have been a remarkable man. In his seventies, and with a serious physical handicap, Mr. Coombes was still able to operate a large dredge, *full time!* Hydrotherapy is often recommended for people with musculoskeletal illnesses, and I sometimes wonder about the effects of weightlessness that one experiences while gold-diving, because of the reduced gravity on aching joints.

For people who might have difficulty walking over rough terrain, there is always *roadside prospecting*. Don't laugh! By stopping at interesting-looking outcrops and exposed gravel beds, you could easily stumble across something important. Remember that Hemlo, Canada's premier gold mine, was discovered right next to a four-lane highway. (In fact, parts of the highway had been cut through the deposit *years before it was found!*). The moral is, don't assume, just because there's a road there, that there's nothing to find right under your nose.

Finally, for those miserable old slobs who just refuse to *get off the couch,* there is always armchair prospecting. I knew one gent in his eighties, still directing a full-blown exploration program from the nursing home were he lived. I believe he was still making some money at it too. But probably, from his point of view, what he saw as important was that he continued to make a valuable social and economic contribution, and he was creating employment for the younger people doing the field-work.

There may be other, more indirect health benefits of gold prospecting. Dr. R.C. Bright, author and practicing chiropractor, reports that in the holistic medicine practiced by some ancient societies, natural, unalloyed gold was considered a great healer, ". . . possessed of a warm energy that brings soothing vibrations to the body and mind." In modern medicine, gold salts have been found to have a powerful therapeutic effect in the treatment of arthritis and some other serious illnesses. Professor Harry Warren, working at the University of British Columbia, made a special study of the medicinal properties of precious metals and their salts. Professor Warren is noted in the literature for his contributions in the field of *biogeological prospecting,* and he is credited with identifying the purple-flowered shrub species, *Phacelia Sericea,* (Mountain Sericea), as a reliable indicator of a nearby gold deposit. What makes this, and some other plants unique, is that their root systems can manufacture cyanide, which effectively fixes, or binds the gold at the molecular level. Most recently, Professor Warren turned his attention to the medicinal properties of platinum and it's effects on the human body.

CONCLUDING REMARKS

I've enjoyed writing and updating this book. I hope you have enjoyed reading it, and I hope you will continue to find it useful as a handy reference when you are planning your prospecting expeditions. There has been a lot of material to cover, but the important thing is to realize that, as part of an exciting, multi-faceted industry, grassroots prospecting will always have an important role. Even the most casual weekend practitioner has a part to play by contributing to the growing database of information, and perhaps one day, in bringing a new mine into production.

We at **GOLD TRAILS** would love to hear from you - your comments, ideas, and your experiences in prospecting and mining. Write and ask to be put on our mailing list in order to receive the periodic newsletters we put out. These include a "Prospectors Referral" section, a sort of public exchange of ideas, information, and local prospecting gossip. Also, if you or a friend has Internet access, try **GOLD TRAILS** excellent website at: http//www.goldtrails.com

Thus completes your basic training in grassroots prospecting. Congratulations, you are now well on your way to becoming a knowledgeable gold prospector. I wish I could be there with you when you find your first *monster* nugget. Your family and friends will be amazed and impressed every time you recount the story of how you cleverly put all of the clues together when you made your first good find. (Have you ever noticed how BIG people's eyes get when you mention the word *goldmine?*)

All the best to you in all of your endeavors. Good luck, see you on the gold trail...

Glenn Leaver

APPENDIX

GOLD FACTS

Scientific Information

Symbol: Au From: Latin root, *aurum*, meaning "shining dawn". Gold is Number 79 on the Periodic Table, between platinum, (78), and mercury, (80). Melting Point: 1945°F (1063.4°C) Density: $19.32g/cm^3$ @ $20^{oC.}$ Mho's Scale of Hardness, (from one to ten): 2.5-3.0 Specific Gravity: 15.6+

Properties

Gold is malleable and ductile; it can be formed into transparent sheets one-quarter of a millionth of an inch thick. A one-foot cube of gold, (30 x 30 x 30 cm), weighs 1187 lbs. - about half a ton! A single cubic inch of gold weighs 8.24 troy ounces, and would be worth nearly four thousand dollars at today's prices. All of the refined gold in existence would fit in a cube measuring only 53.5 feet on each side. Gold is highly stable, and it is unaffected by oxygen or water, and most acids. It can be dissolved in Aqua Regia, (royal water), a mixture of hydrochloric acid and nitric acid.

Uses

Gold is used in protective films, on space-helmet visors, and UV-resistant glass. It is widely used in the electronics and aerospace industries, and has many medical and pharmaceutical applications.

Geology

Gold is formed in veins, lenses, or sheets of mineralized rock, called "orebodies". Where orebodies are exposed at the surface and are subject to erosion, native gold is released, forming concentrations in gravel deposits. Placer deposits of this type, (pronounced plasser, as in "glass"), have widespread distribution throughout the Western Cordillera of North and South America.

"KUNDALINI"

"The Harmonic and Transformative Properties of Gold"

PHYSICAL: Physical Strength; Purification & Regeneration of Body Tissues; Boosts Circulation

ASPECT: Male

MAJOR CHAKRA: The Heart

MINOR CHAKRAS: The Navel, the Crown

PSYCHIC: Balances the Left and Right Hemispheres of the Brain; Enhances Creativity and Imagination; Amplifies Individual Though-Waves

COSMIC ENERGY: Represents the Sun

FORMAT FOR A 'PROSPECTING PROGRAM PROPOSAL'

This document should be typed double-spaced, with the author's name, address, and contact numbers appearing at the top of the first page. The minimum information must include:

A) Project location.
   i) Name of area.
   ii) NTS map sheet number.
   iii) Location map, with an outline of the area to be prospected.
   iv) If the proposed work area is on an existing claim, an up-to-date Mineral Titles Reference Map, or Placer Titles Reference Map, must be attached.

B) Access.
   i) Route and methods of transportation.

C) Prospecting Targets. Must be described by:
   i) Commodity or minerals.
   ii) Deposit Type.
   iii) Geology of Area

D)   The type and amount of work proposed must be clearly defined.

E)   The number of prospecting days to be spent in the field.

FORMAT FOR A 'TECHNICAL REPORT'

A report documenting work performed, complete with summary and supporting data, and including;

A)   An up to date Mineral Title, or Placer Title Reference Map.

B)   A copy of all Notice of Work forms recorded with the Mines Inspector.

C)   An accurate map, or maps, at a scale that will provide sufficient detail, showing: bar scale; true north arrow; location of claim posts and boundaries, or area of prospecting to identifiable geographic features, such as named streams, lakes, roads, settlements, bridges, etc.; location of prospecting traverses; location of all instrument readings with the corresponding values obtained; location of all samples with sample number and type noted; and location and geological description of each outcrop or area of boulder investigation.

D)   Analysis/assay certificates for all samples analyzed and plotted on any of the maps noted in (C) above. The numbering of samples on certificates and maps must correspond.

SELECTED BIBLIOGRAPHY

Books and Papers

Edmond H. Weiss, "The Writing System for Engineers and Scientists" Prentice-Hall, 1982

E.L Faulkner, "Introduction to Prospecting" Ministry of Energy, Mines, & Petroleum Resources, (MEMPR) Paper # 1986-4

R.W. Boyle, "The Geochemistry of Gold & It's Deposits" Geological Survey of Canada, Bulletin # 280, 1979.

"Notes on Placer-Mining in B.C." MEMPR Bulletin # 21, Revised 1980.

"Placer Gold Production in B.C." MEMPR Bulletin #28, Revised 1980. (A good listing of nearly all of B.C.'s gold creeks - gl.)

Jennifer Pell and Z.D. Hora, "High-Tech Metals in British Columbia" MEMPR Information Circular 1990-19.

"Guide to Legislation and Approvals in Placer-Mining" MEMPR Mineral Resource Division, Inspection and Engineering Branch, 1993.

S.S. Holland and H.W. Nasmaith, "Investigation of Beach Sands", MEMPR # 2231, 1958.

"Guide to Mineral Titles in British Columbia" MEMPR Titles Branch, 1996.

Dave McCracken, "Gold Mining in the 1990's" - The Complete Book of Modern Gold-Mining Procedure", New Era Publications, 1993. (Available through GOLD TRAILS)

Herbert Hoover, "De Re Metallica" (Hoover's famous 1912 translation of the original 1556 Latin manuscript.)

"Some Physical and Biological Effects of Suction Dredge Mining" State of California, Department of Fish and Game, 1982.

Journals

California Mining Journal. P.O. Box 2260, Aptos, CA 95001. Published monthly, highly recommended.

The Mining Review. 124 W 8th St., North Vancouver, B.C. Bi-monthly.

RESOURCE LISTINGS

Jewelry-Making

J. Paul Badali, 944 S. 200 E. Dept. GT, Layton, UT 84041.   Offers a complete line of nugget-jewelry

supplies, easy-to-assemble lockets and findings.

Gold Buyers and Refiners

Al Schultz, Box 162, Bronx, NY 10465 Buys and sells crystalline and quartz-gold specimens.

Imperial Smelting & Refining Co. of Canada Ltd.

301-510 West Hastings St. Vancouver, B.C. V6B 1L8

Ph (604)685-2344, toll free 1-800-663-0455, fax (604)685-0103

Training

Yukon/B.C. Chamber of Mines, 840 West Hastings St., Vancouver, B.C. V6C 1C8 Phone (604) 681-5328. "Annual Prospecting and Mining School" night classes. Dubbed, "The School for Future Millionaires" by Saga magazine. Also operates placer-mining classes.

(B.C.) Ministry of Education, Continuing Education Branch, Parliament Buildings, Victoria, B.C. V8V 4W6. An internationally-recognized correspondence course, "Mineralogy 11-Geology & Prospecting".

Ministry of Energy, Mines, and Petroleum Resources, Parliament Buildings, Victoria, B.C. Offers "Introductory", and, "Advanced" prospecting courses, through various colleges around the province.

Remote Sensing

The Canada Center for Remote Sensing, Technical Information Services-User Assistance and Marketing Unit, 717 Belfast Rd., Ottawa, Ontario, K1A 0Y7. Can supply books and indexes of available satellite imagery.

Horizon Research, 134 S. China Lake Blvd., Ridgecrest, CA 93555. Interprets satellite imagery, side-looking radar, for geological applications.

Maps B.C, 110-553 Superior St., Victoria, B.C. V8V 1X5

Information Resources

Crown Publications, 546 Yates St., Victoria, B.C. Phone (250) 386-4636. Free catalog of all government publication listings, maps, geological bulletins, Annual Reports, etc.

Geological Survey Branch, Library Services, Vancouver, B.C. Phone (604) 666-3812. Can help to reference hard-to-find material, old, out-of-print Annual Reports, etc.

Robertson Info Data Inc., 760-580 Hornby Ave., Vancouver, B.C. Phone (604) 683-2037. Listing service for mining properties, annual subscription.

Government Listings

MEMPR - Chief GoldCommissioner, 3rd. Floor, 1810 Blanchard, Victoria, B.C.

MEMPR - Chief Inspector of Mines, 4th Floor, 1810 Blanchard, Victoria, B.C. V8V 1X4 Phone(250) 952-0495

Financial Assistance

MEMPR - Prospectors Assistance Program. To help defray the cost of an approved exploration program. Check with your District Geologist for local availability.

Accreditation

Association of Professional Engineers and Geoscientists of B.C. As of January, 1993, all geochemical, geophysical, and drilling Assessment Reports must be written by a Registered Member, or a person working under a Registered Member. Non-registered individuals may still author Prospecting Reports, and reports pertaining to Physical Work. Call (604) 299-7100 for information on accreditation requirements and training opportunities.

Associations

Gold Dredgers Association of B.C., RR1, S-4, C-23, Kamloops, B.C. Phone (250) 579-8120

The Lapidary Rock and Mineral Society of B.C., 941 Wavertree Rd., North Vancouver, B.C. V7R 1S4 Phone (604) 987-2705. Has chapters in all regions of B.C.

Services

Prospectors Referral, c/o GOLD TRAILS PROSPECTING,   \
"bulletin-board" information exchange, by mail, newsletter, and internet. Also available - consulting services for small-scale placer locating, exploration, and mining programs.

MEMPR Regional and District Geologists. District Geologists and their staffs are very familiar with the deposit types within their respective areas. Individual prospectors may request an initial consultation, at no charge. Smithers: (250) 847-3911 Kamloops: (250) 828-4566 Prince George: (250) 565-6125 Nelson: (250) 354-6132

(US) Prospector's Referral Service, 5785 Hermosillo, Dept. GT, Atascadero, CA 93422. Covers the western US, with some international listings. Keeps tabs on the California scene-the world's hotbed of mineral exploration and small-scale gold-mining activity. Reasonable annual subscription.

For general geoscience information contact:

Dr. W.R. Smyth

Chief Geologist, BC Geological Survey

PO Box 9320, Stn. Prov Gov't

5-1810 Blanchard Street

Victoria BC V8V 9N3

Phone: (250) 952-0429 Fax: (250) 952-0371

The "Canadian Mines Handbook" is the best source of detailed information on mining and mineral exploration companies in Canada. Available at your local library or from:

Northern Miner Newspaper

1200 West Pender Street. Suite 206

Vancouver, BC. Phone: (604) 688-9908

For BC Provincial Government information contact:

Ministry of Employment and Investment

Energy and Minerals Division

Fifth Floor, 1810 Blanchard St.

Victoria, BC, Canada V8W 9N3

Phone: (250) 952-0132 Fax: (250) 952-0291

Another good source of information on prospecting in western Canada is:

BC & Yukon Chamber of Mines

840 West Hastings Street

Vancouver, BC V6C 1C8

Phone: (604) 681-5328 Fax: (604) 681-2363

Ottawa, Ontario K1R 7S8

Phone (613) 233-9391 Fax: (613) 233-8897

The national organization of the Canadian mining and exploration industry is:

The Mining Association of Canada

350 Sparks Street, Suite 1105

Ottawa, Ontario   K1R 7S8

Phone: (613) 233-9391 Fax: (613) 233-8897

Two good national sources of prospecting and mining-related information are:

Minerals and Metals Sector

Natural Resources Canada

580 Booth Street

Ottawa, Ontario K1A 0E4

Phone: (613) 947-6580 Fax: (613) 947-4198 E-mail: sbisson@nrcan.gc.ca

Geological Survey of Canada

601 Booth Street

Ottawa, Ontario K1A 0E8

Phone (613) 996-3919 Fax: (613) 996-9990 E-mail: library@gsc.nrcan.gc.ca

For information on satellite prospecting:

Radarsat International Inc.

3851 Shell Rd. Suite 200

Richmond, BC V6X 2W2

Phone: (604) 231-5000 Fax: (604) 231-4900

For information on prospecting grants, contact:

Prospectors Assistance Program

Ministry of Employment and Investment

Geological Survey Branch

P.O. Box 9320, Stn Prov Gov't, Victoria, B.C.   V8W 9N3

Ph: (250) 952-0388 or 952-0429   Fax: (250) 952-0381

Glossary of Prospecting & Mining Terms

Adit A nearly horizontal passage from the surface by which a mine is entered.

Alloy A mixture of two or more metals, occurring naturally, or man-made, to give hardness or to debase a more valuable metal like gold.

Alluvial Deposits of rock, sand, and gravel which have been transported by the action of running water.

Amalgamation A process in which mercury is combined with another metal such as gold, which mercury has a natural affinity to. The mercury is then removed using an acid, or through burning, leaving behind a pure gold "button".

Ancient Channel See Tertiary Channel.

Arborescent Of tree-like form; Some native gold, silver and copper specimens have an *arborescent*, or a *dendritic* (fern-like) form.

Assay An analysis of a sample of rock or gravel to determine the type and amount of economic minerals present.

Assessment Work The work done annually on a mining claim to maintain possessory title.

Auriferous Gold-bearing

Bar A deposit of sand or gravel lying adjacent to, or projecting into, a river or stream. Some bars can be very rich in fine gold. Hill's bar, south of Lytton on the Fraser River, is said to have produced over three tons of fine gold.

Barren A term used to describe a gravel deposit or rock outcrop that has been found devoid of any economic mineral.

Bedrock The impervious, horizontal-lying upper layer of the earth's crust, upon which alluvial gold settles.

Bench Describes a flat-lying area at some elevation above a river or stream.

Black Sand A dense metallic sand, composed of iron minerals, (magnetite and hematite), and chromium and titanium minerals, (illmenite, chromite, and rutile).

Bleed-Off Natural erosion of bench gravels into a present stream or river.

Blue Lead The bottom stratum of an ancient streambed, turned a blue color from natural leaching, often extremely rich in gold.

Bonanza An historic mining term, derived from Spanish, meaning , prosperity". Used to describe an extremely rich deposit.

Bullion An ingot of gold or silver.

Carat *See Karat*

Cemented Gravels Hard packed stream material, usually found on top of bedrock. Often, but not always, rich in gold.

Cinnabar A red-colored ore from which mercury is extracted.

Claim A legally tenured area of land on which the claim owner has legal ownership to a particular type or class of mineral.

Claim Jumper Someone who illegally mines someone else's claim.

Classification The process of screening out larger sized materials from a body of ore, streambed gravels, or concentrates, using screens of various mesh sizes.

Clean-up Recovery of gold from a concentrate that has been produced by washing a quantity of gravel.

Coarse Gold Gold which is too large to pass through a ten-mesh screen.

Colors A term used to describe small particles of gold. The smallest size visible to the unaided human eye is about one-millionth of an ounce.

Concentrate The accumulated material in a sluicebox or concentrator after washing gravel. Consists of heavy minerals such as black sand, ironstone, etc., and may contain gemstones, gold, platinum, and other metallic minerals.

Conglomerate A rock consisting of other rocks, (usually rounded), cemented together.

Country Rock The earth's crust; ordinary rock surrounding an orebody.

Crevice A crack or split in the bedrock in which placer gold may accumulate.

Dead Work Describes non-paying labour such as stripping barren overburden, or preparing the ground or the mining works.

Deposit A natural accumulation of mineral-bearing sand and gravel, or mineralized rock, in the case of a hardrock deposit.

Dike A narrow section of rock, usually igneous, which has intruded into the country rock. Dikes crossing a river make excellent gold traps.

Dragline The cable upon which a bucket-dredge moves to excavate gravel.

Dredge A machine used to excavate gravel. Usually mounted on floats, employing mechanical means, in the case of a bucket-dredge, or hydraulic means, in the case of a suction-dredge, to remove large volumes of gold-bearing gravel.

Drift A horizontal undercut or tunnel to follow a paystreak along bedrock under the overburden.

Electrum A relatively rare, natural alloy of gold and silver.

Eluvial Deposit A deposit of gold and other lode materials that has been borne away from the original lode, but which have not yet reached running water.

Fanning Sweeping light sands out of crevices and bedrock irregularities while crevicing in shallow water.

Fine Gold Gold which can pass through a ten-mesh screen.

Fineness A system used to indicate the purity of a gold sample or specimen. A specimen having a fineness of .900 would be 90% gold. A fineness of .65 would be 65% gold, and so on.

Fire Assay A method of analysis in which all of the gold and silver is extracted, then separated, weighed and measured in proportion to the original sample, to determine the amount of metal present.

Flake Gold Flattened chips of gold, pounded flat by stream action.

Float (From an eluvial deposit). Loose pieces of gold-bearing quartz or some other gold-bearing rock that has traveled some short distance from it's source.

Flood Layers Some streambeds have different layers of material that were laid down during different storms at different periods. The separate layers may contain gold in varying amounts.

Flour Gold Also known as Very Fine Gold - that which can pass through a forty-mesh screen.

Fool's Gold Iron pyrite or chalcopyrite, which has a superficial resemblance to gold. Beginners are also often fooled by the mineral mica, which has a gold color, but unlike gold, which has a steady "glow", mica glitters and glints as it's angular facets and planes refract light.

Free-milling Applied to ores which contain free gold or silver, and can be reduced by crushing and amalgamation, without roasting or other chemical treatment.

Gangue The non-valuable rock and waste materials associated with the valuable minerals in a body of ore.

Geiger Counter An electronic instrument used to detect radiation emitted by the decay of radio-active elements.

Gossan Hydrated oxide of iron, usually found at the decomposed outcrop of a mineral vein.

Gradient Refers to the dip or grade of a river, or of a sluicebox.

Grains In the Troy Weight System, 24 grains equals one pennyweight, with 20 pennyweights in one troy ounce, and 12 troy ounces in one troy pound. May also refer to small particles of gold in the pan.

Grizzly A device used to allow gravel into a sluicebox while keeping out larger cobbles and boulders.

Ground Sluicing Using running water to direct pay-gravel over a section of low-lying bedrock, or through a channel which has been cut into bedrock.

Grubstake The practice of an individual extending credit to a prospector or miner in return for a share of the find.

Hardpan Also known as "false bedrock" - a hardened layer, usually clay or cemented gravel, which is impervious and may collect gold just like true bedrock.

Hookah Air System An air breathing system used on most gold dredges to supply air for two divers.

Hydraulicing An old method of mining, now seldom used, in which jets of pressurized water are used to blast down deep beds of gravel.

Impurities In it's natural form, gold is usually alloyed with other metals - silver, iron, copper, collectively referred to as impurities, even though they may be quite valuable when separated out.

Jade A precious stone found in many regions of British Columbia.

Junction The confluence of two rivers.

Karat Describes the purity of gold. 24 karat is 100% pure. 20 karats is 20/24ths pure, and so on. Most placer gold is in the range of 18 to 22 karats.

Lay Agreement A working agreement or a subletting agreement between a claim owner and a miner whereby the miner agrees to pay a percentage, (usually 10 to 20 percent) of the metal he recovers.

Lead Refers to a "run" or "paystreak" of very rich gravel, usually found on or close to the bedrock layer.

Lenticular Lens-like.

Lode The original source of in-place, (in-situ), mineral, from which a placer is derived.

Magma The molten material which lies beneath the earth's outer crust.

Malleable The quality of being able to be hammered or shaped into various forms without being broken in the process. Gold is highly malleable.

Mercury (Hg) Number 80 on the Periodic Table, remains in a liquid form at room temperature. Also known as "quicksilver". Highly toxic metal.

Monitor Also known as a "giant" - a large nozzle used to direct a jet of water, used in hydraulic mining operations.

Motherlode The major in-situ source of placer gold in a given area.

Nugget A mass, or lump of valuable metal.

Outcropping The end of a lode which extends out and is exposed to view.

Overburden The low grade streambed material which overlies a placer paystreak.

Paleo-Channel/Paleo-Placer Remnants of extremely old channels which accumulated before the ice ages, in the Paleozoic Epoch, and which are invariably very rich in gold.

Platinum (PGM - Platinum Group Metals) A family of 6 related metals, characteristically white in color. Very valuable.

Prospecting The act of searching for a "prospect" - a location amenable to a profitable mining operation.

Pocket A small body of ore.

Recovery In mining jargon, the act of removing valuable minerals from ore.

Refractory Ore that resists the action of heat and chemical agents.

Retort A device used to separate mercury from gold after the amalgamation process is completed.

Riffles A set of baffles, usually placed at right angles to a flow of running water, intended to trap gold from the gravel that is being washed.

Rim-Rock The bedrock rising to form the boundary of a placer or a gravel deposit.

Rocker An historic mining device, still in use, used as a portable testing machine or for small-scale gold production.

Salting Introducing gold from an outside source into a mine to make it appear richer than it actually is.

Shoring Reinforcing the walls and ceilings of an adit or tunnel with the use of wood beams, to prevent cave-ins.

Sniping Hand-mining crack and bedrock crevices for gold nuggets.

Stake To stake, or legally acquire an area of ground as a mining claim. Also refers to a wooden post, or marker, to delineate the boundaries of a claim.

Tailings Sometimes referred to as "tails". The residual material left over from a mining operation, including large rocks and boulders.

Tertiary Channels Dry river beds which were laid down during the tertiary period, starting 2 million years ago, to the present quaternary geological period.

Tributary A branch or a feeder stream to a river. Old mining superstition has it that the tributaries flowing in from the right , as you look downstream on the main river, are usually the richest.

Values Describes the relative worth of placer gold or other economic minerals contained in the gravels.

Virgin Ground Ground that has previously not been mined.

Weathered Worn by erosion, i.e.: weathered bedrock, or weathered boulders such as "cows tongue".

Wing Dam A type of dam built to deflect a portion of a river or stream to permit mining of shallow in-stream gravels.

Yield Describes the output or production from a given volume of gravel, or the output or production from a particular mining operation. Includes co-products, such as platinum or gemstones.

PROSPECTING & MINING CHECKLISTS

In any critical operation (such as flying an aircraft, for example), the use of a check-list is crucial. The same goes for any mining operation, big or small, and even for prospecting day-trips. Why go to all the effort of researching and getting into a good area, then have the whole thing collapse because some small but vital item was inadvertently left behind? The following listings provide a general format, which you can custom-tailor to suit your own particular needs.

General Prospecting

- Prospecting Journal & Pen
- Maps
- Compass
- Gold Pan
- Trowel
- Shovel
- Pry Bar
- Crevicing Tool (ie: "Gold Claw")
- Magnifying Lens
- Plastic Sample Bags
- Labels and Waterproof Marker
- Sample Vials
- Tweezers
- Snifter Bottle
- Wet-weather gear
- Change of Clothes
- Water and Provisions
- First Aid Kit and Survival Items
- Back-Pack

Optional:
- Classifier Screen
- Pick-Hammer (for hardrock sampling)
- Plastic Pail and Small Hand-sluice (for bulk-sampling of gravel)
- Peeper Tube or Mask-and-Snorkel for underwater sniping
- Suction Gun
- Rubber Mitts in cold weather
- Firearm for wildlife protection
- Snake-Bite Kit

Electronic Prospecting

All of the above, plus:
- Metal Detector or Probe
- Spare Batteries
- Headphones
- Sand Scoop with Sieve

Optional:
- Apron with sewn-in pockets to aid in the collection and removal of metallic trash

Pocket Hunting

All of the items in "General Prospecting, plus:
- Wooden Stakes for marking locations
- Chlorine Bleach and Nitric Acid (or weak hydrochloric acid or oxalic acid) for treating the sam-

- A heavy Iron Bar and a Miner's Pick for breaking up hard ground
- A good magnifier of at least 30x (100x is better for this type of prospecting).

Boulder-Sniping

All of the items in "General Prospecting"plus:
- Come-Along or Portable Hand-Winch
- Boulder-Sling Kit or Choker-Chains

- 100 feet or more of Aircraft-Grade Cable
- Spare cable clamps and Wrench to fit cable clamps
- Wooden Chocks for securing boulder.

Beach-Mining or Mining High-Bench Gravels

Items in "General Prospecting, plus:
- Portable Concentrator or High-banker

- Clean-up Tub and Clean-up Kit (listed below)

Small-Scale Mining or Bulk-Sampling in Small Creeks

"General Prospecting " and "Boulder Sniping" Items, plus:
- Backpack-type Dredge or High-banker Combo
- Fuel and Oil
- Assembly Tools
- Spare Clamps and O-Rings
- Clean-Up Kit
- Tie-Off Ropes
- Rubber Mitts

- Chest Waders
- Dredging Permit or Written Authorization from Claim Owner, as required

Optional:
- Full Wet Suit or Dry Suit, as per conditions
- Inflator pump, if dredge is equipped with inflatable pontoons
- Knee Protectors

Production-Dredging

"General Prospecting" and
"Boulder Sniping" Items, plus:
- Intermediate or large dredge, as permitted
- Wet or Dry Suit
- Air Reserve Tank
- Splitter "T" if more than one diver is to operate
- Air Line for Each Diver
- Quick-Release Weight Belt with 60-80 lbs. for fresh-water operations
- Diving Gloves
- Booties and Boots
- Hood
- Knee Protectors
- Diving Suit Repair Kit
- Low-pressure Air Regulator
- 400 feet of 3/8th poly Tie-Off Rope (1/2" rope is recommended for dredges 5" or larger)

- Clean-Up Kit, Swimmers Ear or similar ear prevention solution
- Engine tune-up Kit
- Complete Tool Kit
- Duct Tape
- Silicon Glue.

Spare:
- Clamps
- O-Rings
- Pump Bearing Seals
- Compressor Belt
- Pump Primer Intake Cap
- Sluice-Box Carpet

Optional:
- Hot Water Heater, if a wet suit is used
- Rubber Raft and Oars or Small Motor for ferrying equipment
- Swivel Nozzle to replace regular suction hose tip

Clean-Up Kit

- Large plastic Clean-Up Tub
- (2) 20-litre Plastic Pails
- Classifier Screens in at least three sizes
- Plastic Funnel
- Clear Plastic Vials in assorted sizes
- Bottle of Detergent or Surfactant to soften water

- Tweezers
- Snifter Bottle.

Optional:
- Clean-Up Wheel or Mini-concentrator
- Mercury Retort
- Chamois
- Jewelry-making Supplies

162

Support Equipment for Extended Operations

- RV
- Tents
- Sleeping Bags
- Folding Cots
- Portable Cook-stove and Fuel
- Fuel Lines and Fittings, etc.
- Portable Heater (i.e.: kerosene heater)
- Cooking Utensils
- Pots and Pans
- Dishware
- Freeze-dried Emergency Food
- Provisions according to a pre-planned menu for the duration of the stay
- Lantern and Fuel
- Extra Mantles
- Survival Knife
- Axe
- Wood saw or Chainsaw
- Can Opener
- Insect Repellent
- Thermos and/or Canteens
- Water Storage
- Ice Chest or Propane Fridge
- Matches and Lighters in water-proof containers
- Candles
- Portable Toilet or Holding Tank
- Waterproof Tarps
- Plastic Bags
- Emergency Day-Pack for each expedition member

Claim-Staking Kit

- Up-to-date Claim Maps and To-pographic Maps
- Air photos
- Hip-Chain and spare line
- Compass
- Flagging Tape and Spray Paint
- Wooden Pickets
- Hatchet for blazing trees
- Axe or Chainsaw for cutting posts
- Prospecting Journal with names and numbers of contact people, private owners, etc.
- Claim Tags and Scribing Tool
- Accurate Watch with Date Display
- Pencils, Ruler and Compass Rose for laying out claim boundaries on the map
- Camera for photographic evidence
- Broad-headed nails to attach claim tag
- Survival and First Aid Kit
- Firearm or Bear Repellent
- Notification of your Trail-Plan to local authorities if traversing remote or rugged locations
- **Optional:**
- GPS Instrument for orienteering and locating
- Metal Detector for Locating Surveyors Pins